Fausta Borja's Beauty and the Beast

Fausta Borja's
Beauty and the Beast

Fausta Borja

BORJA PRESS

For AB,

my Bellamy, my La Bête

CONTENTS

1
BEAUTY

I INSIST ON going alone and my family, relieved, allows it.

Monsieur La Bête sends a carriage to fetch me. I've divided my few possessions between my sisters and packed only a small valise for my new life.

I kiss my brothers goodbye, and bid them to be good, though they are much older than me. Gaspar and Lucio have a tight set to their jaws. They wanted to challenge La Bête, kill him, and bury the family debt along with his corpse. But people whisper that La Bête cannot be killed. That he made a pact with a devil to live forever; and in exchange, he retains the form of a monstrous beast. I think that's superstitious nonsense, of course, but maybe I'm wrong: people also say that La Bête has an insatiable appetite for women and here I am, the latest woman he has bought to satisfy his needs, and I am about to deliver myself to his doorstep.

Lucio's friend, Julian, tries to go in for a kiss as well. I turn my head to avoid his lips and pull back. He looks at me with hooded eyes as I glare at him. Lucio gives me a reproving look but he should've known better than to invite him. Julian is achingly handsome but he is all ugliness inside. He is the one that urged my brothers to challenge La Bête. I wish he hadn't come to see me off.

The rest of my siblings cry as I bid them farewell. Alarico is young, and too genuine to fake his tears, but I can't help but notice that both my sisters look a little self-satisfied behind their handkerchiefs as they blot dry eyes. Fine embroidered handkerchiefs bought with the chests of gold La Bête gave my family in exchange for me.

My oldest sister Fernanda has always tried to take care of me, in her own way. "Remember Inanna's Prayer so that The Beast doesn't impregnate you with a monster," she whispers earnestly in my ear while pressing something into my hand. I pocket it to look at later.

"Remember what we told you about how it goes between a man and a woman," Yesenia says. She and Fernanda exchange looks before eyeing me with pity.

"I'll never forget," I say.

La Bête's driver assists me into the carriage and hands me my valise with a suspicious look. It's heavy with all the metal bits I've collected over the years. He shuts the door.

It's true I'll never forget what Fernanda and Yesenia told me; nevertheless I wonder how much of it they made up to try and shock their youngest sister. My sisters are not yet married and while I know they were chaste in Tierra Rica—the kingdom we lived in when Papi had more riches than he knew what to do with—the other kingdoms have a broader view of appropriate sexual behavior. When Papi lost his fortune in the tsunami of '22, we joined the exodus of others with similar unfortunate fates. We gave up our villa in the capital of Tierra Rica and left the kingdom altogether—I suspect to get away from some persistent creditors. We settled in the town of Orleans, in a kingdom called Arcadia where there were plenty of sloe-eyed young messieurs to comfort my sisters.

What we didn't have was money for my sisters' dowries. Eventually, we didn't even have the money to stay in Orleans and we moved into the outskirts of the Black Forest which is the province of no kingdom. My family hates the small cottage we moved into, but it's grown on me over the years.

I'm sad to leave it.

I take out the item I pocketed earlier from Fernanda—I'm touched that she wrapped it in one of the handkerchiefs she's recently bought—and I stare down at the silver locket strung on a slim chain.

I open it. There's a picture of my mother on the left, just before she died. On the right my father, when he was the same age.

I reach back into my pocket and find the coin I always carry with me—the coin Ahmed left me.

A bright golden coin carved with a four-pointed rose and punctured with a hole. I've never worn it for my family disapproves of my attachment to the old servant but I'm leaving my family now.

I add the coin to my locket chain, clasp the necklace around my neck, and twist to look out the back of the carriage as we drive away from the cottage.

Perhaps my family loves me after all, I think to myself as I wave goodbye. Papi stands behind my sisters and brothers. I tried to say goodbye to him earlier but he avoided me. He's been unable to look me in the eye, or even be in the same room with me for the last month.

Not since he sold me to The Beast.

Yes, my family loves me. They just don't love me as much as they do their riches.

Ahmed hated the Black Forest.

I thought at first it was because he was from across the sea and they had nothing like it in his homeland but it went beyond that.

He caught me once trying to run away from home. This was in Tierra Rica. I was seven-years-old. He clucked his tongue at me in my pink dress, my bag full of the chef's *bolillos*, and my scared eyes; then he invited me over to the little shack he lived in, tucked away at the edge of our estate. There he filled me with tea, smoked his pipe, and told me a story of how he once went wandering from his home. He was exploring a network of caves when he found himself in a strange forest. The Black Forest. He never told me what he was doing in the caves, and what happened to him in the forest; only said that when he finally found his way out of the woods was when he learned the sea separated him from home.

Then he gently suggested that perhaps I wait till I was a little older for such an adventure, and he walked me back to the big house, and helped me climb the tree that I had shimmied down to escape the room I shared with my sisters.

When Ahmed died a couple years later, grief propelled me towards the Black Forest again.

I wasn't thinking about running away. I didn't even pack anything. I was old enough to know how much I didn't yet know, about survival out in the world alone. But I was young enough to fantasize that if I got lost, and found Ahmed's caves; if I magically found myself on the other side of the world, and had no choice but to try and make it alone, everything would be all right.

With no one like Ahmed to stop my foolishness, I found the woods easily. I got lost easily too.

As the sun set, the scariness of my situation set in on me. Not to mention the emptiness of my stomach. But Lady had mercy on me. I came upon a grove of statues. They ranged from human-shaped, to exotic animals, to strange creatures I couldn't believe actually existed.

I found an avocado tree growing next to a hedge of blooming roses and gobbled up my fill. Then I wrapped my cloak about me and crawled underneath a statue of a fearsome lion. Telling myself that the lion would protect me, I laid my head down and slept.

The next morning I found my way out of the woods. To my shock, no one spoke my native language nor the language of my neighboring kingdoms. I hadn't really expected my experiment to work.

But alas, it hadn't: not really. I wasn't in Kurys, where Ahmed was originally from: I was in Boscaterra. It was a western kingdom at least a month's journey from home if you traveled around the Black Forest. But it was still on my home continent. Not the other side of the world. Not far enough to warrant making a go of it alone at nine years of age. Even back then I had an aptitude for calculating numerous outcomes based on set variables: that aptitude does not mesh well with bravery.

Some multilingual pilgrims found and took pity on me. They hired an enchanted carriage to cut through the Black

Forest and take me home to Tierra Rica. I know now that it must have cost them a small fortune.

My family received me with tears of joy and told me I was very lucky. And I suppose I was.

There are dangerous creatures in the woods, and places that call to you, that only lead you to your ruin.

The carriage hits a ditch in the road.

I tumble and right myself, and I wonder, as I often still do, if I should've found the courage to escape all those years ago.

It's night, and raining when the carriage stops and the driver throws open the door.

He assists me out of the carriage, and hops back into the driver's seat.

"Evening, Mademoiselle. Perhaps you will hire me again, should you need to go into a town."

I gape at him. "But don't you work for La Bête?"

The driver touches his cap. "The Beast doesn't employ any servants, mademoiselle. Only his..." he eyes me, "...women."

He snaps his reins and pulls the horses round. We're at the top of a high ridge and they trot carefully down the treacherously steep path we came in on. I'm left alone with the lashing wind and rain and my valise clutched to my chest.

My cheeks are already wet and numb from the cold and my cloak is growing more drenched and heavy by the moment.

I turn to face the Château de La Bête.

It's monstrous. And huge. My family could live comfortably in the gatehouse that rises before me. Fifty—no, a hundred—families could live in the massive stone structure that rises behind the gatehouse. I cannot discern a cohesive roof, only a mishmash lot of jutting peaks, towers, and crenellations broken up by misshapen shadows.

Lightning streaks the sky. In the moment of brilliant illumination I see that the misshapen shadows are gargoyles crouching on the battlements.

Thunder rumbles. I know it's my imagination but it feels as if the very ground beneath me shifts and heaves me forward. The wind propels my back and I stumble to the front gate: huge fortified doors thrice as tall as I am.

Before I can wonder at how I'm supposed to let La Bête know I am here, the gate opens.

I walk through the gatehouse and into a courtyard. The gate closes behind me and cuts off the wind. I see no one but my neck prickles as if someone is watching me.

Another door opens before me and I hurry to it, eager to be out of the rain.

Finally, I'm inside the castle.

No one greets me. Again, the door closes behind me.

Clearly, some sorcery is at work.

I shiver in a long hallway lighted with torches, and my soaked cloak drips onto the narrow carpet lining the stone floor. The air is hushed, as if the castle itself waits for something.

"Hello?" I venture deeper into the hallway.

The ceiling is low, gilded, and supported with rib vaults which give me the impression that I'm exploring a series of opulent caves that form a tunnel.

Murals cover the walls instead of paintings. Arch supports divide the long wall into sections and each section seems to tell the progression of some story. A beautiful couple is the subject of the first few murals. The woman has silvery white hair and the man...I edge closer to take a look when a voice growls behind me.

"You're late."

I whirl around.

At first glance I see only a dark hulking figure and that's enough for my heart to seize. He is enormous. He stands a distance from me but I can tell my head would barely reach his chest, and I am not a petite woman. I notice he is dressed in very old-fashioned clothing: a long jacket with rows of shiny brass buttons over a white shirt with ruffles; trousers tapered at the knees; long boots. The men in Orleans take their fashion seriously and La Bête could be one of their ancestors.

Well, I suppose he actually could be an ancestor for he is rumored to have inhabited this castle for centuries now.

Then he moves forward into the light.

I've prepared myself for this moment, having heard how ugly he is, how unnatural, how *beastlike*.

I manage to calm my breath and force myself to take in the details of his body, thinking that if I examine one aspect at a time, I will not be overwhelmed.

I look, and La Bête stands still in the flickering torchlight. Perhaps he examines me as well.

He is definitely human, or at least more human than whatever else is present in him, so that's already one bit of misinformation I can correct.

But...La Bête is also very definitely something other than human. The line of his legs is...not right. His knee joints do not bend the correct way. His narrow hips and waist are definitely human male—and a fine specimen at that. But they widen up into a great big barrel of a chest. I'm

8

reminded of an illustration of a troll that used to scare me as a child. As for his head... My first impression is that I'm looking at a lion. La Bête has a glorious mane of wavy hair that gleams in the light like copper. It's quite beautiful actually. Even the beard, which is the most overgrown I've seen, to the point that I have trouble distinguishing it from the hair on his head. He has lips—thick but distinctly human—but the inverted triangle of his nose resembles the muzzle of an animal. From the little bit of skin on his cheeks, I determine he is light-skinned, probably a white man considering the lightness of his hair but perhaps mixed since his eyes are warm and dark, and not so round. They are rimmed with thick dark lashes.

He may look like a beast, but I would contest *ugly* and *unnatural*. In a way, he looks like some magnificent creature one might encounter in a magical forest...which I suppose is exactly what he is to me. Intimidating, to be sure. But he fits his surroundings.

"You're late," La Bête says again. "Come."
He spins and marches down the hallway, leaving me to follow.

I take a breath, and still clutching my valise which he did not offer to take, hurry after him.

"The last woman left early," says La Bête as he strides down the hallway. "I've gone two days without—"

He interrupts himself. "You *are* Monsieur Kahlo's daughter, yes?"

"Yes."

"You came here willingly?"

"Yes." I'm practically running down the hallway to keep up with him but I still notice the art on the wall when it changes to...quite scandalizing scenes.

"Your father told you the terms of the agreement?"

"If one of my father's daughters comes willingly to live here with you," I say, "you will cancel the debt he owes you; moreover you will provide him with five chests of gold which you've already bestowed as a gesture of good faith. If I stay for the whole year, you will provide my family with another five chests of gold. Also, you won't kill him for stealing the rose he took from your garden."

The rose was for me, of course. Which is why my family and I decided it was only fair that I be the daughter to fulfill the terms of the agreement. It's also true La Bête only threatened to kill my father until he returned the rose, which my father did. But my family has suffered from debt for too long, and my freedom for their fortune was too good a trade to pass on.

We enter a spiraling stone staircase and climb up. La Bête slows down so that I can haul my legs up the ridiculously high steps but I can tell he is impatient and agitated.

He reflexively reaches for me at one point—I'm not sure if it's to take my valise from me, or to simply pick me up and carry me up the stairs—but he changes his mind and stoically climbs upward without looking at me further.

"That's not all. Did Monsieur Kahlo make it clear what is expected of you here?"

"I'm your concubine," I say baldly. "You have the full right to use my body, whenever you please."

"Yes," La Bête says. His voice is a little strangled. Or perhaps that's his natural growl that I will grow accustomed to. "Yes, that's it. And that will be—often."

We finally reach the second floor landing. The stairs continue their endless spiral upwards but thankfully La Bête leads me into the hallway. This one also has a vaulted ceiling but it actually vaults high. If the hall downstairs is a tunnel of narrow caves, this is a spacious cavern.

A long line of chandeliers light this grand hallway, as well as tall candelabras with drippy wax candles, and a fireplace as tall as La Bête.

"Here," La Bête says, "you're shivering."

He beelines for one of the low armchairs next to the fireplace. "You can leave your cloak here to dry. There's a fireplace made up in your room but this one is bigger."

I set my valise down on the floor and unclasp my cloak. I swing it off my shoulders and set it over the back of the armchair. I rub my arms and step closer to the roaring fire, wishing for a moment's respite to catch my breath.

I turn to La Bête and stop short. His warm brown eyes (they are the color of cinnamon, I decide to myself) are staring at me. I don't know him well enough to judge yet but he looks horrified. Or in pain.

I force myself to approach him—he's really not so hideous, just so ridiculously *large*—and I only have to force myself because I am not accustomed to standing so close to strange men.

I touch La Bête's arm. "Are you all right?"

"No. I am not." Even his breaths have a beastlike timber. But they grow more rapid and shallow by the moment.

"Can I—"

La Bête seizes my wrist. It hurts.

"I'm sorry," I gasp, "I didn't mean to offend you..."

"I'm not offended."

La Bête whirls me around and shoves me forward. I grab the back of the other armchair to prevent myself from falling.

11

"I cannot hold back any longer," he growls. "I need to use you now."

I gasp as La Bête pushes my back. My hands fall on the armrests for support. He grapples my skirts and flips them up over me and the armchair.

"You're not wearing drawers," he says. I can't think of a response.

The *señoritas* of Tierra Rica have no use for drawers, and my sisters and I never took them up when we moved to Arcadia.

I wonder if maybe I should explain this but I have lost my capability for speech.

I hear rustling and then La Bête presses himself against me. Against every part of me. I feel hard flesh meet the softness at the junction of my thighs. His cock. The first that's ever touched me anywhere, much less *there*. A part of me wishes I could turn to see this fearsome appendage my sisters have been telling me about. But the other part is glad I don't have the chance to be intimidated.

I have not quite understood up until this very moment how very...delicately...I have been treated before now. At least physically.

"Is this..." La Bête's voice is strangled. "Are you ready?"

"We might as well get it over with," I say.

I feel the sudden hesitation on La Bête's end which strikes me as exasperating. He's led me to the edge of the cliff and I see no reason to back off from the plunge now.

"I'm ready." I wriggle my hips.

La Bête groans. He bumps his cock against me and thrusts at my inner folds.

I wince as he stabs at my entrance. His cock barely intrudes before my barrier denies it access. Attempts to penetrate farther are unsuccessful.

"Damn it." His cock retreats.

I hear him spit. His cock returns, more lubricated. I wait, frozen, as La Bête swears again, grips my hips tightly, and thrusts his hips once more. He tears through my barrier till he's buried inside.

Oh. Tears spring to my eyes. I grasp the inner ruffles of my skirt and shove them into my mouth to keep quiet.

The Beast's cock splits me open. He makes noises like an animal as he ruts inside me.

I have never been punched in the stomach but I believe that it would be similar to what I'm feeling now.

That's in addition to all the new sensations—if tearing pain can be understated as a sensation—I'm feeling in places no one has ever reached before.

La Bête groans. He sounds a bit like a dying animal. Or am I the dying animal? How do women put up with this, much less *enjoy* it?

It's not that bad, I chide myself. *And you agreed to this.*

I grit my teeth and vow not to make a noise of hurt, and to endure as best as I can. I've had worse pains, I am sure, though none quite so intimate.

The soreness has become really quite unbearable when La Bête shouts and freezes against me.

I think it's finally over.

There's a foreign sticky wetness inside me. His cum.

La Bête slumps on top of me. His hair tickles the back of my neck. I've never felt a man's chest on my back like this. He's hot as a furnace—hotter than the fire roaring next to us. He runs his hand over my back, a fleeting yet soothing touch, as if to apologize for exercising his right over me. At least I'm no longer cold.

La Bête lifts his chest. He shifts his hips and pulls out of me. That's almost as bad as when he pushed himself in.

I force my jaws to relax and pull my petticoats from my mouth. I begin to rise, gingerly.

"Wait," La Bête says. Gods and Lady. What more is there?

Soft cloth skims over my bruised and abraded core and wipes away some of the stickiness. I take another moment before rising, more embarrassed by this gesture than by the whole ordeal that preceded it.

"There's blood," he says. His tone is queer: I cannot decipher it.

"Well, yes." I say. "I'm a virgin."

He is silent.

I turn to face him and immediately blush at my first sight of a cock. I don't get a good look since it's partially covered by the handkerchief. He tucks himself away as soon as I turn. His eyes drop before I can meet them.

"You *were* a virgin," he says brusquely as he laces up his trousers.

I blush harder.

La Bête picks up my valise. "I'll take you to your room now."

More stickiness drips down my thighs as I follow La Bête to my room and I worry that it will progress down to the floor and leave a trail in my wake.

Thankfully, we reach my room before it comes to that.

La Bête looms over me as we stand outside the doors to my room.

"Dinner will be waiting for you downstairs as soon as you are ready," he says.

"Thank you," I say. "Will we be dining together?"

"Yes. I...I have not had my fill of you today, and will need to use you again soon."

I absorb this information. "Then I'll be down shortly."

I wait for him to leave me so I can finally be alone.

La Bête clears his throat. "Which one are you?"

I stare up at him blankly.

"Which daughter?"

"I'm the youngest," I say.

"The one Kahlo stole the rose for."

"Yes."

"Then your name is Linda?"

"No," I say. "*Linda*...is just a word. It means 'beautiful.' I suppose my family calls me that so that they don't have to look beyond my beauty."

The words pop out and I immediately regret them. It's one thing to hold some bitterness against my family but La Bête is no one to me, that I would share such a private thing. I'm also acutely aware that a man called "The Beast" because of how he looks is in a unique position to sympathize with me, and I have no wish to align myself with him.

"Then what should I call you?" La Bête asks.

I look at him in surprise. I realize that I have given my virginity to a stranger who doesn't even know my given name, nor I his.

The soreness between my legs is strong. I remember how he turned me over an armchair for sex before even bringing me to my room, because he could not wait. That he plans to use me again tonight because he has not had enough.

"Call me Beauty," I say.

I go into my room without asking for La Bête's given name.

2
BEAUTY

WHEN IT'S TIME for dinner I return downstairs to the tunnel like entrance hall.

It's darker than before: only a single torch burns in the hallway. The warm light draws me forward towards the silver-haired woman illuminated in the mural panel, but as I reach her, the torch extinguishes itself.

The one next to it bursts into flame: then that dies as the next one lights. The flame moves down the row of torches and I follow it into the next hallway.

In this manner, I am led to an intimate dining room.

There are two chairs around a square table set for two. The table is already laden with covered dishes. I look around the empty room and sit.

I sneak a look under one of the covered dishes—it appears to be pheasant, braised *coq au vin* style with wine and vegetables and garlic. My mouth waters and I cover it again, wondering if La Bête plans to join me soon. My eyes roam the room.

Dark wood panels cover the walls, along with some rich blue and gold tapestries. My slippers sink into the plush blue carpeting.

A merry fire flickers in the fireplace. A chandelier above and two candelabras on either side of the table provide additional light.

"Beauty. You needn't wait for me to begin your meals."

I start.

La Bête stands in the doorway. I marvel that anyone his size could go unnoticed but he has a way of blending into the shadows that I must watch out for.

La Bête approaches the table and sits down. I feel like a tiny doll some capricious child has set down to have tea with a monster.

The candelabra to my right reaches down and uncovers the pheasant coq au vin.

I scream.

The candelabra freezes.

I press my hand to my mouth and will myself to calm down. Sorcery. This castle is filled with it.

"I'm sorry," says La Bête, sounding genuine. "I should have warned you."

"No," I pull my hand down and will myself to pick up the serving spoon. "I overreacted."

La Bête watches as I help myself to the coq au vin.

I've never considered myself a particularly sensitive woman but even I can sense a pall in the air within the castle. I imagine that if someone like my sister Yesenia were in my place, she might even call it the whisper of a malignant presence.

I eye the level of coq au vin left and heap some more onto my plate.

One candelabra uncovers a basket of fresh baguette slices and the other pours red wine into our glasses. A faint rattling noise accompanies the whir of their movements.

"Regarding earlier..." La Bête says. "When we stopped by the fire to remove your cloak and I—"

"Please," I say. "I know what I agreed to. Apologies are unnecessary."

"I'm not apologizing," he growls. "I will never apologize for when I use you. That is simply an aspect of me that you must accept."

I gape at him.

"It will be better for you," he says, "if you understand what you're getting into from the very beginning. I can still look for another woman. If you wish to return to your family."

La Bête holds his hands in his lap in front of him. It is oddly formal, as is his offer to allow me retreat.

I think of being returned to my family. Of their sullen faces as they calculate the loss of the additional five chests of gold they'd be cheated out of because I could not withstand even one year. Of living in the outskirts of the Black Forest when I have been to its heart. And then there are my dreams for the life I have planned after my year is up. My promise to Ahmed.

"I'm staying," I say firmly.

"Very well."

A little bit of tension leaves La Bête. He serves himself the coq au vin and we enjoy the simple meal in silence.

My earlier sense of anxiety recedes quickly with food warming my belly. Malignant presence, indeed. It seems even I can be susceptible to senseless dramatics when cold and hungry. I vow to steel myself against further bouts of hysteria.

As I use a slice of baguette to scoop up the last of the broth on my plate, I wonder if La Bête is going to grab me now and commence with his fucking.

He sets his napkin on the table and rises. "I shall join you in your bedroom at eleven. That gives you a little over an hour to freshen up."

"Thank you," I say.

He searched my face—perhaps for irony—but finds none.

"I suggest you stay in your room till you're more familiar with the castle. Tomorrow my man Bellamy will give you a tour."

"Bellamy?"

"My man, Bellamy. You must do whatever he asks of you."

Another man I must obey? "I thought you didn't have any servants."

"I don't. Bellamy is part of the castle."

I return to my bedroom. It's a suite, actually, a grandiose affair that puts the bedroom I had in the villa at Tierra Rica to shame.

The bed itself is practically the size of a room. It has a dark wood frame with four sturdy posts and a headboard that looks heavy enough to need four men to carry it.

There's a chaise lounge by the latticework windows, upholstered in buttery yellow and pale green patterns that match the ottoman in front of the vanity and high armchairs set against the wall.

An armoire which I rifled through earlier has more dresses than I can count, in all different colors and styles.

A study is attached to the bedroom, as well as a small water closet which includes a compact toilet and sink. I haven't seen a water closet since we lived in Arcadia and I marvel that I have a private one all to myself.

A sharp rapping sounds at my door. I go warily to answer it. It's nowhere near eleven and I hope La Bête hasn't decided he cannot wait after all.

Two animate candelabras are at my bedroom door and they hold a brass copper tub full of steaming water between them.

I stare at them till I come to my senses and allow them inside.

They enter, accompanied by the sounds of clicks and whirs, and set the tub down in the middle of my bedroom. The scent of roses permeates the air.

I observe closely and notice that the candelabras move by some mechanism that allows them to roll seamlessly across the ground. No doubt it helped them move the tub without spilling the water.

I hesitate but decide that modesty in front of objects of home decor is unnecessary, even if said objects are animate.

I undress and slide into the water. It's gloriously hot.

I don't linger in the bath, as much as I want to. I don't want to be caught unawares when La Bête comes.

There's a selection of nightgowns in the huge wardrobe. I skip quickly past the virginal gowns with stifling high necks (I don't have much appreciation for irony), and then the colorful ones with more ribbons and flounces than a wedding cake. I pause to stare dubiously at some filmy scraps of cloth that could only be used as decoration, before I finally find something suitable.

I select a simple, sleeveless nightgown. It's ivory-colored, with a ruched neckline and thankfully only one ribbon circling the empire waist. The rest of the nightgown flows neatly to the floor.

I know La Bête is only coming for one purpose but I make a concession for my modesty by pulling a pale green wraparound over my nightgown.

La Bête knocks promptly at eleven o'clock.

He doesn't bother with undressing me first.

He simply growls and pushes me back until I fall onto the bed. My legs dangle off and The Beast easily lifts me and tosses me to the center of the bed.

He rears back on his knees and quickly unlaces his trousers. His cock springs out.

It's huge. I cannot believe I've had it inside me. I have no others to compare it to but surely it's not supposed to be bigger than a finger or two and yet it's more akin to my forearm.

La Bête has already climbed on the bed when he swears, and quickly scrambles off of the bed.

He takes something from the dresser next to the bed. A slim, tapered jar. He pours a viscous fluid onto his hand and massages it onto his cock.

He returns to the bed and taps my thighs. "Open."

It's the first word he's said to me since he came in my bedroom.

I open my thighs. La Bête rubs the slick fluid into my battered folds.

I must let out a sound because La Bête's eyes flash to me. He stills.

La Bête does something shocking. He dips his head down and places a chaste kiss on my mound. Then he covers it with his hand.

The warmth of his great paw-like hand seeps into my core. I think it actually feels better.

My optimism fades when La Bête removes his hand and turns me onto my stomach.

21

"I promise to get it over with quickly and leave you alone for the rest of the night," he says.

He raises my hips so that I'm on my knees and then he enters me from behind. He slides in more easily this time and I can feel his effort to be more gentle, but I am so sore from earlier that it's hardly a relief.

La Bête keeps his promise. Soon he is done and pads out of my bedroom silently. The door clicks behind him.

I lay awake for a long time, listening to the tick tick tick of a loud clock somewhere in the room and missing the warmth of my sisters in the large, lonely bed.

3
BEAUTY

I WAKE TO a crashing noise.

"Cwoo...hwee! Cwoo...hweee! Cwoo...hweeee!"

I wake groggily and look wildly around our bedroom. Have my sisters gone mad?

I come to my senses.

I'm in La Bête's castle, in the Black Forest.

The mantle clock on my dresser has exploded open and there's a mechanical bird sticking out of it at a crazed angle, heckling me with its wheezing cuckoos.

I scurry to the dresser and stuff the bird back into the clock.

Blessed silence.

It's eight o'clock in the morning. I've slept in later than I normally would.

I dress and go down in search of breakfast. I've gotten used to country life living in the cottage and I hope there is a hearty spread.

Perhaps it's that my sleep was restless the night before, or perhaps I'm still feeling some lingering anxiousness (I will *not* call it dread for I have no logical reason to feel dread), but I squeak when I enter the dining room and run right into a warm body.

"Excuse me, mademoiselle." A startlingly handsome man reaches for my elbow and steadies me. I can't help but stare at him.

It's not just that he is handsome—I dismiss the flurry of excitement that rushes through my body as the natural repercussion of being a healthy, red-blooded, young woman—but there is also something very familiar about him.

"Hello, monsieur," I say politely before extricating myself from him.

He bows. I observe that he dresses in the same old-fashioned manner as La Bête. Perhaps the castle only stocks men's fashions from that particular era.

"Mademoiselle Beauty," he greets me. "I am Bellamy. Please, take a seat. I do not wish to delay the breaking of your fast."

I sit.

"Would you like coffee, tea, a hot chocolate, perhaps?" I had thought the strange short vowels La Bête spoke with were the result of his unique mouth structure but this man Bellamy speaks with the same accent.

"Hot chocolate sounds wonderful," I say. I place where I've seen him before.

"Monsieur, I've seen you in the murals downstairs."

I can see the recognition embarrasses him.

"No, it's but a passing resemblance. The man in the murals doesn't exist."

I see that the subject makes him uncomfortable so I let it go. I don't normally drop lines of inquiry so easily but there is food in front of me now and my stomach growls. I take a croissant from the basket of pastries in front of me, and a deviled egg—and then another egg—and another.

Monsieur Bellamy tacitly pushes the plate closer to me. He's only taken two eggs but I shrug and take the last one as well. If he wanted it, he would've taken it first.

A candelabra sets a cup of hot chocolate down in front of me. I recognize the faint rattling noise I heard at dinner last night and turn an appraising eye on the candelabra. It starts as if noticing my scrutiny, and backs—or fronts?—away. It disappears through the service door, in any case.

That's interesting.

"How is your hot chocolate?"

I try it.

"It's delicious," I say truthfully. Having appeased my initial hunger, my mind begins working again. "Where is La Bête, may I ask?"

The monsieur blinks at me. He has long lashes surrounding his brown eyes. "Didn't I mention? La Bête doesn't emerge during the day. Only at night."

"Oh," I say. "I see."

"I shall give you a tour of the castle once you've finished breaking your fast," he says. "And then I shall need to examine you."

I pause in buttering my croissant. "Examine me?"

"After..." he coughs politely. "La Bête's attentions last night, he wishes to ascertain that you are intact."

"'Intact.' I assure you, Monsieur, that after Monsieur La Bête's attentions last night, I am no longer a virgin. He can tell you so himself. He made quite a point of it, you know."

My face is hot and prickly.

"Excuse me, that was a poor choice of words. I only meant that he hopes you are feeling well, and that I am to ensure you are able to continue receiving his attentions without any...undue pain and discomfort."

I am unable to speak. A local midwife has examined my woman parts before but she is a comforting older woman, not a handsome young man in a castle inhabited by a beast that ravages me at night.

The monsieur gives me a concerned look. "Perhaps I underestimated your discomfort. If you are in pain now I shall take a look straightaway."

"I'm fine," I say faintly.

He's still looking at me with his steady brown eyes.

"In fact," I say, injecting some firmness into my voice, "you needn't examine me at all. I feel perfectly fine. It's not at all necessary."

"It is necessary," he says flatly. "But it can wait till after the tour."

I consume the rest of my breakfast in silence. Better to choose my battles carefully and all that. Monsieur Bellamy must not be very hungry, for he eats only a little, and then settles to read an ancient book.

When I'm finished eating, Bellamy shows me the rest of the wing my bedroom is in, which is mostly empty bedrooms, the grand hall I already saw, and a sitting room with an attached nursery.

Then he escorts me through other parts of the castle. There is a massive library with so many books that I could not finish them if I had a thousand years. There is a room filled with musical instruments. There is even a room that is filled only with mirrors which I think is very strange. As we are about to leave the mirror room something drops from the chandelier above and falls in front of me with a clink.

I crouch down and scoop up the object. It's a ring. It's made of reddish gold metal streaked with platinum white veins—a peculiar alloy I've never seen before.

Excitement grows within me for I can add it to my collection of metal alloys for testing. It's heavy—I suspect it has a high density. I itch to bring out the little notebook and graphite I carry in my pocket to begin some preliminary notes but honesty compels me to catch Bellamy's attention.

"This fell from that chandelier." I show him.

Bellamy leans in to see what I have and recoils back. He bumps into a mirror behind him and has to move quickly to save it from toppling.

"I didn't mean to startle you," I say with alarm.

"You didn't," Bellamy gives me a severe look which strikes me as somewhat comical. But I swallow my mirth.

"You recognize it then? Is it harmful?"

I look up when Bellamy doesn't answer. He is still holding onto the mirror he saved from toppling and his face is ashen. He stares at me, but I'm not sure he sees me. Finally, he seems to notice my expectant look, and shakes himself.

"No...yes. You're safe to hold it. Anyway, it's too late. It's chosen you. You may as well wear it."

I give Bellamy the skeptical look his rambling deserves.

"What do you mean it's chosen me?"

Bellamy shrugs and doesn't meet my eye. "Perhaps it simply likes you."

"What happens if I wear it, will it come off again?"

I only care because I want to be able to test its properties.

"It should come off fine. But it has some juju and could be used as a talisman if you needed," Bellamy says.

Juju. An odd word which I determine means magic from Bellamy's usage. I probably shouldn't try to melt it down then. Probably. Idly, I wonder again where Bellamy and La Bête are from. They have the same accent and use strange vocabulary.

"Sounds useful," I say out loud.

Bellamy gives me a pained smile.

I smile at him tentatively. "Then I can...keep it?"

"You can keep it. Getting rid of it is the problem. It will follow you everywhere you go."

"But it's just a talisman?"

"For now. If it doesn't change its mind."

That sounds slightly ominous but the ring looks more and more appealing to me the longer I hold it. And I rarely have an attachment to jewelry as it's usually made of gold or silver—hardly the most interesting metals.

"The castle obviously intends it for you," he says, as I continue to look at the ring with hesitation and longing.

Bellamy straightens and approaches me. Carefully he takes the ring from me as if it has the potential to explode on him.

He takes my hand and maneuvers the ring onto my finger. It fits perfectly. I stare at it, unsettled. I don't know if Monsieur Bellamy knows it, but he has slipped the ring onto the finger that in Tierra Rica is known as the ring finger. It's where married folk wear their rings as a symbol of their eternal bond.

I can't help but notice that Bellamy has a tattoo that bands around the same finger of his hand.

"You are still forbidden to leave the castle grounds without La Bête's permission," Monsieur Bellamy says.

I nod. Talismans guide their wearer through the changing landscape of the Black Forest. Some people have a natural immunity to the displacement sorcery of the forest but most need talismans to navigate through the wilderness.

Monsieur Bellamy finally escorts me to my room. It's been three hours and I suspect I've seen less than half the castle.

"Thank you for the tour," I say politely as I open the door to my bedroom.

Monsieur Bellamy coughs.

"The examination," he says apologetically when I look at him.

"Oh," I say. I stand there stupidly.

Monsieur Bellamy waits. He studies the hallway instead of my face.

"Come in," I say.

"Thank you." Bellamy's shoulder brushes against mine as he enters my room. He smells of roses. I love the scent of roses and to smell it on Bellamy is both unsettling and soothing.

"Please lie down on the chaise, mademoiselle." He goes to a basin that's already been set up and washes his hands.

I walk over to the chaise and lie down. Light streams in through the latticework windows and throws shards of color all over my dress. I smooth the folds of my skirts down and clasp my hands together.

Monsieur Bellamy pulls the ottoman close to the sofa and sets a wide mouthed jar next to himself.

"I'm going to lift your skirts," he says.

My breath hitches. Bellamy waits for my nod before proceeding.

He raises my skirts up to my waist and taps the knee closest to him. "Open this leg towards me, please, mademoiselle."

The gesture reminds me of La Bête in my bedroom last night. I open my leg and concentrate fiercely on the ceiling.

The ceiling is covered in wood panels and intricately carved medallions.

"Raise this leg, please." He taps my other knee. I raise it. His head is bent over my sex.

My face is red.

"You are no doubt feeling very tender," he says. He sounds grim.

"Mm-hm." I'm busy counting the wood panels in the ceiling. There are intricately carved medallions in the center of each panel and from what I can tell, each one is unique.

Bellamy pulls back and unstoppers the wide mouth jar. "I'm going to rub some ointment into your woman's parts," he says. "It should soothe your aching."

He scoops the ointment into his fingers and bends over me again. My knee reflexively tries to shut. "Sorry," I blurt.

"It's all right," Monsieur Bellamy says. He puts a gentle hand on my thigh to keep it open.

His other hand parts my folds and I can't help a wince.

"You'll feel better soon," he promises.

Bellamy peers at my exposed core. His finger slides in and he rubs the ointment into the walls of my canal. The intrusion hurts but Bellamy is right—I can feel the ointment soothing my flesh as he works.

"All right, then," Monsieur Bellamy says briskly. He tugs my skirts down.

I sit up. Bellamy closes the jar and sets it on the ottoman.

"I'll leave this ointment here for you," he says. "What time do you want your dinners ready?"

I struggle to look him in the eye after he's touched me so intimately. "Whenever La Bête eats is fine."

"You'll be eating dinner alone so it can be set to whatever time is convenient for you," says Bellamy.

"Nine o'clock then," I say.

"Very well. Feel free to explore the castle but remember not to leave the grounds," he says as he rises.

"Ever?"

"Er...I only mean you must first obtain La Bête's permission."

La Bête's permission. Not Bellamy's.

"And if I just want to go outside?"

"As long as you remain on castle grounds, you may explore the gardens and courtyards. Do not leave the outer gates."

"I understand," I say.

"If you need to find me, or should you need something in particular, just say your request aloud and the castle will try to accommodate you."

I clear my throat since it's clear he thinks it's time for him to leave. "And Monsieur La Bête? When he comes back at night to...is there a specific time he will need me? Should I meet him somewhere?"

Monsieur Bellamy looks me in the eyes. "La Bête will find you."

I spend the afternoon dismantling the mantle clock that woke me this morning.

I take the clock to the study next to my bedroom and set it on the empty desk. A round, stained glass window provides the only light but there's plenty of it at this hour so it will do for now.

"I'd like some pliers please, and some turnscrews—very small ones but of varying sizes," I say into the air.

My desk rattles. I open the top drawer to find what I've requested. I happily get to work, making requests for other tools I need as I go along.

My family hates this part of me. The desire I have to take things apart and put them back together again. Even once we were living in the cottage and my skills came in useful, my siblings would always make resentful comments about how I was acting like "the help."

As if that were an insult: to be helpful.

Ahmed was one of "the help" back in Tierra Rica. An old hand who fixed things, he was at the bottom rung of a ladder that was topped by our mayordomo. But Ahmed never shooed me away when I followed him around; he never told me I was too pretty to concern myself with learning how the plumbing worked. Nor did he tell me that my obsession with testing various objects to a score of experiments just to see what would happen was useless: instead he gave me a notebook, graphite, and told me to write down my results.

Ahmed was old and wizened and ugly: the local children called him a goblin and liked to throw rocks at him. I thought he was beautiful. Despite his age, he had an air about him: like a mischievous prankster, and he guffawed like a donkey when he thought I had said or done something particularly clever. We got along grandly.

We might never had gotten away with our odd relationship under normal circumstances but this was just after my mother had died and my father was distraught and the nannies were distracted by all my siblings' demands for attention.

Ahmed taught me that anything that was broken could be put back together again—even if that meant remaking the thing from scratch and with different parts to make it stronger.

All the little turns and gears in the clock are fascinating but after I explore their workings, I turn my attention to the bellows.

I find that the wheezing of my cuckoo bird is caused by a tear in the pigskin. I also suspect the weights on the three bellows are not heavy enough to allow gravity to drop them after the first "coo" so that the second "coo" is lost.

I examine the torn bellow carefully and determine that stitching up the pigskin will not help. I need to make a new one.

"May I have some pigskin please? Or sheepskin will do. About this big." I feel silly as I gesture in the air with my forefingers about a handwidth apart but if the castle can hear my voice, then it's not a stretch to think it can see my actions.

A moment passes and then I check the desk drawer but there is nothing.

I bite my lip. Did the castle not understand?

"I need pigskin or sheepskin, about the size of my hand. I also need some scissors, a small sharp knife, a needle and thread, and some glue," I say.

I think that is clear enough but still the drawer does not produce what I've requested.

Well. I can go searching for those items in a bit. In the meantime I take apart the torn bellow with the tools I have, stretching the pigskin carefully as I note the pattern it was glued down in, in my notebook.

I'm just finishing my notes when I hear knocking.

I look out the window where daylight still pours in. So it's not La Bête. Perhaps Monsieur Bellamy has returned for something? But what?

My pulse picks up as I rise and go into my bedroom to answer the door but it is only a candelabra. It has a wooden crate in its—the appendages I think of as its hands—and it wheels into my room with a faint rattle.

I follow the candelabra into my study where it sets the wooden crate down on the desk.

I peek into the crate.

There is pigskin and the other items I requested.

"Thank you," I say to the candelabra. It nods its upper tier—head—at me but doesn't move from beside my desk.

I get back to work. I've put aside the chair since I prefer to work standing but my back eventually aches as the desk is too low, and I bring the chair back to sit in.

The candelabra—Rattler, I've started calling him in my head, for he's the same one that rattles as he rolls—stands over the desk and seems to interestedly observe all that I do.

Eventually he starts anticipating the tools and items I need and hands them to me as I go. With Rattler's help, it doesn't take long for me to finish fixing the bellow and to reassemble the cuckoo clock.

I test the clock by moving the time forward to eight o'clock and the bird comes crashing out its door.

"COO-KOO! COO-KOO!" It trumpets victoriously.

"Well," I grin at Rattler who claps his hands together. "Perhaps now I ought to build a soundproof box to keep it in."

But I end up bringing the clock back to my bedroom. I move it to the mantel of the fireplace instead of the dresser right next to my bed though.

"I wonder if I might have another bath today," I say to Rattler. He nods at me and leaves.

I have my bath and Rattler helps me into a simple green gown before leaving me alone.

The sun has set and I'm hungry. It's only six o'clock and I regret not going down for lunch earlier before nightfall.

I wonder if I should wait in my room for La Bête but I recall Monsieur Bellamy's words about how La Bête will always find me. I decide that if I must live my life always available to The Beast's urges as it suits him, then I will live my life when he is absent as it pleases me.

"I would like to go down for a snack now," I announce to my room. "I don't care what it is, I just need some sustenance. Some boiled eggs would do."

I leave my room and make my way downstairs.

The torches are lighted now that it's dark.

A flicker of unease licks my insides when I pass the murals.

I'm past the entrance hall and in the slightly larger hallway that leads to the dining room when I hear the growl.

"There you are."

I turn.

La Bête appears from behind one of the stone pillars that supports the vaulted ceiling.

My breath quickens but this time I maintain an outer facade of composure.

"Good evening, Monsieur La Bête," I say. It comes out breathier than I intended. My unease has dispelled despite my heightened adrenaline in La Bête's presence. I puzzle over this but the answer is obvious: my unease (*not* dread) was a result of my irrational fear of the *unknown* and La Bête has made his presence known.

La Bête stalks over to me. I may not fear him but he is an enormous creature and I cannot help taking a step back. He seizes me about the waist and turns me around.

He takes my hands in his large ones and places them on a pillar.

"Hold onto that," he says.

He bends me over and lifts my dress. I grit my teeth. Is this the only manner in which The Beast is going to take me?

Oiled fingers rub into my sex. At least La Bête has come prepared this time.

Despite Bellamy's ministrations and the ointment from earlier, my body hasn't recovered from the activities of the previous night and I hug the pillar for dear life as La Bête enters me from behind.

He plows me and shoots his seed deep into my womb.

Again, he cleans me with a handkerchief afterwards. This time when I rise and turn around, he is already walking away from me.

Well. I do appreciate the lack of false affection at least.

My face red and my chin high, I make my way to the dining room as I had originally intended.

A spread of boiled eggs, nuts, fruit, and bread awaits me.

I eat mechanically as I feel La Bête's seed slowly seep out of me and soil my skirts.

I decide I'm going to have to start wearing drawers.

4
BEAUTY

LA BÊTE FINDS me again later when I'm in the library and bends me over a table and takes me there. Then he comes to me in the night and takes me again. He leaves and visits me again near morning. I wonder why he doesn't just stay in my bed or bring me to his.

My days at La Bête's castle pass in this manner:

I breakfast with Monsieur Bellamy and sometimes he shows me a new bit of the castle, or more often we split to spend the day in our own endeavors.

I spend my days working on my catalogue on the properties of metal, but with all my free time now that I'm not doing all the chores around the family cottage, I soon go through all the bits of metal I've already collected.

So I take to reading or exploring. I disassemble clocks, and inspect dumbwaiters, the plumbing, and an old bell pulley system that must've been in use before the castle sorcery made it obsolete.

I find the plumbing of particular interest and Rattler and I poke about the pipes in the basement of the castle while I fantasize of running hot water directly into my room. The water is already directed there for the water closet so it wouldn't be such a stretch to divert it for my baths. I'd have to think of a way to heat it though.

As soon as night falls La Bête finds me wherever I am (I don't avoid him, exactly, but I don't make it easy for him by waiting in one place either), and takes me. I find out that my first night where he only used me twice was an anomaly. Since then La Bête always takes me three to five times in the night.

He never brings me to his room. He never sleeps in mine. I doze next to him in my bed sometimes but I think he just watches me while I sleep, and then wakes me to take me again, (and again) before he's finally sated enough to leave me and return to his bed.

Each time he turns me over and ruts me from behind like an animal.

I find that I actually don't mind it so much, especially now that the initial soreness has passed. It's only that...well, I'm curious is all. I was the sort of child that, upon being taught how to skip rocks across water, meticulously collected rocks of all different sizes and various shapes, and tested and noted my results for skipping each one.

My methods have only grown more meticulous with age.

Of course, sexual intimacy with La Bête is not an experiment...but as long as I am here for a year...and I'm having sex with him anyway...

One other constant that I have contemplated measuring is the occasional odd feeling of unease—anxiousness—perhaps even the touch of fear (not dread), I feel when exploring the castle on my own.

But such ethereal emotions are hard to quantify, and when I go looking for these feelings, they elude me. They only catch me off guard, unaware, when I am not paying attention.

I've taken to noting these instances in my notebook, a preliminary step to setting up a proper experiment, but so far I have been unable to discern a basic pattern beyond the fact that it usually happens at night, and only when I am alone.

I've noticed it doesn't happen when I'm in my room which I think supports the conclusion that there is no "other" presence in the castle, malignant or otherwise, only my own irrational fear flaring up.

That is a part of why I deliberately choose to leave my room every night. To defy my irrational fear. Or invite more evidence to support that I should do a proper experiment of some sort.

One night La Bête finds me in the music room where I'm (very badly) picking out a mournful tune on a guitar.

I falter when I see him but he doesn't immediately seize me for once, only leans against the doorframe and nods. So I continue my clumsy strumming. After a few chords and a shy look at La Bête, I begin to sing.

My voice is no great instrument—it's too husky for that—but I have perfect pitch which always impressed our musical tutors, and the melancholy tune I've chosen suits my voice.

"Your voice is beautiful," La Bête says when I'm done. I appreciate that he doesn't lie about my guitar playing.

"Thank you," I say politely, more for his patience than his compliment. My voice is like my physical beauty: it's just something I was born with so it always puzzles me when people think I've accomplished something by having a beautiful voice or a beautiful face. Although I suppose some skill and training went into modulating my voice.

I decide it's a better compliment than saying I'm beautiful.

I rise and return the guitar to its setting.

I'm startled when La Bête grabs me (though I shouldn't be), and I clutch his arm instead of turning around and bending over like he wants me to.

"Wait, don't," I blurt out.

I crane my neck up at his face and see his eyes widen. The black pupils dilate within La Bête's cinnamon irises and his nostrils flare.

"Are you...refusing me?"

His arm tightens around my waist and I suddenly realize this is the closest I've been with my face to his. I smell that whiff of forest he always carries about him: the sharp scent of juniper trees over earthy loam, and warm animalic musk.

"I'm not," I say tartly. "I just wonder if we can't...do it another way."

His warm breath stirs my hair as he stares down at me.

"In a different position," I clarify, in case he doesn't understand. "Perhaps...facing each other?"

"You would look at The Beast while he fucks you?"

I think he says it like that to make me flinch, but I meet his stare straight on.

"I would look at you while you fuck me," I say.

La Bête growls.

He backs me into the wall. A painting crashes to the ground. He raises my skirts and—

"What is this?" he says in a deeply affronted voice. His clawed fingertips carefully finger the skimpy drawers covering my nether region.

"They're called 'panties,'" I say. "There's a seamstress in a small hamlet that makes all this—"

Lingerie, I'm about to say, but the sound of La Bête tearing through the panties interrupts me.

Oh well. I can always ask the wardrobe for more.

La Bête has already yanked down his trousers and he tosses me up and says, "Put your legs around my waist."

I do. The wall and his hand supports my back while his other hand guides his cock to my entrance. It's the first time I've seen the actual penetration act and I'm mesmerized at the sight of his large member disappearing into me.

La Bête groans.

"You forgot the oil," I gasp.

"Don't need it anymore," he grunts out.

He's right. He slides right in. My body has learned to lubricate itself in defense. He pulls out and smashes into me again.

My hands are on his shoulders but I feel off balance with my entire body resting only on his thrusting cock so I throw my arms around his neck.

La Bête's eyes sear me as he pounds into my slit. My back is going to be bruised tomorrow. Other parts are going to be bruised tomorrow.

With La Bête lifting me up I'm nearly eye-level with his face for once. Our noses are practically touching. His mouth is slightly open as he uses me and I can see his teeth gleaming. He has pointed fangs on the top and bottom. I wonder what they are for. Does he eat raw meat? Does he have to hunt like an animal?

"Am I satisfying your curiosity, *Beauty*?" He bares his teeth at me. "Does it please you to look upon the horrible, monstrous, *beast*?"

"I wouldn't say...it pleases me...per se," I gasp out in response. Something about this new position makes me feel so odd. "But of course...it's only natural...to be curious."

It's hard to keep track of my thoughts and to say them aloud while La Bête is thrusting but I try to finish answering him. "So yes...I suppose I am pleased...to have my curiosity...satisfied."

La Bête stops. His arm behind my back tightens. His other arm reaches across my bottom and I squeak as he hitches me closer and tighter against him. I'm squished between the hard wall and his harder body. His cock spears my center and somehow I feel it all the way up through the tips of my breasts, the top of my head, and down to my toes.

Instead of thrusting, La Bête grinds his hips against me in slow circles. He's widening me and it should hurt but instead I feel...unsettled.

"What are you doing?" I ask, trying to sound normal and polite, and not like his cock is unraveling my body.

"I'm satisfying your curiosity," he says. He eyes bore into me. They are warm cinnamon once more, and they practically glow.

"Oh," I breathe. Not in response to him, but in reaction to all the chaotic signals my body is flinging at me.

Then he starts to pound into me again.

I clutch his mane of hair in my hands and bury my face into his neck.

I'm amazed at how slippery I am, how easily La Bête slides me up and down on his huge cock. I flex my legs and help him sink deeper into me each time.

It still feels like his cock is punching me in my womb but instead of being painful, or only painful, it's also making me feel...relaxed? No! I'm the opposite of relaxed! It's like I have a clenched knot deep inside of me and his cock is forcing it smooth, like a pestle grinding something to pieces inside of a mortar. And the little bits are going to fly off at any moment...

My eyelids flutter at the sensation. I realize I'm moaning continuously. (How strange when the previous times hurt so much more and I was able to keep quiet!)

The friction against my inner lips is unbearable—and then my core catches aflame.

A guttural moan falls from my throat as the flame brightens and spreads. It rushes throughout my whole body and I cry out.

My sex clenches around La Bête's cock and it's like the rest of my body decides it can let go. My arms release La Bête's neck and my legs slide down his waist. La Bête catches me though, he draws me in tighter while he ruts through my body's surrender.

My body flails loosely against him—I probably knock my head on the wall behind me a few times because La Bête suddenly buries a hand in my hair. He uses his other hand to prop my bottom up against him and presses into me. His cock thrusts deeply into me, so deep I think it's going to go through me and through the wall behind me.

His hot seed gushes into me as I shudder around him.

Suddenly I can hear our gasping breaths in the still air.

Gods and saints, he smells *good*. And he's so *warm*.

No. No, he doesn't smell good. He smells like an animal that's been roaming the woods. And of course he's warm: he's a great big hairy beast.

His cock flexes inside me and I whimper.

"Shh..." He makes soothing sounds as he gently removes himself.

He keeps a hand on me to prop me against the wall but I make a noise of protest and he withdraws.

I slide down the wall till my bottom hits the floor. My head falls back against the wall and I realize he is staring down at me.

I turn my face away.

It's not enough. I bring my knees up and bury my face.

"Beauty?" His voice is still rough with his spent pleasure.

I try to contain my own rough breathing. "Yes?"

He doesn't say anything and finally I look up.

His eyes are fathomless. "Are you all right?" he says.

"Yes." My voice is brisk though my throat is oddly prickly.

I look away from him again.

"Are you sure?"

I realize my legs are still exposed and push my skirts down though I'm still messy with his seed.

He offers his hand and I take it.

La Bête pulls me to my feet—too hard and I bump into him. He grabs my waist to steady me. I yank my hand away and stumble back.

He doesn't say anything, just watches me.

I back away, unable to look into his cinnamon brown eyes.

"Please," I say, unsure of what I am asking.

I turn and flee.

If there is indeed a malignant presence that watches over me, it leaves me alone that night as I escape to my room.

I suppose even malignant presences must choose their battles.

5
BEAUTY

I'M IN A ROOM full of clocks and a bird smashes out of one of them, screaming "Coo-koo, coo-koo," and then suddenly birds smash out of all the clocks, and they all shriek, and then water bursts out from the clocks—(where does the water come from?)—gushing in huge sprays across the room that soak me, and then someone seizes me from behind and covers my mouth and whispers in my ear, "Coo-koo."

I wake with a gasp and sit up in my huge bed. My eyes search out the mantel clock and I see the time: 9:01.

I adjusted the cuckoo clock to the later time since La Bête's demands on my body keep me up at night.

Now it rouses me in the morning and signals dinner time at night.

I arise for the day and breakfast by myself for Monsieur Bellamy is nowhere to be found. I'm relieved for I feel on edge and need some solitude to sort myself out.

I return to my study to work on my current project.

Pipes lay everywhere: different lengths and colors including copper, red brass (which is really brass mixed with copper), yellow brass, silver steel, as well as other parts like fittings and valves.

I'm designing a new supply line for hot water. I've discovered there are underground hot springs beneath the castle from which the candelabra have been hauling up water for my baths.

I'm poring over my latest sketch on the floor (for there's no room left on my desk) when Rattler comes into my study. I've told him and the other candelabra they may enter my rooms as they wish, without knocking.

Rattler tugs on my sleeves and rolls back to the door. His rattle is more discreet now: I took a look at his rolling mechanism and tightened a bolt that was coming loose but I put in an extra washer so that he could keep the sound as an ornamental touch. He seemed pleased that the issue was fixed and doesn't seem to mind the continued rattling.

Anyway, I'm not convinced he couldn't magically make the sound go away if he really wanted to.

Rattler impatiently rolls back and forth by the door. He obviously wants me to follow him.

I rise.

He rolls down toward the old nursery as soon as I step out into the hallway.

I haven't been in this suite since Monsieur Bellamy first showed it to me weeks ago.

He's here now and greets me with a bow and curt words that do not do justice to the sight that awaits me: "Your new work suite, Mademoiselle Beauty."

I gape.

Bellamy stands next to a massive workbench that takes up the middle of the room. Light pours in through a window that takes up nearly an entire wall from about waist high, up to the ceiling. No stained glass here—the window is so clear I can see the precise outline of trees outside. A long table is built along another wall, with tools hanging above it and an assortment of drawers stacked underneath, presumably storing more knick knacks.

"All this..." I gaze around in amazement and uncertainty. "This is for me?"

It cannot be.

But I can't help running my hand along the wooden tabletop. It's almost a foot deep. Incredibly sturdy.

"All this," says Bellamy, "and the two connected rooms so you can use them for additional tools and storage."

I stare at him, stunned. "But why?" I should be grateful but the words blurt out of me: I sound suspicious, demanding.

I drop my eyes and try again. "I mean, it's very nice." *Nice* is such a weak word for how perfect it is.

My eyes have landed again on the workbench and I notice it is placed high enough that I can comfortably work standing up. I see stools for me to sit or lean on when I get tired.

"Why?" I repeat.

Bellamy looks uncomfortable. "Because," he says.

He's usually more eloquent.

"It's a gift from La Bête," he adds.

At the mention of La Bête's name my mind goes straight to what happened in the music room.

Being pinned and rutted against a wall. My intense reaction.

My face flames.

Is this a *reward* for my especially good performance?

"How thoughtful," I say in a strangled voice. I sound like I mean the opposite.

Bellamy eyes me with alarm.

Flashes of the intercourse with La Bête are still hitting my senses. I cannot stop them. His eyes, dark when angry, warm otherwise. His heat. The softness of his hair. I can practically smell him now. The intense—I admit to myself—*pleasure* as I came. I don't remember how his face looked afterward (I was busy trying not to meet his gaze) but I imagine it now, filled with that smug expression males get when they think they've bested you.

I *hate* him.

"Yes," I say. My voice has smoothed. It's silky now with venom. "I'll have to thank him later. I'm sure he'll *appreciate* that."

"Ah," says Bellamy. "Er, that may only make him uncomfortable. Consider your thanks already noted."

His words give me pause. I consider that this is actually a gift from Bellamy and that La Bête had nothing to do with it. After all, how would La Bête even know of my hobbies if Bellamy hadn't told him?

But then what reason does Bellamy have to treat me with such kindness?

I eye him. He looks more flustered under my scrutiny than I've ever seen him. Is he...attracted to me? Well, every man that is attracted to women is attracted to my physical beauty...but is he attracted to *me*?

He's very good looking but that's worthless. He seems kind which means more. If I'm honest with myself I do find Bellamy very attractive but there's nothing I intend to do about it.

I already have La Bête to deal with and even if I didn't, I don't want to waste my time with beaus when I have plans for my life.

I thank Bellamy again: it's honest gratitude but I'm carefully reserved when expressing it.

I don't want to encourage the man in any way.

He leaves me alone to organize my new work in solitude.

Which is just fine. I like nothing more than being left alone.

I'm in the library when the sun sets.

I'm not reading, or browsing for a book. I'm looking out the window. More clear glass.

The valley that lies below the castle is awash in orange and red, like a fiery sea.

"What are you thinking?"

La Bête has found me.

His sudden appearances no longer surprise me and I don't bother turning.

"In the land of Kurys, the sun sets over the sea. I would like to see it one day," I say matter-of-factly. I add, "Also, the trees have lost their leaves. Soon it will be winter. We ought to go to the nearby villages for supplies before the snow sets in."

"We have everything we need in the castle," La Bête growls. "There's no need to leave."

"Still," I say absently. "There may be a few things I wish to obtain."

"You need my permission."

I finally turn.

"Is that a gauntlet you've thrown?" I ask mildly.

"No," he says. "Just reminding you of the...necessary protocol."

I raise my brow. Today La Bête wears the same clothes he does everyday. His mane of hair is brushed and shiny. Something about the meticulous care he takes to dress so neatly tugs at me. No! Why should it? It just means he is vain. Besides, the candelabras probably dress him. I ignore the voice in the back of my head that observes that their "hands" would not be able to do up his buttons.

"Where did you hear of this land of Kurys, and why would you want to go to there?" La Bête says gruffly.

"An old friend of mine was from Kurys." I touch my necklace where Ahmed's coin is strung.

"'Was?'"

"He died," I say repressively. I don't want to talk about Ahmed. Not to The Beast.

"I'm sorry," La Bête says.

I acknowledge his statement with a nod.

We stand there awkwardly, me by the window, La Bête in the center of the room.

He clears his throat and strides over to me.

The scent of the forest overwhelms me as it always does when he is near. It makes me want to sink my hands into the earth—or into The Beast.

He stops short of touching me.

I realize I've stepped away from him. My hip digs into a desk next to the window.

As a matter of fact, it's the same desk he took me over in one of our earlier ruttings this week.

I gesture nervously towards it. "Should I...?"

"No. The couch."

I look around La Bête to the couch behind him.

"Lie on it," says La Bête.

He moves aside for me and I make my way over.

I sit gingerly on the couch, then lie back. I'm reminded of Bellamy.

He hasn't tended to me on the couch since those first couple days, which is just as well.

My body—specifically, my sex—is embarrassingly wet almost all the time now. Sometimes just walking from room to room and feeling the slide of my nether lips running together is enough to make me feel...ready for La Bête's attentions. In truth I haven't needed the oil for a few days now though last night in the music room is the first time La Bête hasn't used it since the beginning.

La Bête places a heavy knee on the couch next to my legs.

I turn my face to the side. Our last coupling is still fresh in my mind though I try to banish the memory.

"Perhaps you would prefer over the couch," I hear La Bête say.

I sit up. "Whatever you wish," I say woodenly. I'm trying not to think of what is to come. Of how I may react. Again.

La Bête rises me and maneuvers me around the couch.

I follow compliantly and automatically bend over the back of the couch.

I expect to feel his hands rustling up my skirts so I jump when I feel them on my shoulders instead.

"You're very tense," says La Bête.

"Sorry," I say. I clutch the back of the couch. Now I'm reminded of our first coupling when I arrived at the castle, wet and bedraggled.

I endured rather than enjoyed the taking of my virginity but if La Bête were to take me now in the exact same way—

I suck in a deep breath to try and calm myself. I'm a jumble of emotions and sensitive nerve endings.

I'm not even sure of what I want or don't want right now. I need a moment to think. But La Bête requires my services: this is why I'm here.

I realize La Bête hasn't touched me or said anything for a while.

When I look over my shoulder he is farther away from me than I thought he would be. He must have stepped back.

I rise in startlement.

"Are you all right?" I ask.

I'm already stepping forward and reaching for him when I feel the echo of my words and action in memory.

My eyes flash to his and I know that at that moment he is reliving the exact same memory of when he couldn't hold himself back any longer and took me in the hallway that led to my bedroom.

La Bête jerks back though my hand has stopped in midair.

I realize he is breathing like he has just climbed up the mountain to this castle.

Without a single word of explanation, La Bête turns on his heels and leaves me in the library.

Alone.

Again.

6
BEAUTY

I MOPE ABOUT the library for a bit, fidgety and unable to relax.

Finally, I choose a book and settle onto the couch.

A few minutes later my face is red and my breath uneven. I close the book.

Not in the mood to research my project and looking more for escape than enlightenment, I chose a red leather bound book with gold letters on the spine proclaiming: Fausta Borja's Fairy Tales.

But I'm taken off guard by the intimate acts portrayed within its covers, as well as the level of minute detail the author discloses of those said acts.

I decide the book deserves closer scrutiny in a more private place. I take it upstairs to my room where I...scrutinize the first few stories.

It's late when I fall asleep, exhausted and vaguely dissatisfied. La Bête has not paid me a visit.

The next day, I wake from my restless sleep with a headache.

Bellamy is nowhere to be found at breakfast.

For some reason, this puts me out.

I pour myself some coffee and wonder what Bellamy has got up to. He wasn't at breakfast yesterday morning and then presented me with the gift of the workroom later.

Is he preparing something now? Did La Bête put him up to it?

I hear a distinctive rattle and Rattler appears in the dining room—he has a stack of books.

He deposits them next to my eggs and backs (I've discovered that he does have a front he always presents himself with) away from me with a bow.

There's a note on top of the stack: I pluck it.

Beauty,

After last night it occurred to me that you might make use of these books. There are more in the library but I selected a few I thought you might enjoy.

It's unsigned.

My face flames as I remember the sort of book I was reading the night before and wonder if this is a recommended reading list based on that one—but I settle down when I reach for the top of the stack and see its title: *The People and Customs of the Land of Kurys.*

I go through the stack: a catalogue of the flora and fauna of Kurys, a book on Kurys's history of architecture, a translation of a work by a famous Kurysian philosopher, another translation of a work of poetry, and lastly a book of Kurysian fables: *1001 Nights.*

I sit back in my chair, flummoxed.

The note isn't signed but it seems clear that La Bête wrote it. He is the one I mentioned Kurys to.

I settle in to read the book on architecture, and wonder what La Bête's game is.

I'm invigorated after a leisurely morning of reading. I spend the afternoon tweaking my hot water infrastructure designs. The sun is beginning to angle down in my workroom when I decide to set off for the outdoors for a well deserved breath of fresh air.

I'm forbidden to leave without La Bête's permission but the castle's outdoor grounds are vast.

I've explored two of the gardens thus far: one is a no-nonsense herb garden, and the other is a sparse yet beautiful affair. Instead of neat rows or groupings of flowers, it features single exotic plants surrounded by rocks or sand or twigs so that they look almost like strange creatures in a distant ocean or landscape. It's unlike anything I've seen before.

But there's a third garden I've recently discovered.

It's brisk out and I tug my cloak closer around me as I step along a winding path. It leads me to a maze constructed of tall hedges twice my height. Inside the maze, the air is more still, the cold less biting. My world is reduced to the lush green of the hedges, and the brilliant sky.

I made quick work of the maze the other day but spent extra time memorizing the whole of it so as to truly appreciate the work of whoever engineered the puzzle.

This time I follow the most direct route to my prize.

The scent hits me before I find the center.

I eagerly navigate my way through the last turn and there I see it.

One last hedge lies at the center of the maze: it's circular and uniformly green like the other hedges, giving no hint to its inner lushness.

I circle around it, looking for the little gap I found the other day. There it is: I duck and squeeze through the narrow entrance.

Bright, blooming spots of red surround me: I'm in the secret rose garden.

Unlike the two other gardens I've seen, there is no discernable order to the rose garden here, besides the encircling hedge. Bushes grow wildly and with abandon. There is no standard of size: some rosebushes are small—small as the lapdogs that are famous in Arcadia, and others are monstrously huge and overgrown and overlap with others.

And also unlike the other gardens, where the coming winter has stripped them of their colorful blossoms, this rose garden blooms in defiance of the cold.

A single stone bench is haphazardly placed in the garden. It's not in the center, it's just off to the side like someone threw it in and left it where it landed. I like that it too seems to have grown from the garden. For all I know in this magical place, it did.

I lay back on the bench. The fading sun bleeds streaks of pink, orange, and lavender through the sky.

I soak in the lush scent of the roses, the chill in the air. Peace settles over me.

A whiff of junipers alerts me to his presence. I turn my head.

La Bête lumbers over to a clear spot not far from my bench. He wears a cloak over his usual outfit and simply sprawls back on the ground and stares up at the sky. Eventually I turn my eyes back up as well.

But I hear his breaths: they echo in the wind that caresses my skin.

We say not a word but I feel La Bête's presence acutely.

The tranquil air of the garden seeps deep inside me, and in turn, it's as if my being extends out of me, acknowledging no bounds of flesh and skin. I inhabit the rose garden as surely as I inhabit my blood and bone. I consume the dying sunlight with the green of my leaves. My red petals exhale scented breath and La Bête inhales it. He is soothed. I know it somehow—how can I not know when he inhabits my rose garden?

I feel La Bête's person as clearly as if notes of music were playing in my ear. The melody of La Bête's mood as he relaxes is strangely familiar to me. I try and place where I've heard this melody before but I am distracted by a discordant chord: a gossamer web of malice veiling La Bête's core.

I examine this web: it is a separate thing from La Bête. It comes not from within him, but was laid over him. It doesn't belong there. I try and tug the web off and it's slippery and slides around a bit before settling back around him. Determination floods me. I want that thing off of him.

La Bête stands abruptly.

I realize I've sat up and am staring at him expectantly.

But he turns away from me and lopes out of the garden without a word.

My breathing is hard and unsteady. My connection to the garden is suddenly severed and the disorientation leaves me feeling dizzy. It takes me a few minutes to steady myself, find my balance once more inside the limited boundaries of my skin.

The sky has darkened. The sun has probably sunk below the horizon.

And then I understand that this is the first time I've seen La Bête out in the light of day.

7
BEAUTY

I LIE IN MY enormous bed, alone for the second night in a row.

My reverie in the rose garden has cleared my head. I see a couple things now with clarity.

One: I hesitate to call it a "malignant presence" but something plagues this castle, and La Bête. I have seen it visualized as a gossamer web that traps his soul.

Two: I can now admit that I was perturbed by my sexual encounter with La Bête in the music room the other night.

I have erroneously viewed myself as somewhat of a martyr: a beautiful maiden, sacrificing herself for her family. Nobly enduring her suffering under The Beast.

But what sort of sacrifice is it if I feel the most intense physical pleasure of my life? What sort of martyr am I when my "enemy" is not a vicious monster but simply a strange looking man of average churlishness? A man who I find magnetically attractive and who, in less than a week has shown more consideration for me and my interests (in his own boorish way), than my family has in my entire life.

And what exactly have I saved my family from? A life of cleaning up after themselves and doing honest work for a living?

Most laughable of all in my deranged fantasy of martyrdom is the plethora of ulterior motives I have hidden from everyone, including myself. I wanted to escape my family. I have fierce ambitions that could never have been fulfilled if I had stayed under their guidance.

I'm not a martyr, I'm a gambler.

And if I want to win, it's time to take some risks.

"I never see you out during the day," I say. "Yesterday was the first time."

La Bête grunts.

I've come across him again in the rose garden. This time he was already there when I ducked through the bushes into the inner sanctuary. La Bête is sitting on what I've come to think of as "my" bench.

He did not visit me last night. That's two nights in a row he's avoided me.

I sit down next to La Bête. He stiffens. His hair is a bit tangled today and I note that some of the buttons on his jacket were done askew. It's midday but the sky is grey and heavy with clouds and the purple air feels like dusk.

I'm curious about La Bête's diurnal habits—does he normally sleep through the day? Or is there another explanation for his usual absence? Curiosity usually inspires me to ask what my family would consider rude questions, but right now I want to put La Bête at ease.

"Thank you for the books you sent me," I say instead.

Another grunt. I'm not sure he's even heard me. He's staring straight forward with a pained, almost glazed look in his eyes.

I put my hand on his bare forearm. His sleeves are rolled up and the considerably numerous hairs on his arm seem to stand up on edge. "It's fascinating to read about other lands," I say. "Though not as fascinating as visiting them, I'm sure."

Yet another grunt. He's starting to sound panicked.

I'm debating whether I should bring up the topics of other lands he may have visited when La Bête hurls himself off the bench.

I stare at him in surprise as he bounds across the rose garden and gets about as far from me as he possibly can, squeezed between the outer hedge and a trellis which supports an uncomfortably thorny looking rose vine.

He stares back at me from behind the safety of the thorny trellis.

"You must like roses," he says. It's an innocuous supposition that sounds, to my rational ear, like an accusation. He goes on in this vein, firing off each line like a tense rifleman fires warning shots from behind cover. Stay back, the shots say. "You requested your father to bring you one. You visit this garden. You wear a coin engraved with a rose around your neck."

I rise from the bench.

"*You* must like roses," I retort. "You have a rose garden, you spend time here, and you threatened my father's life when he dared to pluck one."

"This is *my* garden," The Beast snarls.

I approach La Bête. "If you don't want me trespassing in here, you should've mentioned that it's forbidden. I can leave you alone."

61

"No." This is said as forcefully as the rest. "Stay."

I'm in front of the trellis he's hiding behind. I stare at him through the mass of green tendrils. La Bête looks unsure of whether he wants to attack me, or run away.

He closes his eyes. I let him maintain his distance, with the rose bush between us.

"The scents here soothe me," La Bête says. His eyes are still closed. "Besides their magical properties, I can almost imagine, here, that I am among others. Among humanity."

I blink. First things first. "You imagine the roses are like people? I think you have been living alone in this castle for too long."

The Beast is silent. I taste the hurt in the air, and regret my words.

But then La Bête opens his eyes and speaks.

"I believe it's in Kurys where they believe that the scent of roses symbolizes human souls," he says. His words may seem like a rebuke after mine but he recites them like an offering.

He continues. "When I am here I imagine that I am surrounded by the souls of all those I once knew. Not just the ones I loved. People I've hated. People I don't even remember meeting. Before the curse I knew so many people. I had no idea."

This is the first La Bête has confirmed that there is a curse. I'm excited for I believe this curse could be what I envisioned as a web trapping La Bête, but I'm also in thrall to La Bête's unusual monologue, so I don't interrupt. This is the most I've ever heard him speak.

"I would never have guessed that after all this time it is not my lover I miss most, or my parents who are long dead. I miss the baker just as much. I remember an argument I once had with her when she changed her recipe for beignets—I

remember it nearly word for word—but not her name. I
relive that argument sometimes just to remind myself what
it's like to have normal connections to the outside world—
connections that aren't just desperate folk who want to
borrow money. And then there was the milkman. The postal
worker who delivered our mail."

I don't know what these people are—milkmen and
postal workers—but La Bête's words affect me. I can feel the
black hole of loneliness inside him—if I'm honest, it's inside
me as well.

"And the women," La Bête says. "Every woman who
has accepted an invitation to spend a year in the monster's
castle. I'm a blight in their lives and each of them is as
precious to me as the scent of these sacred roses."

His voice turns low, almost imperceptible but carried
over to me between stems and leaves and blossoms.

"I truly *am* the monster they say I am. I wasn't at first
but look at me. Those women couldn't wait to get away and
here I am, imagining that their poor souls are still here,
trapped with me."

He stops speaking. But my mind whirls and I know
that it has been swept up in the exact same line of thought
as his:

A part of my soul will be left behind to soothe him
when I've moved on.

I'm not sure which part of that sentiment disturbs me.

"It was my friend Ahmed who was from Kurys," I say.
"He gifted me with this coin. I was a child, and he an old
man but we were connected in that rare way that some
disparate people are."

I touch the engraved coin around my neck.

"I didn't learn the significance of it till after Ahmed
died. It's a symbol of the Banu Warda: they're a group of

scholars from Dar al-Sakan recognized for their particular brilliance."

"Dar al-Sakan: the university?"

"Yes." It's the most famous learning institution in the world. The prestige of being a scholar there is high, but the prestige of being one of the Banu Warda is unparalleled.

"Was Ahmed one of your tutors?" Clearly, La Bête is both impressed and incredulous that a famed scholar from Dar al-Sakan could be a mere children's tutor.

I snort. "Ahmed was one of our hands. He fixed things about our estate in Tierra Rica and lived in a little shack. He never once told me he'd been a scholar."

"Incredible."

"When Ahmed gave me this coin, he told me that if I ever found my way to his home, that I would find welcome there, with this. He made me promise that if I remained unhappy at home, that I would leave for Kurys. I found out more after he died. The Banu Warda each receive only one of these coins and they bestow it upon someone they've closely mentored. This coin signifies that Ahmed chose me as his protégé. And it guarantees me a scholarship to study at Dar al-Sakan."

"But that's..."

"Incredible," I finish for him. I can tell that La Bête understands the honor, that it impresses him. I am gratified, not for my own ego (or not only for my own ego), but because no one else I've told has cared.

"I'm amazed that you remain in the Black Forest lands," La Bête says.

"Well," I say. "Passage across the sea costs money, money my family doesn't have." I add belatedly, "Didn't have."

"That's why you're here," La Bête says, "here with me. You accepted my offer so you could go to Kurys when your year is over?"

"Oh no," I say. "That money is for my family. They don't support the idea of me going across the sea to some foreign university. They expect me to stay here and marry."

"Marry?"

"Or at least they *did* want me to marry. I expect they thought my beauty would bring in a rich suitor and that they could live above the poor means to which they never grew accustomed to when my father lost his fortune."

"I see."

La Bête's voice carries a frost so tangible that for a moment, I think I see crystalline shards form on the vines between us. Certainly a small fraction of the five chests of gold my family now possesses would cover my passage to Kurys. But they've made it clear they will not support my dreams of attending the university.

"It's all right," I tell him. "I have a plan to get there."

"You do?"

"Yes. Step one was getting away from my family. I've done that."

"What's step two?"

"Step two, I'm still formulating. Recently I've been considering becoming a courtesan."

Silence.

I hurry to explain myself in case La Bête is doubtful of this course of action, or the wisdom of me pursuing it in light of my current level of proficiency.

"I'm beautiful so I expect that will interest a number of men to begin with. As for my bedroom skills, it wouldn't be fair to judge them as they are now," I say. "I was relatively inexperienced when I came to you after all, and you've been, erm, what is the term they use? 'Wham bam—'"

"*Wham bam—?*"

"'Thank you, mademoiselle!'" I finish triumphantly as I remember.

More silence.

"But," I say tentatively as I edge around the trellis, "given all the time that we have left together, I don't see why I can't build up an impressive skill set. Assuming you're willing."

Apparently La Bête has lost his skills to make speech.

I capitalize upon his silence and spring my attack.

I touch his arm.

I lean into his warmth.

I tilt my face up towards his.

When he still stands there, unmoving as stone, looking down at me, I take the last step forward and press my mouth to his in a kiss.

La Bête comes alive.

He growls deep from his throat.

His arms come up around me, hard, strong, vise-like. I ought to be scared that he'll crush me but I'm excited.

We've copulated numerous times, all over the castle, and yet this is our first kiss: my mouth to his.

La Bête's lips press bruisingly upon mine. My lips part and his tongue dances with mine.

His mouth is searingly hot. Our teeth mash in that first desperate kiss as I try to invade his mouth in turn. His fangs give me pause but I gain entry into his mouth and revel in the slide of our tongues tangling together.

I clutch at his mane, at his beard, and the crush of my skin to his sets off explosions of his scent in my nostrils.

I twist my face against his, rub my cheek into his beard, intent to mark him as surely as he marks me.

I realize I'm being carried. La Bête holds my legs around his waist as he walks, and his cock is hot and urgent through his britches.

I bite his ear and press my mound tighter against his hardness but La Bête lifts me away.

He sets me on the bench on my back.

Eagerly, I lift my skirts but instead of undoing his britches, La Bête falls to his knees in the dirt.

"What—*oh*." My breath leaves me as La Bête's hot mouth covers my sex through the panties I continue to wear on a regular basis.

Right now I'm not sure if I'm glad of the material that separates me from direct contact with La Bête's tongue, or curse it.

My sex comes alive as La Bête breathes onto it. I arch back and moan. My skin feels tight, my nipples chafe against my dress.

La Bête's fingers run across the edge of my panties, right along the sensitive ridge next to my sex. The pads of his fingers skim the thatch of hair that surrounds my folds, back and forth, back and forth as I shiver and arch my back farther.

La Bête's hands jerk against my pelvis and I hear a rip. Another set of panties, ruined.

La Bête's mouth locks onto my sex and my mind goes blank, ruined panties forgotten.

His tongue delves into my folds. His tongue is large, rough, and scratchy, and it scrapes against every nerve ending along my core.

La Bête runs the tip of his fingers along my inner petals, traces my slippery desire up to the nub of pleasure.

All it takes is a gentle press and I arch my sex against his mouth in release.

I cry and hear a satisfied chuckle—I feel the hum of it too, down there against my lips.

I protest when La Bête continues to lap at my sensitive sex.

"I would taste you," I say.

La Bête shoots to his feet so fast I feel the disturbance in the air. Or is that the wind? I feel a cool droplet fall on my cheek and realize my face is hot. My body burns with desire.

So does La Bête's. His desire is more obviously apparent: he's already undone his trousers and his cock sticks straight out of his body. The sight of the large blunt phallus bobbing in the air is almost comical—certainly if passion wasn't my foremost emotion at the moment, I might even laugh.

I sit up from the bench and then I do have to laugh, a little, when he swiftly maneuvers in front of me and presents his cock some mere centimeters from my face.

La Bête glares down at me, but I see the desperate plea in the look and take mercy on him.

I grasp La Bête's cock. He groans—the noise fills the air so dramatically I have to laugh again.

"Beauty," La Bête growls, equal parts warning and plea.

His desperation amuses and titillates me so I take my time as I pull back on his foreskin till the crown of his penis is revealed. I lean forward and tentatively touch my tongue to him.

La Bête whimpers.

I'm eager to taste him but I go slowly as I drag my tongue against the tiny aperture at the tip of his bulging crown.

Precum coats my tongue and I swirl it around the head of his cock.

La Bête groans again but my mirth is rapidly receding in the face of his obvious passion. My own desire rises again and I feel my swollen sex throb.

I grind my greedy sex into the bench as I explore La Bête's cock with my mouth.

My skirts are still rucked up about my thighs and I see La Bête's eyes glaze over as he sees my legs rubbing against each other.

He pulls back. I make a noise of protest as he lifts me off the bench.

"I need to taste you again," he says.

But this time he lies on the bench himself.

"Get on top of me," he says, and turns me the other way when I try.

I end up over him with his cock poking my face and his head between my legs. He throws my skirts out of the way, winds his hands around my thighs and pulls my center to his mouth.

Droplets of rain hit my bare bottom but I don't care. I lower my mouth over La Bête's cock and take him in.

I've heard from my sisters and read in the erotic fairy tales of how women can take cocks deep into their mouths—all the way into their throats but whenever I try to go that far I can't control my gagging. I settle for massaging the base of his enormous erection with my hands as I bob my head enthusiastically up and down at its tip.

My method seems adequate, for La Bête constantly interrupts his worship of my sex to groan into my inner thighs. My own desire builds up and teeters on the edge as he continues this pattern of licking and fingering, caressing and groaning his hot breath across all my sensitive parts.

To be honest I felt a bit scandalized when La Bête first poked his head between my legs, a little shocked by the blatant sexuality of the gesture.

But soon I find myself clenching my thighs around his head: his tongue presses insistently against my nub and his fingers slide easily in and out of my slit.

When I explode with release I jerk my mouth off of La Bête's and scream in pleasure. My hands clutch reflexively at his cock.

I realize that cold rain is pouring down on us when the gobs of La Bête's hot seed hits my face.

My scream ends with gulping gasps. When I close my mouth I taste his salty cum mixed with sweet rain.

La Bête recovers before I do and picks me up and carries me back to the castle as the storm overtakes us.

We strip off our sopping wet clothes in my bedroom and as I stand naked and shivering before La Bête, I realize we've never seen each other completely nude.

But I don't get the chance to thoroughly examine La Bête since we dive under the covers to warm up.

Soon La Bête's arms go insistently around me, and I rub myself against him.

My back is to him and I arch as his cock, already hard again, seeks out my core.

His hands grab my breasts and massage their hard peaks as I accept the thrust of his cock into me.

When we're done we lay like that, exhausted by our pleasure. I fall asleep with the rain lashing against the windows, La Bête's arms tucked around me, my back against his chest, and his cock still inside me.

8

BEAUTY

THE STORM has abated when I open my eyes.

It's still day out—late afternoon by the angle of the light streaming in through my colorful windows.

I'm alone in the bed but I hear La Bête rummaging around in the water closet.

I stretch and feel the delicious soreness in all my muscles before hopping out of the bed to clean up by the wash basin.

I've considered where to place the running hot water in my plumbing designs. In Arcadia we had a central water closet in addition to an outhouse, and water was also run to a bath and sink next to the toilet.

While this arrangement is more convenient for plumbing, I think for outgoing sanitation purposes, I would prefer to divert the hot water into the bedroom instead, or perhaps build another room entirely solely for bathing.

Building an entire other room is a longer project though, and I regretfully put it out of my head as I finish up wiping up the last of La Bête's slick deposit with a piece of flannel.

I hear the door to the water closet open and turn to greet La Bête—only to shriek in startlement when Bellamy enters my bedroom.

Naked.

"Beauty!" Bellamy puts his hands out in front of him and backs away. "This is not what you think, please let me explain—"

"You're La Bête," I interject, as I will myself to stop trying to cover my breasts and sex with my hands. "I've suspected as much."

And yet it's hard to feel comfortable in front of Bellamy when it is his beastly form that I have been having intimate relations with.

I back away towards the bed, and like a coward, I hop into it and peer out at Bellamy with the covers drawn up to my chin.

I study his body with interest as he approaches the bed. I scoot over so he can get in and stare at him when he lies next to me.

"How long have you known?" Bellamy asks.

"I've had vague suspicions for a while which I usually dismissed. But my suspicions grew stronger as I began to realize that La Bête—you—were not quite the callous beast you pretended to be."

Bellamy flushes. I scoot in a little closer to him until our knees touch.

"It wasn't until yesterday in the rose garden when I saw you—La Bête—during the day when it really occurred to me. I had the hypothesis that a lack of intimate relations has a negative effect on you, but I had no idea what that effect was. When we stopped—"

I blush.

"—our sexual activities I knew you—La Bête—must be affected. When Bellamy failed to make his usual appearance during the day, then my hypothesis grew into the theory that it is the lack of intimate relations that turns you into The Beast. Is that correct?"

"Yes," says Bellamy (for it's hard to immediately transition into thinking of him as La Bête in this form), "that's the gist of the curse."

My ears fairly twitch at the mention of the curse. I hesitate for it must be a sore subject for him, but I think we are friends enough, or at least allies at this point, for it to be acceptable of me to ask:

"How did you get cursed?"

Bellamy sighs and turns to lie on his back.

I bite my lip and worry that I have overstepped my bounds but Bellamy's hand seeks mine out and holds it in a warm grip.

He speaks while looking up at the ceiling.

"You know the Black Forest is a magical place?"

I make a noise of assent. It's not a real question: I recognize that he is easing himself into a story with painful memories.

"Well, I'm not from here. 'Here' not just being the Black Forest, or this continent; but I'm not from this world."

Ordinarily this sort of statement would inspire many questions from me but right now it is tangential to what is really important. I keep my silence and squeeze Bellamy's hand for encouragement.

"Where I am from, there was a caste system. The starlings made up the ruling class—you might call them sorcerers. Starlings were born with juju—magic—and the

73

magic gave them power; and the power made them greedy; and they kept all the magic and power for themselves.

"I was born of the earth. Not a starling. No magic except a talent for growing things.

"I created gardens and they were different and eye-catching enough that even the starlings took notice. I was hired as the chief gardener in a starling household—a minor house, but a proud one, as they all were.

"I created gardens for their palace and impressed my masters enough that they showered me with privileges. I was given my own room in the servants' quarters and an outrageous allowance. Of course I was only a possession, or at most a favored pet, but not a person in their eyes: yet I let the attention go to my head. When Beka made overtures of sexual interest, I reciprocated."

Beka. For some reason, the sound of her name makes me shiver, even in the light of day. My mind flashes to the beautiful silvery-haired woman in the murals downstairs.

"Beka was a young starling about my age. We were perhaps just a little younger than you are now. We carried on in secluded parts of the estate whenever we found the chance. We declared our undying love for one another."

Bellamy is tense, his brows lowered and eyes fixated on the ceiling.

"It was stupid of me to get involved with Beka but I grew even stupider: I grew careless. I brought her to my room. Soon we were conducting our affair in my room every night. It wasn't long before one of the servants tattled, or perhaps one of her brothers followed her one evening, and we were caught.

"They put me on trial. They put Beka on trial too: she defended our love at first but after a while I suppose the pressure grew too much for her. She renounced me, said she'd made a mistake, that she'd been seduced by my earthiness but had come to realize that she was as far above me as the stars in heaven are from the dirt on the ground.

"As soon as Beka admitted she was disgusted by her liaison with me she was forgiven and taken back into the fold. I believe she married almost immediately after. I was not given a chance to say I'd made a mistake. I could only wait as Beka's family deliberated and handed down my sentence.

"I was punished with a curse that showed everyone my 'true nature'—because all people of the earth were no better than beasts, and I was exiled from the only world I've ever known. They put me in a castle with all the trappings of what I supposedly aspired to when I dared to fuck a starling. I was set up to live like a king, yet look like a beast, and to crave the touch of a woman or else go mad from my beastly desire. And that's how I ended up here."

He turns to face me.

"I thought after all this time," he says, "that what would hurt the most was Beka's betrayal."

I meet his eyes steadily as he continues.

"But it was easy to forgive her after a time. I barely even remember her. And I can't blame her if she did what she had to, in order to survive."

"And," I say, "it's entirely possible that she made a deal behind your back, saved you from some other worse fate, perhaps execution, by denouncing you."

I'm not feeling kindly toward Beka (that feeling of *not-dread* increases exponentially when I turn my mind towards her), but it's in my nature to point out all probabilities.

Bellamy considers. "It's true: it was within their rights to kill me. Though sometimes I think that would've been more merciful."

He is silent, and contemplative.

"Ahmed was old when he died, but it wasn't old age that took him," I say. I'm not sure why I say anything at all. Perhaps my sense of fair play demands that after Bellamy shared something so intimate, that I return in like.

"The young took him," I say. "Rash young boys set Ahmed's shack afire and the old man burned to death inside of it."

Julian was one of those boys. Lucio was friends with him even then which threw me into a black rage. My entire family said I was overreacting. Julian was only a boy. Julian was very popular. Julian came from a good family. He couldn't have known the harm he would cause.

I was nine by then, but my family's betrayal made me feel ancient.

Bellamy squeezes my hand which still lies in his grip. It doesn't lessen the enormity of my heartache, but to my surprise, it bolsters something inside me, that helps me stay aloft.

"There was a midwife who witnessed the incident," I am able to continue. "She identified the boys who committed the deed but our mayor deemed them too young to understand the consequences of their actions."

Fury rises in me, as it always does when I relive the memory. "They were put in the stocks for a couple of hours."

A couple hours of discomfort for my best friend's life.

"That's all?" Bellamy says when I stop. "For what they did?"

"That's all," I say. "I'm sure it helped that they all came from prominent, influential families. And Ahmed was just a stranger, an ugly foreigner."

I say the words and feel the uncomfortable reminder of who else is considered a strange, ugly foreigner.

Bellamy leans forward and kisses me. It's not seduction: comfort, rather.

I accept his comfort and offer my own. It's not long until our arms wind around each other and tighten.

I find that sex with Bellamy the man, is just as interesting as sex with La Bête The Beast.

Bellamy retreats before sunset.

"Will you not need to return as soon as you've become La Bête?" I ask with some amusement.

"Some processes should remain a mystery," he declares as he shrugs back into his clothes. White shirt. Tapered trousers. Blue velvet jacket with brass buttons. Somehow I've never noticed before that they wore the same clothes, and I'm a little surprised that La Bête's clothes fit Bellamy.

"How is it, do you think," I muse, "that the starling's curse still holds here, so far from your world?"

"The roses," Bellamy says simply. "They're from my world, and they power juju from my world. Perhaps even juju of this world.

"Hmm," I say. "Have you considered letting them die?"

Bellamy gives me a scandalized look. "Let roses *die*? What sort of monster are you?"

I smirk at him from the comfort of my bed. "The practical kind. Perhaps the magic would disappear and lose its sway over you."

Bellamy shakes his head. "The roses cannot die. They don't need to be watered. I barely tend to the rose garden at all, I only let it grow as it pleases."

"What if you tried to kill them? Set them on fire?"

Bellamy's eyes bug out and he nearly chokes. "You are a ruthless woman, Mademoiselle Kahlo."

His comment stings for moment for that is an accusation I've heard often—but then I remember that he is teasing.

"You mean 'rational,' don't you?," I say primly.

"Yes, and I see those gears in your head turning so let me tell you before you begin devising experiments to murder my poor roses, that burning them only increases their power. They will boost any enchantments from my world. My curse."

He gestures at me.

"Your ring."

"My ring?" I finger the ring Bellamy—La Bête—put on my finger on my first day here.

"It's a talisman that can guide you in the right direction," he says. "But with the sacrifice of a rose? You could transport yourself from anywhere you please—in the blink of an eye."

"Anywhere?"

"One rose won't get you across the ocean," he admits. "But from a nearby kingdom back to my castle..."

Arcadia is a nearby kingdom. Tierra Rica is not much farther.

"Hmm," I eye my ring, impressed. No wonder La Bête zealously guards his roses. Such power can be dangerous in the wrong hands. "So you sacrifice a rose by burning it?"

"Yes," he confirms. He pauses by the door on his way out and gives me the gimlet eye. "And Beauty, don't even think about torching my rose garden."

I laugh since that is exactly what I'm considering, while running various hypotheses on what might happen as a result through my head.

I throw a pillow at Bellamy's head which he catches with a grin.

"Get out," I say to him. "Go undergo your mysterious *process*."

He leaves and I lie back in my bed and consider how I really don't mind the curse of his beast form at all. In fact...

I grin as I stretch.

I'm looking forward to seeing La Bête.

9

BEAUTY

"SOME COIN FOR food, mademoiselle?"

I turn and see the beggar woman at my elbow.

I reach into my skirt's inner pockets and draw out a coin for her. It's not a lot, for it's part of the small pool of pocket money I have from my previous life, but it's enough to feed her for the day if she's frugal.

The older woman curtsies gratefully and disappears into the crowd.

Orleans is no city, but pilgrims from every kingdom travel here every year for the festival of Our Lady of Orleans. I made the trek once with my family when I was a child. Santa Inanna is very popular in Tierra Rica and my mother was a devout follower.

The mid-size town is boisterous and bursting with people this close to the festival which is next week. I'm dazzled after all my quiet and seclusion at Château de La Bête.

I stroll down blacksmith row examining the metalwork on display but food vendors hawk their wares on foot, carrying their goods in boxes strapped around their necks.

They scream at me as I pass, offering meat pies and bao, rice wine and mead.

"Pomegranates, milady? Juicy pomegranates for a juicy lady!" The vendor's eyes glitter at me and I ignore him for his cheek though I dearly love pomegranates.

"Hoity toity, she is!" he cries after me in a bitter tone. "Can't take a compliment, that one," I hear him spit and hope he didn't aim it at my cloak. "That's rich considering she's a whore for The Beast."

My face reddens and I whirl around to confront the odious vendor. I descend upon him in my fury and he backs away, surprised. I jab my finger against his chest.

"That's right," I say. "I'm a whore. I exchange my services for money. If that's what makes me a whore, then you're a whore too. A pomegranate selling whore!"

The man sidles away with his box of pomegranates, all his vitriol melting in the face of my sudden aggression.

A blacksmith covering the stall next to me snorts in amusement. She is a brawny woman who looks like she could arm wrestle La Bête. She has a magnificent sort of beauty I've always envied: the sort of beauty that arises from her inner strength, rather than a fortuitous arrangement of symmetrical features.

"That's a lass," she says approvingly. "Don't take no mouth from him. I'm sure you got enough to deal with living with that monster up there."

The blacksmith jerks her head back toward the Black Forest mountain behind her, where La Bête's castle sits looking down at us.

It seems I'm famous.

Or infamous.

"He's not such a monster," I feel compelled to say in La Bête's defense. "He's only cursed with a beastly form. His outer form has no bearing on his inner character."

She eyes me dubiously. "But he was cursed for a reason, no? Had to have been some nasty business to be cursed to look like *that*."

"Have you ever seen him to know what he looks like?" I demand. "Do you actually know him to judge his character?"

The blacksmith narrows her eyes at me. Her indulgent good humor is gone. "You're a naive young thing, so let me give you a piece of advice. Men will say anything to get into a pretty girl's good graces—and between her thighs."

"I believe actions speak for themselves."

The blacksmith snorts again, but now with contempt, and it's directed at me. "I suppose throwing gold at you was enough to get you to spread your legs, so maybe my words are wasted on one like you."

She turns away and ducks under the awning of her stall before I can think of a response.

My cheeks redden. Not with embarrassment. With anger and frustration. Who is she to judge us when she knows neither of us? And her judgment bothers me more than that pomegranate man for she reminds me of some I grew up with. If people like the blacksmith were only a little more open-minded...

"It's no use trying to bring some people around," a soft voice says behind me. I turn to see the beggar woman again.

"My advice?" she continues though I've not responded to her. "Say he's disgusting and you can't wait until your year of misery is over."

"But he's not disgusting," I say, trying to remain reasonable in the face of yet another person who thinks they have a right to meddle in my business. "He was cursed and he's trying to live with it as best he can."

"I know," she says. "I was like you once: I was one of La Bête's women."

Taken aback, I reassess the woman in front of me. Her greying hair is well kept for a beggar's, and her clothes have that worn, mended and re-mended look that I am all too familiar with, but they are clean. Her lined face is kind but must have been plain even in her youth.

"A beauty like yours is rare," she says wryly. "And La Bête never made looks a prerequisite for his arrangement. He only requires a woman that is willing."

"I do not judge your inner character by your outer plainness," I assure the woman. "I only reassess your looks because I am trying to determine whether you really are a beggar."

She laughs. "'Plain *and* a potential liar,' I'm flattered!"

Her summary of my assessment is truthful but I remain silent in case she is offended despite her seemingly good cheer.

"I may have been slightly ingenuous when I asked you for coin," she says. "I confess I was curious to meet La Bête's new woman. I make a small income from selling potions and minor spells—"

"You're a witch?"

"Not a very good one!" she says and laughs again. I'm starting to like this woman despite her wiliness, or perhaps because of it. "I've had to rely on the mercy of others now and then. So I *am* a beggar."

"What happened to all the gold from La Bête?" I ask. She seems old enough to have potentially had a lot of time to spend all that money, though I have no idea if she was already old when she served La Bête. And it is an awful *lot* of money.

"Do you remember Genevieve Duval?" The old woman deflects my question with one of her own.

FAUSTA BORJA

I play along to see where she is going. "Genevieve Duval was the sorceress who was caught poisoning children in the small villages and towns of Arcadia. She was burned alive for her crimes."

This all happened when I was a little girl in Tierra Rica, so it was something I heard of when our family moved to the kingdom of Arcadia.

The woman nods. "Genevieve was another one of La Bête's women."

That is not something I knew, or if I've heard it before, I do not remember.

She continues, "When Genevieve's year with La Bête was over, she returned home to her village where her family and friends were ready to accept her back into their arms. They were sympathetic to her plight, you see. Perhaps it helped that Genevieve was known as quite a beauty in her time—though I don't think she was quite as beautiful as you—" the woman's wink to me is sly, "—and people thought of her as a tragic figure. What a shame, they thought, to sacrifice such a beauty to a horrible beast."

I nod in understanding. I am very familiar with this general tone.

"But Genevieve did not act the way the villagers expected her to. Instead of being traumatized by the way The Beast used her, and being suitably distressed enough for one of the village's handsome young men to save her with marriage, Genevieve was contrary when the villagers tried to sympathize with her. She defended La Bête. Said he was just a man like any other, only he was cursed with an ugly exterior."

I nod vigorously—I don't agree with the "ugly" necessarily: I mean, objectively speaking, La Bête's features are not without charisma and appeal, but I understand Genevieve completely.

"When Genevieve wouldn't play along with the tragic damsel role, the villagers began to turn against her. She couldn't walk down the street without people spitting on her, or calling her a whore. They said she was a depraved slut who enjoyed The Beast's perverted attentions. Too soiled for a real man. Her family was ashamed of her. Tried to get her to shut up and stay shut in their home till the scandal died down and people forgot about her. But Genevieve was never much for caving in to others. And then there was the sickness going around at the time."

"The one that killed the children?"

"Children, some adults, but children were especially vulnerable. Genevieve had some knowledge of healing and thought it her duty to help people. And there were families that were either too desperate or never cared what others thought, who accepted her help. Some got better with Genevieve's treatments. Some didn't."

I have a sinking feeling in my stomach. The story of Genevieve Duval has always struck an uncomfortable chord with me, for my thoughts turn inevitably to poor Ahmed in his burning shack. But this is the first I've heard her story where she wasn't painted the villain. And it's probable that my emotions are contributing to my assessment, but this version rings truer to me.

"Then the accusations started. They came from all over. From families Genevieve had never met, from villages she'd never visited."

"*Linda!*" I hear a familiar voice. "Beauty! Someone said they saw you here, why didn't you tell us you were coming into town today?"

My brother Gaspar bounds to my side. The beggar stops speaking and Gaspar looks her up and down coldly.

Another body sidles next to my other side. Julian.

The woman grabs my arm and leans in to my ear. She whispers, for me only: "After they burned Genevieve at the stake, it was her family that got her gold. Remember that."

The old woman kisses me on the cheek and walks briskly away before I can stop her, and tell her she is welcome to stay and talk to me.

It would be a lie. Gaspar and Julian are eyeing the woman's back with distinctly unwelcome looks. Julian has possessively put his hand at my back and I move deliberately away from him.

Gaspar catches this and gives me a reproachful look. He nudges me with his elbow back towards Julian.

How typical of my brother. Saving me from people I don't need saving from, and foisting suitors on me who I would rather be saved from.

"I can't believe you let that disgusting old hag get close enough to kiss you," Gaspar says distastefully as he hugs me and carefully kisses my other cheek.

Julian tries to go in for a greeting kiss as he always does but I put my hand up to halt him. "And I can't believe you're friends with this monster. Isn't it enough that Lucio has remained friends with him all these years? Are you under his spell now too?"

"Beauty!" Gaspar chides me, and shoots a nervous look toward Julian who of course wears the same bland smile he always does. A charming mask for an evil creature. Lucio always laughs when I attack his friend, and Julian simply smiles, but my honesty makes Gaspar uncomfortable.

I don't care. I will always think of Julian as Ahmed's murderer because I will not be fooled by his friendly demeanor and status as a respectable citizen.

And I don't understand my brothers and my family. Even if they don't believe that Julian murdered Ahmed, don't they see how he hangs about me like an annoying fly when I consistently and persistently make it clear that I want none of his attention? Do they not find it disturbing that Julian only smiles when I say horrible things to discourage him, and generally acts like I mean nothing I say?

"Beauty," Julian says smoothly as if I have not just called him a monster and meant it. "What a relief to see you looking healthy and acting like your usual incorrigible self. We've been worried about you, holed up in that beast's castle."

Gaspar nods.

"I'm perfectly fine," I say irritably. I direct my words to Gaspar and try to ignore Julian. "I've been treated fairly by La Bête so there's no need for our family to worry. How is Papi doing? And our *hermanos*? Is our cottage holding up?"

The structure was dilapidated around the edges but I have lovingly restored parts of it over the past few years so that it is a sturdy construction, if humble.

Gaspar laughs heartily. "We're not living in that old shack anymore! We've moved back to town!"

I gape at my brother. Back to town? But...I calculate the cost of renting even a cheap townhouse in Orleans, add in salaries for a minimal staff to maintain such a residence, and consider the fine clothing my siblings like to wear.

My family will be out of all the money La Bête gave them in less than a year.

"Oh Beauty," Gaspar hoots at me. "Your face is priceless. Don't worry about us, we're doing fine. We're seeing old friends and having a grand time."

I look from Gaspar in his velvet jacket to Julian who is wearing a wool ensemble that is so perfectly tasteful, I perfectly hate it and want to cut it to pieces. It is studded with bright gold buttons and tailored perfectly to his fit form. Even someone like me who doesn't usually notice fashion statements understands that Julian's ensemble is costly and signals that he has a lot of money at his disposal. Julian's family has always been well off but they had heavy investments in one of the ships that were lost in the great tsunami of '22—the same tsunami that depleted my father's fortune.

Julian's family fared better than mine but they took a loss at the time. It looks like they've found better fortune since I've been gone.

Gaspar pulls my arm into his and leads me in a stroll down blacksmith row. Julian falls in behind us which is smart because there is no way I would tolerate walking alongside him.

"But what about you, Beauty?" Gaspar says. He looks down at the worn trousers and tunic I've worn under my cloak. I avoided pants at first with La Bête, thinking he would mind the extra work of taking them off but it turns out, he doesn't seem to mind at all.

"You would think that with all his riches, The Beast would clothe his concubine better," Gaspar says.

My face reddens. Strange that I don't like my brother calling me La Bête's concubine, when I was called La Bête's whore less than an hour ago. Both are accurate descriptions of my role.

"I chose this ensemble," I say to Gaspar. "There is a magical wardrobe that simply conjures up whatever I wish to wear and I thought this would be the most practical for a day trip."

Gaspar eyes me uncertainly, but I am not known for making jests.

"A magical wardrobe and you choose *that*? Beauty, I think living in that cottage in the middle of nowhere touched your head. It's not as if you still need to do chores, or fix things in La Bête's castle."

My brother must see something on my face for he pauses and peers at me. "You aren't still fixing things, are you, Beauty? Like some old hand? You are! And no doubt still trying to drown rocks for your book!"

"Well at least I am not wasting money I do not have! Or will not have if I continue spending it like you! What were you and Papi thinking, moving the entire family back to Orleans?

"We have connections in town," Gaspar says condescendingly. "We need to spend money if we are to make money. Besides, our fortunes might change. Did you hear that the Montserrats have recovered one of their ships?"

The Montserrats are Julian's family. So that is why Julian looks like he's dripping with money. He is. "But the tsunami was over a decade ago," I say in disbelief.

"Exactly. You never know when our luck will change," Gaspar winks at me. "And yours too, Beauty."

"What does that mean?" I say. "Explain." The conspiratorial air about Gaspar makes me nervous.

He looks behind us, presumably at Julian, and then leans in towards me. "Now that Julian has come into his fortune, you and he can finally get married."

I come to a complete stop. Gaspar is forced to stop as well or else drag me down the street.

"Are you mad?" My voice is loud, perhaps even slightly hysterical (can you blame me?), and passersby stop to look at us curiously.

Julian bumps into us and I whirl to take them both in with my glare.

"Listen to me for I will say this very clearly," I declare loudly. "I am *not. Ever.* Going to marry Julian."

Julian crosses his arms and gives me his bland smile as if I am not rejecting him in full public view.

Gaspar lurches forward and pats my shoulders awkwardly while trying to shush me. "There, there, Beauty. You don't have to be ashamed of your servitude to La Bête. You've done what you had to do, for family."

"What does that have anything to do with anything?" I ask in genuine confusion.

"It's understandable that you don't want to bring shame to Julian," Gaspar says. My eyes bulge but for once I cannot express in words my current feelings towards Julian.

"But he loves you, he's loved you since you were children, just as we think—if you could only admit it to yourself—you love him too.

"*No*," I finally find my voice. "*No*."

I stare at Gaspar, stunned, for I did not realize the extent of my family's madness. "I am not secretly in love with Julian. I *hate* him. He murdered Ahmed—"

"That's enough!" Gaspar says sharply.

"He *murdered* Ahmed and feels no remorse—"

Gaspar slaps me.

The sound cracks in the open air.

My brother and I stare at each other, frozen. Gaspar has never raised his hands against me: no one in my family has crossed this line before now.

I realize my vision is blurring and I panic for I'm not used to tears and don't know how to stop them from welling up.

A strong hand grips my arm and a gentle hand touches my cheek before I can elude it. "Beauty, are you all right?" I hear that hated voice ask sympathetically. "Gaspar," Julian continues sharply, "you go too far."

"Beauty," Gaspar gasps and reaches out for me, "Mi *hermana, lo siento!* I'm so sorry, I don't know what came over me—"

I pull back before Gaspar can touch me and yank my arm out of Julian's grip.

My eyes leak and I swipe angrily at my hot tears.

"Stop," I say shakily. "Just stop. I'm going home."

Gaspar looks at me in confusion.

"I'm going back to La Bête's castle," I clarify.

I turn on my heels and, ignoring the curious and scandalized looks of those around me, flee from blacksmiths' row and back towards the carriage that will take me home to La Bête.

10
LA BÊTE

I FEEL THE acute lack of Beauty's presence when she goes to Orleans.

I always feel the lack of a woman—the lack of sex with a woman—being cursed as I am, but I miss Beauty with more than my cock.

I'm in love with her.

I tend to the gardens while she's gone. The roses don't need any tending for they have a will of their own, but it's time to prepare the other two gardens for the coming winter.

First, I attack the herb garden: I pull up all the plants like basil and tarragon that cannot survive the frost and put them aside. I'll save some for Jenny in case she could use the extra. I know she grows her own herbs but most of it is used for her potions and she might want some for her kitchen.

I use evergreen boughs to create windbreaks for the lavender, chamomile, and winter savory.

Then I cover the remaining herbs in the ground with mulch, and add extra protective layers to the rosemary and lemon verbena which are more sensitive to cold.

Working in my gardens always gives me a simultaneously micro and macro view of time that's dizzying. On the one hand I feel my every inhale and exhale; on the other hand I grasp that the winter is one breath of the earth, and spring its next.

When these plants bloom again, Beauty will still be here living in my castle, honoring her word as women like her always do, and fulfilling her perceived duty to her horrid family. In another breath, she will be gone.

There will be no woman in her place. I've waited centuries for Beauty, for the woman I'm destined to love, and when my ring showed up to mark her, I knew she had arrived.

But her presence is a double edged sword.

Her absence today is a cruel dart from next autumn's breath, a foreshadowing of the desolation she will leave in her wake.

I realize I am overmulching and throw down my shovel.

The fragrant and colorful witch hazel shrubs will bloom for a while yet, so I leave them be.

I should mulch the other garden for the winter but I leave my shovel and mulch behind and find myself stalking towards the maze: towards my sanctuary, the rose garden.

If I were a good man I would let Beauty go now before any harm could befall her. For someone so maddeningly rational and driven by logic, Beauty's every emotion and feeling is transparent. I see her falling for me.

Well, I am not a good man and cannot let Beauty go. I should at least make her hate me. Continue acting like a boar, a reviled monster.

It's what I've tried to do with every woman since Genevieve. Genevieve, whose empathy destroyed her.

But when you've been with as many women as I have, and loved more than your fair share, you immediately recognize someone like Beauty for what she is: in no small part because you realize it is the absence of her that you've felt for centuries.

I need her. I need her through the winter, the spring, through every season of every century of the rest of my cursed life.

Besides, even if I were too stupid to realize I loved Beauty, the fact that the ring chose her says it all. She's the woman for me.

But I love her too much to shackle her to me.

A part of my curse is that I am held back from revealing the extent of it. It's true I'm cursed with a beastly form that demands the charms of a woman, but I am also trapped in my own castle. It's not that I choose not to leave (which is what Beauty believes for she invited me to go to town with her), but that I *cannot* leave. Furthermore, not only am I cursed to need a woman's intimacy to survive, but now I need Beauty in particular.

The starling who cursed me said that if a woman came along that I fell in love with, that the ring would find its way to her, and that she would become the only woman that could satisfy me. And if that woman were to declare her love for me in return...then we would both be bound to each other forever.

I'm not sure what that means, but I know the starlings and their malice. I'm afraid it means we would *both* be forever trapped in this castle. Perhaps it would even mean Beauty would be cursed with her own beast.

How can I do such a thing to someone like Beauty? Someone who dreams of traveling to the other side of the world? Someone who deserves everything she's ever dreamed of and worked for?

I'm sitting in the rose garden, depending on its soothing fragrance to hold The Beast at bay until nightfall when I feel her presence approach.

My breath quickens, my heart hammers, (my cock throbs), and I rise to greet Beauty.

I fix my dirty cuffs and feel a twinge of regret that I didn't change into a fresh ensemble before she arrived. Considering how ugly I am half the time, it's the least I can do to maintain an appearance of neatness for her.

She appears, ducking cautiously through the hole in the hedge. If I were in my other form I could not resist immediately snatching her, tugging down her trousers, and taking her here but I am not in that form, and I have enough presence of mind to see the striking uncertainty in her eyes when her gaze meets mine.

"What's wrong?" I say promptly, for it's obvious something is wrong.

Beauty lowers her eyes, a rare gesture from her, and mumbles at the ground. "Nothing."

I stare at her. Her cheeks are red with cold but she looks otherwise healthy.

She notices my scrutiny and elaborates, "The carriage ride was bumpy and I feel a little nauseous. I thought maybe the scent here would calm me."

For a dizzying moment I consider that Beauty might be pregnant but I discard the foolish notion almost immediately (with some regret). In my world, people of my caste are sterilized at birth, and must petition a starling court for the privilege to bear offspring. Even if that weren't the case, Beauty is a smart and resourceful woman who plans for everything.

"Please, sit," I say hurriedly when Beauty remains standing.

We sit side by side on the bench.

"Did you find what you were looking for at the market?"

Beauty hesitates before responding. "Not quite. There were no unusual alloys to be acquired and I would have to spend a good deal of money to commission something to my own specifications.

I could strike myself down. I had forgotten that the bulk of Beauty's money had gone straight into her family's hands and that she likely had very little spending money.

"About that," I temporize as I think of how to fix this. "It occurs to me that since you're working on renovations for the castle, I should hire you and pay you a fee. I think five chests of gold would be fair."

This is actually a fair solution to compensate her for her work, and I could kick myself for not thinking of it sooner. This way Beauty will be set with her money to travel to Kurys when her time with me is done.

But Beauty stares at me with...dismay?

"We could negotiate a better rate if that doesn't seem fair to you," I say.

Her brows draw in even farther. "But I wasn't even in town to find materials for renovations. It was for my own private project. You don't need to compensate me."

"Of course I do," I say. "You still deserve payment for the work you've been doing."

Are her cheeks reddening? They were already so red to begin with, it's hard to tell.

"I don't know...I don't know that I'd even have time to implement anything before my time here is up."

She stands abruptly. "Perhaps we can discuss the specifics later, I need to freshen up before evening."

Both our heads tilt up to the darkening sky. Inanna, the bright evening star, glitters near a barely visible moon.

"Very well," I say.

I let her hurry away from me, wondering what is going on her head.

11
BEAUTY

"TAKE OFF YOUR clothes."

Night has fallen. La Bête has appeared.

He stands in my room, making it seem much smaller.

I shiver with anticipation but hesitate.

I want nothing more right now than to lose myself in the purely physical sensations that La Bête can provoke within me but we still haven't had a chance to examine each other naked yet and I'm feeling queerly exposed already.

I pull my tunic off, push down my trousers and step out of them.

La Bête takes in my thin chemise and panties.

"Take everything off," he says softly.

I pull the thin chemise off and stand before La Bête with my breasts bare for the first time. I cannot look at him so I look down where I can see the flush overtake my chest and know that it covers my face too.

I slip my panties off before I can overthink it and stand naked before La Bête.

His eyes perform a most thorough examination of my form.

He takes a few steps towards me: his hand reaches for but stops short of one of my breasts.

"Very nice," he breathes. My breasts are fairly large for someone as slim as I am. They're capped by puffy nipples that are mostly areola and usually give my breasts a conical shape, but they've hardened for the occasion so that little nubs point straight at La Bête.

He pulls his hand back and holds it with the other as if to keep a tight rein on himself.

"Pull your hair down," he says.

I reach up and pull my long hair out of the simple ponytail it was drawn back in. Wavy locks of dark hair fall to my shoulders and down my back.

"Turn around. I want to see all of you."

I obey him—but slowly, slowly. I sway my hips as I turn to show him my backside and feel my hair brush my back as I come full circle. The look on his face is gratifying.

He sighs—a gusty, happy noise.

"Now get on the bed and lie on your back."

I glance down La Bête's body. I see his erection straining his trousers and I'm amazed that he still hasn't pounced me. I shake my head at him.

His eyes darken. "You dare defy me?"

I smile at him, slowly. His beast is excited by the prospect of someone to subdue. But I want my fair share first.

"I would see The Beast," I say. I let my eyes speak for me in clarifying *how* I would see The Beast: naked.

La Bête's nostrils flare.

La Bête shrugs off his blue velvet coat and tosses it to the side.

He unbuttons the shirt underneath—slowly, slowly.

I should have known La Bête would be the eye for an eye sort.

But The Beast loses his patience halfway down his shirt and simply tears apart the rest of his shirt.

Buttons fly everywhere. One dings my knee and I'm thankful it didn't catch a more sensitive spot.

His bare chest is covered in a thick down of fur. His arms are huge and muscular.

My pulse quickens—and La Bête's eyes beeline to my bare breasts—but I force my breath to even out.

I raise a brow at him, coolly.

"Take everything off," I say softly, throwing his instruction back at him with the same intonation he used.

La Bête's eyes glint at me as his hands move to his trousers.

Quickly he undoes his trousers and pushes them down. His now familiar cock juts out at me.

Ah.

He looks glorious.

Like some fantastic creature from the woods, perhaps the result of a coupling between a forest god and human woman.

I can no longer stop my chest from heaving as I struggle to contain my excitement.

La Bête's gaze on me is pure animal lust.

I turn away from him, feeling the hair on the back of my neck prickle as ancient instinct screams at me not to turn my back on a beast, and I move onto the bed.

I hear only his panting as I crawl into the middle of the bed, conscious of how my sex must be peeking at him.

I flip onto my back.

To my surprise, La Bête doesn't immediately spring upon me and begin rutting.

He stalks forward and comes to a stop at the foot of my bed.

I wait for him to climb on top of me but La Bête remains standing.

"Spread your legs so I can see your pussy," he says.

Pussy? Like a pussycat, I think to myself. I remember the word was used in the fairy tales too.

I draw my knees up and open my thighs for him.

He gazes into my core. I know that I am wet for him and wonder if he can see or smell it. I think he does.

"Touch your breasts, Beauty," He says. "Touch them the way you like to be touched, the way you touch yourself to feel pleasure."

I suck in a breath. This is unexpected.

"Don't make me say it twice."

I don't.

I reach up and lightly run the palms of my hands over my nipples. They've already turned puffy again after I took off my chemise and I continue running my hands lightly over them until I've coaxed my nipples into pointing again. My head pushes back on my pillow and I stare into the ceiling as my breath quickens.

Once my nipples appear, I work my thumbs over them. I caress lightly since they are very sensitive. I feel the pleasure shoot straight down to my sex.

"Now touch your pussy. Touch yourself the way you like to be touched."

I reach down with one hand while the other continues to massage my nipples.

I lightly touch my "pussy" and run my fingertips lightly against the trim hair covering my outer lips like La Bête did the other day. The sensation makes me shiver.

Then I take the wetness leaking out from my core and drag it up to the little pleasure nub nestled above my folds. I don't touch it directly—here too, I am sensitive, but I lightly run my fingers up to the flesh that forms a hood over my pearl. I rub there and my head falls back into the pillow again as I moan.

"Touch yourself inside, Beauty. Feel how slick you are. Show me."

I peek down at La Bête. His cinnamon eyes are practically glowing. I know my face is red from arousal and embarrassment but I force myself to meet his eyes as my hand ventures lower.

I find my damp center and dip my finger in and out, gathering more moisture to coat my finger till I can slide it all the way in.

La Bête's nostrils flare. He starts, but stops himself. He stays at the foot of my bed, watching me.

I slip in another finger and arch my back. Lady, that feels good. Before La Bête I could only ever fit in one finger without hurting myself.

My two fingers slide easily in and out of my passage. I feel my pussy clamping tightly around them and the thought of my pussy clamping down on La Bête's much larger cock makes me moan.

I look down at him again.

Though La Bête stands there like a mountain, his monstrous cock is bouncing from its effort to reach me.

"Make yourself come, Beauty," he growls.

I remove my fingers from my tight slit and rub frantically over the hood that covers my pearl of pleasure.

It doesn't feel as good as having my fingers inside but I want to come quickly so I can have La Bête fill me instead.

My breath hitches as I feel the warmth catch my core and spread throughout my body.

I stiffen as my climax overtakes me and sigh out my pleasure.

La Bête climbs atop me.

He enters me and I moan. My sex protests his entrance so soon after my climax but it's slick and La Bête glides all the way in and fills me with his engorged flesh.

La Bête's massive chest tickles my face as he slowly plunges fully inside me. He rests his forearms to either side of me and crouches his upper body over mine.

I bury my hands into the fur on his chest and raise my legs. He's too big to wrap my legs around from this position so I have to settle for digging my heels into the bed as he rocks inside me.

He goes slow when he normally pounds fast and hard and I writhe helplessly against his onslaught of leisurely paced thrusts.

My back arches against him, my hips rise to meet him, my sex weeps her desire, and still he maintains his slow, provocative rhythm.

He delves deeper inside with each piercing thrust.

The tide of another climax approaches and recedes as La Bête stubbornly resists the urging of my frantic hips. He annihilates the faster tempo I try to establish, ignores my restless shifting: I feel the tide approach once more and La Bête ruthlessly presses my writhing hips into the bed.

My climax ebbs away again before it can crest.

Helpless noises fall from my lips. I feel my long locks of hair tumbling over my face as I shake my head back and forth.

La Bête's eyes catch mine and I am helpless before his gaze. His eyes pin me as surely as his cock does. He plunges inside me, a relentless invasion that fills me to the brim, leaves room for no thought, and finally the sensual waves crash over me.

I buck wildly against La Bête as I convulse around him. He pins me against the bed and slowly rotates his hips as I cry out my pleasure.

He's thrusting again before I've recovered.

I fall bonelessly back on the bed as he grinds into me. I stare up at his face and see The Beast overtake the man.

His tempo increases tenfold. He seizes my ankles and shoves my knees up to either side of me to accommodate his ferocious thrusts. His eyes are slit nearly shut.

I can only lie beneath him, hostage to a raging beast as he jerks violently into me. My center is open and slick from his plunder.

Suddenly he stiffens against me with a harsh groan. My ankles drop from his slack grip.

Warmth pours into me. The wet gush triggers something inside me and I lose control once more to my passion.

I claw at his back and La Bête gathers me into his arms and we shudder through our final moments of ecstasy together.

La Bête releases me.

He carefully extricates himself and flops onto his back next to me.

We lay there side by side. Our pants fill the room.

I close my eyes. I'm sweaty and sticky and sore but I want to memorize every detail of this moment. I suspect I will not find another man like La Bête if I search the entire world; if I search all the worlds. I want to savor this for I will never find it again.

I hear La Bête shift and his breath ruffles my cheek.

"What is that?"

His voice sounds peculiar.

I open my eyes and turn to see what he's looking at but he's looking at me.

"What is what?" I ask.

La Bête props himself up on an elbow and reaches for me—reaches for my cheek.

"Ow," I say, before I can stop myself. My cheek is tender where Gaspar slapped it earlier.

"You have a bruise here forming," La Bête says. His voice is deceptively even, but I am not fooled. I feel the coil of his muscles as he tenses, and I sense the rage simmering inside him, ready to boil over depending on my response.

"Oh...that," I say, searching my mind for a way to recount what happened that doesn't sound like I got into a dramatic fight with my brother...and then I search my mind for a convincing lie for there's no way to truthfully play down the incident.

"Someone hit you," La Bête says. He sounds accusing, and I flinch.

"It was just a slap," I say.

"Who?" La Bête rears up. His question is a roar.

I quickly sit up and draw the blankets up to cover my breasts.

"It doesn't matter," I say.

"Then you will tell me," La Bête hisses.

"I won't because...because I'm not sure that person would be safe from you."

"That is the point!"

"Just forget about it," I say.

"It was one of the villagers," La Bête fumes. "They take their hatred of me out on the women who come to serve me."

"If you retaliate, they will only hate you more," I say.

"Or," La Bête say, "perhaps they will learn a lesson not to fuck with The Beast."

I secretly agree with him—or I would, except this is my brother we're talking about.

I appeal to his reason for I know Bellamy is inside The Beast somewhere. "We are outnumbered," I say. "We cannot afford to retaliate even against those that deserve it. They will storm the castle one day and tear you apart."

"I will tear many more of them apart first."

"And what will happen to me?" I say.

La Bête growls.

"Or whichever new woman you have up here with you? They will tear her apart too and you'll be too dead to stop them."

The breath goes out of La Bête as surely as if I punched him in the stomach.

He hangs his head.

La Bête sits that way in silence for so long I tentatively reach out to touch him.

Ignoring my hand on his shoulder, he slowly drops his head into his hands.

I feel his shoulder ripple beneath my hand as he shudders.

"La Bête?" I whisper. I'm afraid to see his face but I cannot stand not seeing his face.

"La Bête?" I plead.

La Bête raises his head and swivels his head to me. We stare at each other.

Abruptly, La Bête tugs at the sheet I hold against me. I relinquish my grasp and bare my breasts to him.

La Bête pushes me back on the bed and lowers his mouth to my aching mounds. My arms encircle him and I clutch tightly at his back.

His hot tongue laps against my nipples. It is the first time he's put his tongue to my breasts. I explode with longing—no—*need*.

I desperately need to have La Bête inside me.

La Bête reads my mind.

His cock probes below and suddenly he drives himself fully into my hot core.

When it's over La Bête tears himself off of me and pads out of the room without bothering to take his clothes with him.

It's just as well for I do not think I can withstand another post-coital conversation.

I turn onto my side, press my hurting cheek into my pillow, and draw the covers over myself.

If my eyes leak tears tonight, there are no witnesses to prove it.

12
BEAUTY

OVER LA BÊTE'S objections, I return to town a week later.

Gaspar wrote me a letter apologizing for the incident at blacksmith row and begging to meet with me in person to tell me how sorry he was.

La Bête thinks I am not safe. Not from Gaspar, not from other people who hate La Bête.

Perhaps it's true but I need a break from the exhausting cycle of fighting and fucking that La Bête and I have fallen into.

When I finally admitted to him that it was my brother who had slapped me, La Bête was silent on the subject for a day and I breathed a sigh of relief, thinking he had finally laid the issue to rest.

But the next day he sat me down (he in his human Bellamy form) and outlined his plan for me: La Bête would give me some money, and I would pack my valise and purchase passage to Kurys. Immediately.

I don't know what sort of woman La Bête thinks I am, but I am not about to renege on my word, nor am I going to take his money which I have not earned, only to escape by myself and leave him behind to deal with the consequences.

For what does he think will happen if I go along with his plan?

Right now the villagers are only mildly agitated about the women they "sacrifice" to La Bête every year—but all of those women emerge from The Beast's lair a year later perfectly unharmed. Some are perhaps...*enlightened* by the experience though they are smart enough not to say it.

If a beautiful young woman like myself were to disappear without word from his castle, people would be suspicious. Combined with the rumors that Julian and my family are no doubt spreading, about how much I abhor The Beast, the villagers would work themselves into a frenzy. The story the old beggar woman told me of Genevieve Duval still runs through my head.

Though I wonder at the witchery skills of the "old" beggar woman who could have the ability to disguise her looks and age. They say they never found the body of Genevieve Duval in the ashes of the fire though there is usually at least a skeleton.

Nevertheless, her story still rings true.

In any case, my brother has reached out to me, and even if I am not ready to forgive him, Gaspar is my family. I cannot ignore his request to see me.

Two bodyguards lumber alongside me as I walk down tailor row. La Bête hired them.

We reach the end of the row and the shop that Gaspar requested I meet him in.

I suggest to the bodyguards that they wait outside, but they refuse.

The tailor isn't surprised to see me though he gives the two men behind me a sidelong glance before escorting me to a private room in the back.

The "private room" is the size of my wardrobe in La Bête's castle—large for a wardrobe, but tiny for four people, two of whom are the size of elephants. My bodyguards inspect the room, its sparse furniture, and Gaspar, before showing themselves out.

To my exasperation, one of them loftily warns Gaspar that they'll be waiting right outside.

Gaspar gives me a pained smile when I take a seat at the small table across from him.

"I'm sorry you think you need guards to have a visit with your brother," he says.

"They were La Bête's idea," I say. I immediately regret my words after they leave my mouth for although they are the truth, they imply that La Bête and I are at odds.

"And perhaps it wasn't such a bad one, considering how our last meeting went," I add coolly.

Gaspar narrows his eyes. He seems to reconjure his smile with some effort. My brother takes a moment to pour the tea set up on the small table between us.

I grab my cup and hesitate before bringing it up to my lips. I blow on the hot surface of my tea and an aroma of roasted seaweed wafts up to my nostrils. Hojicha. My favorite.

I set down the cup without taking a sip.

"I received your letter," I say. I want to get on with the reason I came. Being in such a small room after the spaciousness of La Bête's castle is making me feel claustrophobic.

"About that," says Gaspar. He sets down his tea and gives me a serious look. "Beauty, first, I want you to know that I am very sorry about what happened. I must remember that even if you are my baby sister, you are also a grown woman, and I had no right to discipline you in public that way."

"'Discipline' me?"

Gaspar pinches the bridge of his nose. The lacey ruffles of his shirt spills frothily out from the edge of his sleeve. The vanity I find endearing in La Bête is annoying in my brother.

"Beauty," he says. "You must stop making these hysterical accusations at Julian. Now that Julian's family has regained a portion of their fortune, Julian is poised to become one of the most influential men in town—and in the kingdom. A whisper of a scandal, no matter how untrue, could seriously damage his reputation. I take it upon myself to tell you this because Julian has been overly indulgent of your behavior. He loves you. And if you would only stop being so stubborn, you would see that you are right for him."

I'm in thrall of fury at Gaspar's words but his last sentence makes me shudder. I don't know why my family does not believe me about Julian. It's one thing to dismiss my accusations of murder but another to act as if I have not made it clear that I loathe him.

I stare down at my tea and wonder, as I always do when I'm around my family, whether I'm losing my mind.

I haven't had a sip of tea and it's not because it's too hot. It was perfectly steeped at a hot but not scalding temperature.

I am paranoid that the tea is drugged.

It doesn't make sense. And I don't really think the tea is drugged, I just have a vague paranoia about drinking it.

I search my mind for a logical reason for this and find none. Only my feelings of discomfort, and a vague distrust of my brother since he slapped me. But if anything, I should be worried that he will physically hurt me again: I am not.

I am uneasy that he is trying to get away with something.

Am I truly mad? It's true I've always been considered odd. And most people dislike me. With the exception of La Bête, who is gratifyingly straightforward, and Ahmed, who was endearingly puckish, I rarely get on well with people. I don't know how to talk to others: most of the time I have nothing to say. I am mostly unaffected by the frustrations others feel when they believe they have been slighted and I've found that many people bond by complaining about something.

I've always believed that I am a rational person who sees things the way they are, and that others' beliefs are tainted by their emotions. But I have felt a tumult of emotions in my life as well. I just try not to let them affect my reasoning faculty. But perhaps they have, to an extent I am unaware of. If I am honest, Ahmed's death was traumatic for me at that young age.

What if I see things differently, not because I am logical, but because *I* am the one tainted by emotion? What if everyone else is right?

Is Julian truly innocent of murder?

Julian was there. There was a witness. He and the other boys admitted to setting the shack on fire. Is it possible that he really was young and stupid enough to believe that he could set the shack on fire, and not hurt Ahmed?

I believe that Ahmed was locked into his shack—based on the fact that he did not make it out. But perhaps he was asleep. Perhaps he never woke up. There is no evidence that the boys deliberately locked Ahmed into the shack to trap him there.

So it's possible that Julian was malicious and stupid, but not murderous. Is it possible my love for Ahmed, and my grief at his death made me overly hateful towards Julian? I imagine how I would think of the situation if it were a stranger. Say, Genevieve Duval. What if she had been burned, not at the stake, but in her home?

My mind wrestles. Malicious and stupid, or a murderer—is there such a big difference if the end result is the same? If the perpetrator is not remorseful?

What about Gaspar's belief that I am secretly in love with Julian? My logic is easy to examine for its strength but I rarely look at my emotions.

I look at them now. That's easy.

No.

I am not secretly in love with Julian.

I know because I am secretly in love with La Bête.

"Beauty?"

I blink.

Gaspar has lowered his head and peers up at me. I'm still staring down at my tea.

"I can see that you're considering what I've said," he says gently, "that's good. Very good."

I blink again, trying to remember what we were talking about before I fell into my reverie.

"You've never given Julian a fair chance," Gaspar says, "and it's high time you did. He wants to marry you, you know."

This again.

"Gaspar," I say firmly. "I am not going to marry Julian."

Gaspar's lips press together.

"I am going to serve out the rest of my term with La Bête and then I am going to Kurys: I am going to Dar al-Sakan."

"Beauty!" Gaspar pounds his fist on the table. I jump. "It is just like you to be so selfish! I don't know if it's because you're the youngest, or whether your beauty has made you vain, but it is my burden to remind you that you have a duty to our family."

"What do you think I'm doing, Gaspar?" I ask, baffled. "You've received the chests of gold from La Bête."

"And now you can come home!"

"But what about my agreement with La Bête?"

Don't you want the rest of the gold, I think but do not say aloud for Gaspar is antagonized enough.

"He is a beast! Agreements with beasts need not be honored. And what will he do? He has no influence outside of his enchanted castle. Let him find another woman—or not. Perhaps it's time we addressed the situation and got rid of The Beast that's been terrorizing our women for generations."

Gaspar's words blow a cold breath of fear through me. This is what I have dreaded would come to pass. This is why they don't care about the rest of the gold if I serve out the rest of my year. They want to take what isn't offered, what isn't theirs.

I don't understand why people want to destroy those who are different, but I know from past experience that if they have enough majority, enough power—and hold aloft the lure of money—they will succeed in spreading their hatred.

I'm scared. I'm utterly infuriated too. But for survival, I must pretend I am neither.

"Do you think that's possible?" I ask, as if I am only mildly interested. "To...kill The Beast? So that he could never bother anyone again?"

Gaspar sits back in his chair. If I read my brother correctly, he is surprised by my reaction, and pleased.

"I think so," he says slowly. "There have been a few dissenters who argue that he is harmless and say he is no different than the men here who visit—forgive me—whores in brothels. But they are becoming the minority. You know. You've had to endure. He is a beast. Not human. He has no right to our women."

I swallow and nod. "I could help you," I say. My tongue feels thick and my heart is in my throat. "Whatever your plans are, I'm already there, inside La Bête's castle. I can help you carry out whatever it is that you plot."

Gaspar gives me a keen look. I am a terrible liar but I try to look as guileless as possible.

"Thank you for the offer," he says. "But as your brother I'm more interested in keeping you safe. I'd rather bring you home. There's a carriage outside, in the back. And an exit, under this table."

Gaspar taps the carpeted floor with his foot.

"I..." I try and think of something to say. "This is unexpected. I have projects—tools and materials I've left back at La Bête's castle..."

I must go back to La Bête. I have to warn him and...I have to spend as much time with him as I can before my year is over. Even if he doesn't love me back, even though I am just another woman in a long parade of those who have served him, I don't care.

"Beauty," says Gaspar, tapping his foot. "You are obsessed with things that don't matter. Who cares about your projects and tools? They are not important. I didn't want to bring it up and worry you when there's nothing you can do about it, but Papi has been sick."

"Sick?" I think my heart has permanently lodged itself in my throat. It makes my voice come out in a squeak. I try to clear my throat. "Sick with what? What's the matter with him?"

"The physicians don't know," Gaspar says smoothly, "and I'm sure they'll figure it out. But just in case...Beauty, don't you think you ought to see him? Would you ever be able to forgive yourself if Papi died while you were up in that enchanted castle, flipping your skirts for a beast?"

I'm beyond being insulted by Gaspar's crude phrasing but his posited scenario of my father's death while I'm away makes me flinch.

I rise. "All right," I say. "But let me write a note for La Bête."

Gaspar's face darkens and I add, "It will buy us some time in case he comes after me or tries to punish us for breaking the agreement. If he thinks I'm only visiting Papi because he's ill, he's more likely to wait for me to come back."

"Very well," Gaspar relents. His eyes already gleam with his triumph. I'm too worried about Papi to care that I am also doing exactly what Gaspar wants. Gaspar thinks that once I am home, I am going to stay but he's wrong.

I will find my way back to La Bête.

I write my note but Gaspar doesn't allow me to give it to my bodyguards directly. He insists I leave it with him and he will give it to them once I am gone.

I acquiesce and we move the little table and the little square of carpet that was underneath the table, and Gaspar opens the trapdoor for me.

I climb down a rickety ladder, and make my way through a dark tunnel to the end where I see sunlight poking through. I climb another ladder that leads up along a wall, to a window. I shimmy out the window and drop to the ground in the alley behind the tailor's shop.

A carriage waits for me, just as Gaspar said.

13
LA BÊTE

I WAIT FOR Beauty's carriage to return her to me.

When it arrives, two shamefaced guards give me a note from her instead.

I read the note and when I am done roaring at the guards, I dismiss them and retreat to the library to brood.

What other choice do I have?

I am trapped in this castle and the woman I love is outside of it where I can't protect her.

Less importantly, without Beauty to calm me, I will be lost to my beast.

And I will die.

14
BEAUTY

MY FAMILY'S new townhouse is in the fashionable Hill District—so named for the hill my carriage climbs up to deliver me to my family.

I stare down and think I can see the smaller district where we lived previously below me.

I'm dropped off in front of a red brick building. A majordome answers the door and eyes me in my worn traveling ensemble.

But someone must have informed him of my arrival for he takes my cloak and escorts me to the parlor where I'm momentarily stunned by the flock of young women gathered there in an array of brightly dyed dresses, like gaily colored swans.

Two swans emerge from the flock with squeals of joy—Fernanda and Yesenia. My sisters seize my arms and drag me to a loveseat where they squeeze in on either side of me. I'm drowning in their excited chatter and voluminous skirts spilling over my legs, while the other swans stare at me with facial expressions ranging from curiosity to disdain.

"But Beauty, what on earth are you wearing?" Yesenia pulls at my loose tunic. "I can't believe The Beast had the gall to clothe you in rags! The least he could have done was provide you with a decent wardrobe."

There are so many things wrong with Yesenia's statement, my brain stumbles in trying to formulate a response.

"No matter," says Fernanda. "You're back home now—we're so happy Gaspar was able to help you escape!"

"I came to see Papi," I manage to get out.

My sisters' faces are blank.

"Papi?" says Fernanda. "He's at his club right now with Lucio and Alarico but they'll all be home later. We weren't sure if you'd be able to escape the castle to see Gaspar—it's not like we could sit at home waiting for you in case you made it."

"But...is Papi well enough to be at his club? Gaspar said he was ill."

Fernanda and Yesenia exchange a swift look I find impossible to decipher.

Fernanda leans into me. "That's a family matter," she whispers, "let's not discuss it front of these girls."

She sits up and winks at me.

Yesenia hands me a fluted glass. I sniff. Expensive champagne. Served in expensive crystal.

My sisters both glare at me for they can read my thoughts and I sigh and take a sip. I'll take up Papi's condition and their extravagant spending with them later when we're not surrounded by strangers.

I endure the rest of the afternoon, trying to converse politely while I agonize over whether La Bête has received my note yet, what he must be thinking, and how badly he'll need me tonight. He can go a night without me, perhaps two or three. But is there a point that he can reach from which there is no return from The Beast? I wish there could be a backup woman in place to serve his needs...then I'm surprised by the wave of jealousy that washes over me.

How irrational of me.

My sisters keep looking at each other and going into the corner to whisper and I'm relieved when they announce to the other women that I look tired and they're taking me upstairs to my room for rest. I'm not physically very tired but I'm mentally exhausted by the presence of so many excitable people after the solitude of La Bête's castle.

I follow my sisters, grateful that they sense I'd rather retreat to our room.

But to my surprise, they show me to my own bedroom.

"We know you'd probably rather not share room or bed with us," Fernanda says.

"Thank you," I say, blinking. The room is sparse with only a bed and a small, narrow window, but there is an attached water closet. I notice the wash basin with its own plumbing and crouch down to examine the S-shaped pipe.

"Huh, you'll have to show me to the water source for these later," I say to my sisters absently.

There's no response. I rise and wander back into the bedroom. It's empty.

I go to the bedroom door.

It's locked.

I have a sinking feeling in my stomach which I ignore. I take a deep breath and rap loudly on the door.

"Fernanda! Yesenia! You've locked me into the bedroom," I say.

"It's for your own good, Beauty." Fernanda's response is immediate—she's waited on the other side.

"Fernanda," I say, trying to sound patient and rational. "What are you doing?"

121

"We'll discuss this later, Beauty," Fernanda says. "But we want you to give Julian a fair chance. Gaspar said he would tell you Papi was ill if it seemed you harbored any loyalty to that beast."

"Papi isn't ill?" I say. My relief over this piece of news turns the sinking feeling in my gut into a ball of fury. "You lied to me?"

"For your own good," Yesenia says. The imploring tone of her voice infuriates me. "Julian wants to marry you! You're perfect for him! Why can't you see that?"

I raise my fists and bang on the door with all my might. The door is heavy but my landing fists boom and I hear a squeal.

"Let me out right now," I say loudly. How on earth my family thinks this will convince me to marry Julian is beyond my scope of understanding. They are mad. They, not me.

Or rather, they are greedy, shallow, selfish—and deluding themselves if they think I'll come around.

"I will never marry Julian Montserrat!" I shriek at the door. "Never! He's a murderer!" I hope all the swans downstairs hear me and are scandalized. I hope one of them has a smidgen of conscious and tries to free me.

There is no response from my sisters and I can only assume that they've hurried downstairs to clear out their guests before little sister can further embarrass them.

I quiet down for there's no pointing in further screaming or pounding. The door is too heavy to break down and I've already tried to make my voice heard.

Now it's time to plan, and think of a way out.

15
BEAUTY

JULIAN COMES to visit me that evening.

I've searched every centimeter of my room, tried squeezing my head out the window and through the little opening at the bottom of my bedroom door that's meant for lapdogs—for that's what I've figured out my room is, with the haphazard bed thrown in its corner. A room for pets.

But I am too big to escape through those exits.

My family has shoved food through the lapdog door but no one has had the courage to visit me.

When Julian comes into my bedroom I'm standing by the window, analyzing the stability of the sill.

I turn to face the monster.

He is handsome, I won't deny that. Dark eyes, dark hair, a masculine jaw and a noble nose.

Julian's eyes consume my form greedily. He makes no attempt to hide his desire for me as he normally does in front of my family.

His blatant desire and the darkness of the room make me uncomfortable so I move to light a lamp.

I almost immediately regret it when we are bathed in an intimate, romantic glow.

"What do I have to do to convince you to marry me?" Julian gets straight to the point.

This aspect I appreciate about Julian: he knows that I am not fooled into thinking he is a decent human being, so he drops the act when we are alone.

"There's nothing you can do, Julian," I say calmly. He is unaffected by empathy so I try to appeal to his reason instead.

"You can have other beautiful women, Julian. Women who are more receptive to your charms. Women who would complement your ambitions."

"I know that," he says impatiently. "Of course there are other women, perhaps not quite as beautiful, but more skilled at navigating through social circles, and who are certainly more interested in maintaining their appearances, in public or otherwise."

Julian gives my tunic and trousers a pointed look.

"Any of them would be infinitely more appropriate," he says. His gaze turns intense and he approaches me with slow, measured steps.

"But I'm not interested in a woman who is fooled by my charms. I want you. There's only ever been you, Beauty. Ever since we were children, I've been obsessed with you. Not because you're beautiful—or not just because of that. You *see* me. The real me."

Julian stands so close to me his breath flutters my face as he speaks softly. "And I see you. I've always seen in you, what you refuse to admit."

"That I secretly love you?" I inject as much scorn and contempt into my words as I can. I want to step away from him but don't wish to appear weak.

Julian smiles. "That we are more alike than you admit."

His hand reaches for my hair and pushes a lock behind my ear.

I shudder and take the step back after all. I back into the wall.

"You're wrong," I say shakily.

Julian observes me against the wall. He folds his arms and maintains his distance. But I'm not fooled into thinking that makes me safe.

"When others let their emotions cloud their judgment, you are the voice of reason. You see things the way they are, not the way you want them to be when you're feeling optimistic, or the way you think they are when you think you've been treated unfairly. You are the most cold, most logical, most *rational*, being I've ever encountered—other than myself. You have some weaknesses but I can help you with those."

I'm silent for Julian is going to tell me what he thinks my "weaknesses" are whether I want him to or not.

Julian smiles at my silence and continues. "Your first weakness is that you don't know how to pretend interest when others are prattling. People love validation. If you give it to them they will be grateful, and think of you fondly—and be more receptive to taking your side in disputes, or providing future favors."

Julian finally releases his arms and moves in toward me. He grasps my shoulders. "Your other weakness is that you do fall occasionally, to that irrational hammer of emotion. Witness: your love for Ahmed."

I close my eyes at the mention of my dead friend.

"It was somewhat understandable that you would feel some attachment to the man for the way he took pity on you and became your mentor. But your love for him was all out of proportion. And he cared as much for you."

Julian sounds perplexed. "I admit it made me jealous. I had thought up until then that you were exactly like me. I was disappointed when I realized otherwise. But I thought I could fix it."

My heart stutters. "Fix it how?" My voice croaks out.

Julian purses his lips and studies my face. "Well, I realize now that I cannot change that aspect of you. But perhaps I can help you channel it towards me."

"My capacity to love?"

He nods. "I can provide you with a comfortable home. Elevated social status. You would have the money to buy all your rocks and continue your studies in peace. I would only ask in return that you occasionally act the hostess for appearance's sake. Accompany me to some gatherings. I will teach you how to interact with people so that they like you. And we will share in the intimacies of marriage, of course."

He says this last coolly but his breath has sped up and I easily recognize the signs of arousal. "You remain untraumatized by The Beast's attentions so it's reasonable to expect that you can adequately handle mine."

I choke.

Julian frowns. "Where is the fault in my proposal? It should appeal to you. Why doesn't it appeal to you?"

"Julian," I say, and although I am certain he has all but confessed that he murdered Ahmed to me, I have no rage left to feel over Ahmed's death. I've always thought Ahmed's legacy to me was his mentoring of a brilliant mind from an equally brilliant mind—but his real legacy was his love.

"Julian," I say again as my voice breaks. "Love is not proportional."

He stares at me. This is the most empathy I've ever felt for him. Perhaps we are more alike than I admitted to myself. Only I had someone like Ahmed early on, to teach me that love is worth the heartache. And then when I met La Bête, I learned I was capable of falling in love as well.

"Love is not proportional," I repeat. "Not to favors. I cannot channel my love towards you if you provide me with money and comfort. I want *love* in return. I want—"

I stop myself. I want La Bête. And I realize that I know without a doubt that La Bête loves me too. My heart aches for having this realization when I am trapped and unable to connect with him.

"I want companionship," I say instead, for La Bête is already in danger. "I have no need of the finer things in life."

Julian stares at me. "Being married to me would mean you have my 'companionship.' As for love, I don't believe I am capable of the emotion, but what I feel for you—I believe that is the closest thing to love I can feel. Is that not enough?"

I think quickly. "Perhaps it can be," I say slowly, as if reluctant to admit it. "It would certainly be nice to be with someone who understands me and doesn't believe I'm wasting my time with rocks like La Bête and my family."

Julian smiles triumphantly.

"But," I say, "I don't appreciate how you've trapped me here against my will."

"You weren't giving me a fair chance," Julian says reasonably. "I just wanted you to listen to me."

"And I have."

"What would you do, return to The Beast?" Julian looks at me sharply with his hooded eyes.

I must go carefully. Julian knows me better than my own family does. He is more difficult to lie to.

I attempt a careless shrug. "My family interprets my reluctance to renege on my agreement with La Bête as a sign that I feel some affection towards him, but they are projecting their own motives onto my actions. I believe in keeping my word. That's all."

"I've noticed that," Julian says. "But surely you can see that La Bête is not worth your consideration? He's less than a man."

I take a deep breath. "Even so," I say. "While I'm willing to bow out of my agreement with him, I feel I must give him notice that I don't intend on returning. So he can find another woman to fill my place. Otherwise, he will simply wait for my return. Or perhaps he'll think something happened to me and come looking."

"Then you are amenable to my proposal?"

"Yes," I say simply. "Let me write a letter to La Bête, and once I've received his confirmation that he received my...resignation...we can—" I try to keep my voice even, "—we can announce our engagement. I don't require a lavish affair so we can marry whenever my family deems it appropriate."

My family, and polite society, will consider the usual two-month wait appropriate considering I've recently been with another man.

Julian's eyes gleam. "Very well. Write your letter and I will deliver it to La Bête myself. And I will bring his response to you myself. Then we will announce our engagement."

16
LA BÊTE

A MAN COMES to visit me, the day after I receive Beauty's note that her father is ill.

He is handsome and I smell Beauty's scent lingering on him and I want to tear him in half and smear his entrails on the walls.

Instead I receive him in the library where he politely waits for me to read Beauty's letter and pen a response.

Dear Monsieur La Bête,

This letter is to inform you that I am requesting release from my contract. The man delivering this letter to you, Julian Montserrat, is an old family friend who has recently made his feelings known to me.

I am to marry him.

I know you'll understand it wouldn't be appropriate for me to continue my service to you.

I wish you the best and hope that you can find another woman to fill my place posthaste.

Regards,
Mlle. Kahlo

P.S. I regret I will not be there to see the
blooming of next year's roses.

I read the letter through twice before I set it down.

The man who delivered it, Montserrat, stands at a nearby bookcase, ostensibly browsing its titles but I suspect he is observing my reaction out of the corner of his eye.

Since I was deprived of Beauty last night, I'm stuck in my beastly form despite the light of day. My rage is hard to swallow, but swallow it I do.

Beauty's safety depends on it.

"My congratulations are in order," I say to the man. He turns. My voice is growlier than usual but he would expect me to be put out. I give him a pained smile that conveys annoyance, but nothing more. "I wish you and Mademoiselle Kahlo the very best."

Montserrat smiles coolly. "Beauty requested that I bring her your reply."

"Of course."

I rifle through my desk and find some fresh parchment. I carefully grab my quill with my large hand, dip it in ink, and pen Beauty my reply.

"Oh!" I say, as if I've just thought of something. "She mentioned how she will miss the roses and I still have some in bloom. I will let her know that I'm sending a rose along with this letter—that is, if you don't mind?"

Montserrat gives me a tight smile. I'm already adding my postscript to inform Beauty.

It is a risk to allow one of my roses to leave the castle, but I will take that risk for Beauty. I doubt Montserrat knows that my roses are enchanted, and even if he does, I don't think the roses would cooperate with this world's magic. Since I mention it in the letter, hopefully he will not withhold the rose from Beauty out of jealousy.

Speaking of jealousy.

It is all I can manage to fold up the letter and insert it into an envelope for Montserrat.

I've already plucked a rose from the garden—I wanted one next to me to keep me company in Beauty's absence and I carefully extricate it from my lapel.

I hand Montserrat the letter and the rose. "There," I say. "Please give my regards to your betrothed, along with this rose."

I force myself to turn away from him, dismissively, as if it were that easy for me to pass Beauty on to him.

"Now, if you will excuse me, I will have to put the notice out that I'm in search of another woman. My servant will show you out."

I grin wolfishly when Montserrat eyes the candelabra Beauty named "Rattler" with dismay.

Rattler leads Montserrat out of my library and I fall into my chair and put my head in my hands.

Again, I am helpless to save Beauty.

But she is smart. She is resourceful. And I've given her the means to save herself.

17
BEAUTY

I'M LET OUT of my prison to accompany my family to the Our Lady of Orleans festivities in town. My sisters dress me up in one of Yesenia's gowns and do up my hair for the outing with my family. My father doesn't come with us—I haven't seen him at all since my return to town.

Julian is supposedly delivering my letter to La Bête today so at least I'm spared his presence. I don't know how long I must endure our sham of an engagement. I need to escape.

But even if I can slip away when Fernanda, Gaspar, Yesenia, Lucio, and Alarico are constantly shadowing me; even if I make it out of the crowds without someone recognizing me and alerting my family; even if I make it to the Black Forest and use my ring talisman to guide me to La Bête's castle, how long will it take me to travel on foot? I don't have enough coin to hire a carriage from one part of Orleans to another, let alone through Orleans and deep into the Black Forest. And supposing I survive this journey through the dangerous woods full of *bzou* and Lady knows what else, what will greet me when I arrive?

The longer La Bête goes without a woman, the deeper he descends into his beast, and the harder it is to bring him back.

How far gone will he be if it takes me weeks to return home?

No. I have to figure out a way to get to him sooner.

We make our way slowly towards the basilica at the other edge of town.

Musicians pluck merry tunes on their *conchas*: stringed instruments made out of armadillo shells. The *concheros*—dancers—hop around the crowd and throw beaded rosaries at those who win their favor.

Lucio and Gaspar grab each of my arms when one of the dancers tries to start a jig with me. They herd me back into the fold and Gaspar mutters, "We should have left her at home."

"And have her miss the celebration? Of Santa Inanna herself? What would Mamá say?" Yesenia's eyes flash. My siblings had an argument about letting me out today. Yesenia and Alarico were my defenders.

Gaspar doesn't retort. If there is anything sacred in my family besides money, it is the memory of my mother.

When we get to the basilica the crowds are too large for us to make our way in, but we join the throng of pilgrims in the plaza outside.

I stare at the eight-pointed rosette that decorates the front of the basilica and am reminded of Ahmed.

I clutch the coin that dangles from around my neck and offer a quick prayer up to Our Lady.

The day passes.

I smile coolly when my siblings tease me about "playing hard to get" with Julian all these years, and laugh at the street artists' skits in the plaza.

But in my head, I plan my escape. It will be tonight. My family expects me to try something now, while we're out: they will relax when we return home and I haven't budged from their side. They will think me exhausted from the day's activities and loosen their guard.

Julian will have returned from La Bête's castle, hopefully with La Bête's response. If I can get rid of Julian, I will make my escape then. I'm dreading what Julian will consider appropriate affections for us once we are officially betrothed.

I'm distracted from my scheming when the crowd gathered in the plaza roars.

I look up. A mob of perhaps thirty men carries the Lord of Misrule over their heads—a huge figure constructed of wood, straw, and cloth.

I gasp when the men set down the figure and prop it up in its customary pedestal in the plaza.

This year the Lord of Misrule has been dressed in a white shirt and old-fashioned blue jacket with brass buttons. I would have chalked this up to coincidence but they've also given him a mane of lion-like hair—and I hear some of the men screaming, "Kill The Beast!"

Yesenia turns swiftly to gauge my reaction and I manage only to raise a brow.

But my heart pounds.

"This is new," I say carelessly as several of the men light torches. I recognize local townsmen. They hold the flames up to the figure and it catches instantly aflame.

It's an old custom still observed in some places to burn the effigy of the Lord of Misrule but that hasn't been done in Orleans in years. The plaza is just too crowded, and it wouldn't be safe.

Mothers pull their curious children back and I'm heartbroken to hear the cry of a few get taken up by many: "Kill La Bête! Kill La Bête!"

I can't help but remember my lessons my from history tutors: the Lord of Misrule used to be a real man that was burned as a sacrifice at the end of the festival of Our Lady.

I turn away from the effigy, not caring what my family thinks. I don't have to like La Bête to find the hatred in this town sickening.

That's when I notice her. The conchera—shell dancer. She's younger. Prettier. But recognizably the "old" beggar woman I spoke to last week.

The conchera winks at me. I draw closer to her.

"Look at those beautiful scarves," I say inanely when Lucio sees me stray. I can't judge if her scarves are any more aesthetically pleasing than the other dancers' but I am lucky when Yesenia "oohs" and flounces over with me.

I desperately want to speak to the conchera in private—she said she was a witch with some minor skills and I hope that perhaps I can get a potion from her—but my sisters flank me. I smile and toss my head back and dance with them, hopping from side to side while I twitch my skirts, and trying to make eye contact with the conchera when my sisters aren't looking.

"She has rhythm," shouts the conchera, and she throws a rosary at me.

I put up my hand and catch the beads.

She puts her hands on her hips and tilts her head at me. "You have the eye of a maid that will soon be married," she says slyly.

My sisters laugh.

"A fortune-teller," Fernanda claps her hands in delight. "Tell me mine!"

The conchera turns to Fernanda and purses her lips. She sashays over to my elder sister and whispers in her ear. Fernanda's eyes widen and still the conchera speaks. Yesenia giggles at the myriad of expressions that pass over our sister's face: doubt, startlement, and finally when the conchera pulls away, awe.

Fernanda gives the conchera a coin.

"Now me," Yesenia demands. She holds up her coin for the conchera's attention though the woman is already turning to Yesenia.

She whispers to her for a while and Fernanda is too lost in her own thoughts to tease Yesenia in turn.

Yesenia blushes and seems pleased with her fortune when the conchera is done.

Finally she turns to me.

I've composed my plea and am ready to present my case when the conchera grabs my arm and leans in close, but she speaks first.

"The rosary beads are enchanted with poison. They dissolve quickly in liquid, though the poison will still work without it. One or two beads will put an average-sized man to sleep but more than ten will kill him."

Her words brush my ear and I shiver.

"Thank you," I say.

"Consider this repayment for last week," she says.

The conchera pulls away. Music bursts from the nearby musicians and her solemn look is wiped away by a wide grin. She hops back to her fellow dancers without another glance my way.

"Yours was so short, Beauty," says Yesenia. "You should have offered her coin, that's the way to get them to talk."

"I'm satisfied with my fortune," I say, clutching my rosary beads in my fist.

And I am.

18
BEAUTY

JULIAN IS WAITING for me when we get home.

My family scatters and leaves me alone in the parlor to receive him.

At least I am not forced to receive him in my bedroom again.

"I've done as you requested and delivered your letter to La Bête. Here is his reply." Julian hands me a letter.

I take the envelope from him and study it in dismay. It's addressed to "Beauty" in a familiar spiky, sprawling hand, and sealed with red wax. La Bête's seal imprint shows a lion.

"Is this all?" I ask casually.

"What else did you expect?"

I look up at Julian's bland face and I regret asking. I am dismal at subterfuge. Well, it's too late now to take it back.

I shrug carelessly and open the letter.

"He took the news as well as expected," says Julian as I scan La Bête's letter. "He seemed annoyed that I took you from him but resigned. He must have been expecting something of the sort."

I peek up to see Julian's self-satisfied smile. My eyes return to the letter. My heart races when I get to La Bête's postscript. He understood my plea. I hold up the letter.

"La Bête says here that he included a rose from his garden as a keepsake. Did he give it to you to pass on to me?"

"Oh that!" Julian smacks his head. "He did. But I didn't want to tuck it away into my bags in case that would crush it, and I'm afraid I lost it on the way over here."

He is channeling the sort of self-deprecating gentleman we both know is a false facade.

"I hope that's not too much of a disappointment, is it?" Julian says. His hooded eyes dare me to say that it is.

"No, not at all," I force out.

"Well, then. Beauty. I have delivered your letter to The Beast, and brought you his reply. Will you keep your end of the bargain?"

I take a moment to reply. Julian knows I don't really want to marry him. He will see through my falsehood anyway if I act thrilled by the thought of our matrimony. Better he see my resignation and think me honest.

"Very well, Julian. Let's call my family members in here and announce our engagement."

My father finally makes an appearance with the rest of my family.

Julian announces our engagement to all and my siblings make a ruckus of joy while I die inside.

Fernanda actually cries tears of happiness.

Yesenia and Lucio are jubilant and they bounce excitedly up and down and call the servants for champagne to celebrate.

My father sidles over to me: happiness crinkles the corners of his eye.

"I'm so happy for you, *mi hija*," he says as he hugs me for the first time in months.

"Thank you," I say automatically. My cheeks hurt from holding my mouth in a forced smile.

His smile fades. "Are you—"

He's cut off as Yesenia cries, "Here's the champagne!"

"Let me help you," I call out to my sister as I brush past my father. I dismiss the pretty maid who wheeled in the champagne cart. No need to subject her to family drama.

Yesenia and I pour the bubbling liquid into fluted glasses. The others gather round Julian. Lucio and Gaspar pound his back as they congratulate him.

"To the bride and groom-to-be!" Gaspar toasts once we've passed out the glasses.

"To Julian who finally won over our prickly sister!" Lucio.

"To our *beloved* sister," Yesenia says with a pointed look at Lucio, "who was finally able to get past her stubbornness to see what she had right in front of her!"

"If your marriage lasts as long as Beauty's stubbornness, that'll be longer than most," Alarico jokes.

Everyone laughs and sips deeply of their champagne.

"And look," says Lucio, who has made his way over to me. He holds up my left hand. "He's already claimed her in the Tierra Rican tradition with a ring!"

My sisters "aw" and I smile faintly at the look on Julian's face.

"Not too fast," Gaspar says to Julian with mock sternness. "The ring is for married people and you're not there yet."

Julian's face has lost his mask of geniality.

"Take it off," he says in a soft voice that nevertheless cuts across the room.

Gaspar laughs. "I was just joking, brother, it's all right to break with tradition sometimes."

Julian doesn't even acknowledge him.

He stalks over to me and looms threateningly. "Take it off, I said."

"No," I say.

"What's going on?" Fernanda says with a nervous twitter.

"Take it off," Julian says again.

"I won't," I say.

"It's just a ring, brother," says Alarico.

Neither Julian nor I spare glances for my family. Our masks are off and we glare at each other with the full force of our dislike and displeasure.

"Take it off or I will chop off the finger you wear it on," Julian hisses at me.

I hear the breaking of a dropped champagne glass. I hope it was empty.

"I feel dizzy," Yesenia says. No one pays her any mind but from the corner of my eye I see her hand go to her forehead—and then she slumps to the ground.

"Yessy, this is no time for your dramatics," Fernanda says sharply.

My father is at Yesenia's side, he pulls her lax head into his lap. "She's really fainted—"

My father is once again interrupted, this time by Fernanda as she goes limp and thuds to the ground.

141

My father looks up at my siblings in horror as one by one, they faint to the ground.

Julian and I are left standing. Beads of sweat are forming on his forehead and I see understanding dawn in his glazed eyes.

"You will pay for this," he says, "you will both pay." Julian finally drops to the ground.

"*Mi linda hija*," my father says in a choked voice. "Is this your doing?"

"Yes, Papi." I did miss one of the champagne glasses that were passed out but I managed to get the rest.

"What have you done?"

I take the empty champagne bottle and brandish it at my father, though he makes no move to rise.

"I poisoned them with a sleep spell, Papi, but they'll wake up fine," I say. "I'm leaving here and returning to La Bête. Don't try to stop me. Don't call for the servants to stop me."

"Why would you do this?"

"I tried to be reasonable," I say, still trying to be reasonable. "I explained that I was not interested in Julian. How could I be when he killed Ahmed?"

For once my father doesn't dispute that Julian killed Ahmed. "You cannot fight men like Julian. They are charming snakes that win everyone over to their side. Publicly accusing them of murder only makes you look mad."

"It's too late for that advice, Papi," I say. "In any case, now I've done what I've had to in order to escape."

"Why are you returning to La Bête?"

"I love him," I say defiantly.

My father shakes his head. "Even if he is not the monster people say he is, people believe he is a monster.

When I was younger we just thought of La Bête as an ugly, shy man. Women went willingly to him from all the kingdoms, have always gone willingly. Never thought it was my business to interfere between consenting adults. That's how most people thought. But these days those sentiments have changed: at least in Orleans. Men like Julian have noticed the endless stream of gold at La Bête's disposal. They will take up the cause of defending their women although the women aren't theirs to begin with. Anything to justify storming that castle and looting it."

My mouth goes dry. "You think they will storm the castle?"

"I've overheard Julian and your brothers and what they plan. There's a mob of them ready to move on the castle. They have transport, weapons, maps, a sorcerer. They mean to destroy La Bête tonight, during the height of the Santa Inanna festivities."

"Then I must go immediately," I say. I set down the empty champagne bottle for it's apparent my father will not physically stop me. "I'm sorry, Papi. I love you. And my brothers and sisters. But you must let me go."

My father pleads with me as I head out of the parlor, even calls me by my actual name.

My heart breaks to leave him but staying would only lead to further heartbreak. Eventually there would be nothing left of me but a beautiful and empty shell.

19
BEAUTY

I DON'T LEAVE the house immediately.

I return to my room to gather my cloak and things I don't wish to leave behind.

Then I look through the guest rooms until I find one with Julian's bags.

I rifle through them until I find it: the enchanted rose La Bête sent me.

I don't know why La Bête didn't come for me himself but I suspect that his curse has to do with it.

That, I will deal with later. For now, he has given me the means to get back to him.

I take the cover off one of the burning lamps.

Holding the enchanted rose by its stem I touch the blossom of the flower to the fire.

It catches flame immediately.

Instead of burning through the petals and dying, the fire envelopes the rose blossom completely.

I bring it up to my face, enchanted by the sight. I've no natural magic myself but I feel the tingle of the rose's magic strongly. A power has built up in it, and it's ready to be used.

I bring my other hand to close it over my hand with the ring. The power of the talisman zings through me.

I close my eyes. *Take me home. Take me home to La Bête.*

A strong wind gusts from nowhere and the flame goes out with a whoosh.

A great roaring fills my ears.

I drown in the scent of roses.

20
BEAUTY

I THINK I pass out for a while.

When I come to, pinpoints of light form a mantle around me.

I blink.

I realize that I'm on my back, staring up at a blanket of stars.

I'm in the rose garden.

The sound of low growling sets the hair on the back of my neck prickling.

I rise to my elbows and freeze.

La Bête is crouched low near my feet. His mouth is formed into a snarl that exposes his fangs. I look into his eyes and see no recognition register there.

"Easy," I say softly. I edge back away from him, slowly. "Easy," I repeat as La Bête's eyes narrow and his growling intensifies.

"La Bête?" I say. "Bellamy? Are you in there?"

La Bête has his hands on the ground before him as if they are the front paws of his legs, rather than his arms.

Dear Lady. I finger my rosary. He looks like he wants to kill and eat me.

But I did not poison my entire family to return to the man I love, only to die at his hands.

I snarl back at La Bête.

La Bête leaps.

I bring up my hand with the rosary beads I've torn off. It's a good chunk—I don't know how many since I had to blindly fumble with them in the dirt—and I hope it's enough as I shove it into La Bête's mouth.

His teeth scrape my hand and leave it torn and bleeding.

I scoot swiftly back as La Bête coughs and rears up, clawing at his throat. I crouch behind the stone bench.

But La Bête doesn't come after me.

He collapses to the ground and lays there, still.

I scramble over to La Bête.

I find myself hoping now I didn't use too much. La Bête is much larger than an average sized man.

I find him lying on his back, panting up at the sky.

Probably very similar to the position in which he found me moments ago.

I think of La Bête, reduced to a wounded animal, crawling to the rose garden to go mad or die in peace.

I touch his face. His silky hair is so soft.

He's not passed out like my family was earlier, but neither is he cogent and present with me.

His eyes stare blindly up at the sky.

The drugs have calmed him, put him into a stupor, but he is still awake. Still stuck in beastly form that is driving him mad with bloodlust.

Well, there's another kind of lust I can satisfy, that may still calm his beast.

I bury both hands in his mane and bring my face to his unresponsive one.

I snuffle my breath into his nose and he stirs. His eyes move over me. I breathe into him again and he looks again and this time his gaze stays on me.

"That's it," I say. "Remember me?"

I move my hands down his body. I stop to rub his chest and feel the vibrations there like a giant cat rumbling with pleasure.

I move over La Bête and straddle his body.

His hardness presses against me.

I lean down and put my mouth to La Bête as I grind my center down on his cock.

He gasps and I jerk back in case he tries to bite me but he only throws his head back.

My hands move down his body to his trousers and I scoot farther down his legs.

I press my hand against his cock and it strains to reach me through the restrictive material.

I tug at his pants. His erection springs out.

I take his eager cock in my hand and squeeze it tightly.

I roll back his skin and dip my head down to suck on his head.

A loud vibration rumbles above me—more beastly purring.

This is no time for sweet exploration. I swallow as much of La Bête's cock as I can.

His musky scent and the feel of his cock—velvet over hardness—arouses me and it's not long before I lift my skirts.

I notice for the first time the chill of the air against my bare buttocks, but soon I've lined his cock up with my sex. I drop my skirts again and slowly lower myself down.

I sink gingerly down on La Bête's erection till it is buried inside of me. La Bête throws his head back and lets out a guttural moan.

My knees dig into the dirt as I ride La Bête.

I sink my hands into his chest for balance as I move up and down his length. I come down harder each time, and for each time I sink down onto him, La Bête seems to regain more and more of his awareness.

Soon he is looking up into my eyes as I bounce wildly up and down. His hands come up to my hips and grip me there.

My sex is slick and squeezes tightly around him each time I drop down.

La Bête grasps my hips and pushes them down against him as if to keep me still against him but I jerk wildly.

His body seizes in that familiar way and his grip goes slack.

Ruthlessly, I clench my sex around him as I continue milking him through his orgasm.

I feel the warmth of his seed flood me and he is crying out but I continue until I feel my own pleasure burst out of me.

I cry out and La Bête grabs my back and pulls me down to lay atop of him.

His arms wind around me, his hands touch my hair, and he looks up at me with wonder in his warm cinnamon brown gaze.

21
LA BÊTE

"YOU CAME BACK," I say.

She gazes down at me with her dirt-smudged face, her hair a wild tangle about her head, and I think I have never seen a being so magnificent in all my centuries.

"I came back," she says, her usual perfunctory and matter-of-fact tone sounding somewhat breathless. "And—" her brows draw downward, "—and now we have to leave."

I sit up and wince as Beauty abruptly detaches herself from my throbbing cock and stands.

I notice her hand.

"What happened?" I demand as I take out my handkerchief and wrap her hand in it. Her hand is small in mine and luckily only a few drops of blood bloom through the cloth as I awkwardly tie it with my large hands.

"You happened," she says with some asperity.

I stare at her, chagrined.

"It's just a minor wound," she says when she notices my face. "I had to get you to swallow the rosary beads so you wouldn't try to kill me. I practically shoved them down your throat."

"Then Jenny was able to reach you?" I say with relief.

I take her hand and pull her out of the rose garden and through the maze. We need to get back to the castle so I can summon an enchanted carriage for Beauty.

"Jenny? The witch who was disguised as a beggar, and then one of the festival dancers?"

Beauty's strides quicken to nearly a run in order to match mine.

"Yes, she's a friend of mine."

"Did she visit you then, while I was gone?"

I sense another question under the obvious one, in Beauty's sidelong glance toward me.

"She just stopped by to give me some news and tell me she'd seen you in Orleans. I asked her to give you the rosary in case you came back and needed it to tranquilize me."

"It came in handy," Beauty says. "I can tell you about my escape later, but now we have to pack our bags."

"Beauty—

"La Bête, please listen to me: there's a mob planning to storm the castle tonight."

This is in line with what Jenny told me. "I understand but I cannot go. You must go without me. I've already packed your valise, including your metal collection." Beauty shoots me a sharp glance. "I apologize if it's not organized to your liking but I didn't want any time wasted in case you were fool enough to return."

"Fool enough to return? I saved you from your beast."

"And put yourself in danger," I retort.

"Of course I returned, we had a deal!" Beauty says angrily. "You paid my family, and I owe you one year of servitude."

I whirl to face her.

"I don't want your servitude," I roar. "I want you tucked away somewhere safe."

151

As usual, Beauty is cool and unflappable in the face of my passion.

She crosses her arms. "So you already know about the mob that's headed here," she says.

"Yes."

"You have to see that you cannot stay," she says, using her damnable *I'm being very reasonable while you are acting hysterical* tone of voice. "I know you want to defend your home but Julian is a man of power, and privilege, and influence. And now the mob has chosen his side. There is no reasoning with them. And you are severely outnumbered. Sometimes you have to run away to fight another day."

I grab her by the shoulders. The stars shine down on us: their clarity almost hurts. Now that we're out of the maze, there are no high hedges to protect us from the biting wind.

I have to raise my voice.

"Listen to me," I say gruffly. "Please trust me when I say I have a sense of self-preservation. If I thought that the two of us would have a better chance to defend the castle, I would allow you to stay. But this castle was built to show off wealth, not to defend against an angry army of townspeople. You have to leave."

"Why can't you come with me?" Beauty asks. As usual, her piercing gaze is an exclamation point to every question. "Why don't we both just leave then? Why didn't you come to town, even when you knew I was imprisoned?"

Her words are like blows. She deserves a man that can come to her rescue. Not a half man, half beast that is trapped in an indefensible castle about to be set upon by a mob that will devour her if they find her here.

"You're trapped here, aren't you?" Beauty looks aggrieved. "Why didn't you tell me sooner?"

Because I was afraid it would come to this. And I knew how you would choose. And I can't let that happen.

"What makes you think it's any of your business?" I say, injecting as much hostility into my tone as I can muster. I just think of what the mob will do to Beauty and it's not difficult. "And why should I take the trouble to rescue you from a situation you were foolish enough to fall into? Perhaps I'm tired of you, and want another woman. And now I find I'm sick of your questions."

I pick her up and bodily haul her into the castle. I think she is too surprised to argue. I've noticed her tendency to go silent when she's computing inside her little head, as if she's redirecting all her energy into formulating a fresh solution. As soon as we are inside I dump her back to the ground. Beauty stumbles and I don't help her as she finds her feet.

"There are your bags," I say coldly. I've already set them by the door. "Wait here while I go and summon you a carriage."

I turn my back on her.

Beauty's voice finds and strikes me. "La Bête! Don't you walk away from me!"

I falter without meaning to before I come to my senses and keep going down the hall.

Something crashes into my back. Hard.

I turn with a roar. I can't help it. I'm The Beast. I don't take well to being hit.

Beauty's bag lies on the ground near me and she stands a few feet away with her hands clenched by her sides.

"I am *not* leaving," Beauty says.

Her words are dangerous. I cannot help but plead, "Please stop, you don't know what you're saying."

"I see what you are trying to do, and it won't work."

"You know nothing. Stop talking!"

"You say horrible things but it's because you want me to go. I know you love me—"

"A wild assumption!"

"—I know because—"

I leap forward and put my hand over her mouth. "Don't say it!"

Beauty's hand comes up and slaps me across the face. It barely stings but the hurt and anger on her face does. I remove my hand by reflex.

"Don't you ever try to silence me again," she says quietly.

And I obey her, for as much as I want to cover her mouth again, as much as I need to stop her from saying her next words, I stand there, helpless, as Beauty declares:

"Bellamy La Bête, I love you."

22
BEAUTY

AS SOON AS the words leave my mouth, I feel a searing pain on my hand—not my injured right hand, but my left one. It's the ring.

It's white hot and burning me.

I yelp and try to take it off. But—there's no ring.

I gasp when I look down at my hand.

Where there was once a metal ring, there is now a tattoo. I realize it's the same as the one I've seen on Bellamy's finger. Which means it's the same as the one on La Bête's.

"Let me see your hand," I demand.

La Bête has his eyes closed. He opens them and regards me with his pained gaze but lifts his hand to me without protest.

I brush aside the thick hair covering his knuckles—and there I see it. I never noticed it before because he's so hairy. I hold my hand with the matching tattoo next to his.

"What does this mean?" I ask, in what I think is a heroically even tone of voice.

"It means you're trapped here with me in this castle," La Bête says.

I mislike his defeated tone.

"Why?" I ask.

"It's the curse. I couldn't warn you. The ring I gave you as Bellamy, that belonged to my mother. It's the ring I intended to wed Beka with. We don't have the same tradition there as you do in Tierra Rica: it was simply the only piece of jewelry I owned, and the thing most valuable to me. I wanted to give it to the woman I love. When I was cursed, this mark imprisoned me in the castle. And my mother's ring...they told me it would appear when a particular woman came along. The woman I would fall in love with."

La Bête looks at me. His eyes are luminous. "You."

He seizes me and kisses me, hard. He pulls back before I can twine my arms around him.

"I'm sorry," he says. "I love you too, though you've already figured that out. I've loved you from the beginning. And I've had to fight the urge to want your love in return. Because of this."

He gestures at my hand. "The ring marked you. According to the terms of the curse, if you were to ever return my love, then we would forever be entwined, cursed to live out our lives together."

"But that doesn't necessarily mean we are both trapped in this castle," I argue. "If anything our love should break the curse. At least according to every curse I've heard of."

La Bête smiles faintly. It's bittersweet. "I'm not of this world. My curse is unlike any you've heard of. Our love has probably only strengthened it."

I shake my head. "Then there must be some other way to break it. It doesn't make sense if there isn't."

"It's magic."

"There is a logic to everything," I insist. "Even to magic. Even to your world's magic. A curse cannot exist without a means to break it. At the very least we should test the new parameters of your curse."

La Bête follows me as I charge back outside. We bend into the raging wind.

I have never been a foolish enough woman to think that love alone solves everything (I've seen firsthand how my family's love for each other solves *nothing*), and I am undeterred by this new twist. We will find a way to be together, and to be free.

"If this doesn't work," he says to me urgently, and I can tell he already thinks that it won't, "there's a secret passage tucked behind the shelves in your workroom—what used to be the nursery. I will show you there after this but just in case…"

He cuts himself off as the sound of distant shouts reach us.

We come out the gatehouse and come to a halt. We behold a snaking line of lighted torches below—no doubt supplemented with pitchforks and blunderbusses.

"They're already so close," I gasp.

"The magic of the castle prevents their sorcerers from landing within its grounds, but it looks like they've managed to maneuver just outside it."

"They'll see us if we go out these gates," I say.

But it's too late.

"There they are," a magically amplified voice carries over the mob. "The Beast and his brazen whore have come to greet us! They cannot hide from my sorcery!"

A roar goes up.

La Bête grabs my hand and we step back. The jagged line of torches bobs towards us and I'm beginning to pick out faces in the front of the mob.

"Your reign of terror is over, Beast!" A chill goes down my spine. This time the magically amplified voice is Julian's. "Make way for justice! No mercy for traitors!"

A huge fireball shoots out from the night—and right towards us.

La Bête shoves me down. I taste blood and dirt on my lips as a loud explosion rocks the ground. La Bête is sprawled over me but I still feel the impact when he takes the brunt of some sort of strike.

I peer up through my mess of hair and see a gaping hole where the black iron gates once stood. Shards of metal bars lay scattered around us.

"Come!" La Bête lumbers to his feet and hauls me up. We flee with the wind at our backs, back towards the gatehouse.

"The secret passage?" I yell to him.

"No, it's a dead end and they've already seen us! If we go back to the maze, you—we—can escape into the forest behind the castle."

We run past the inner courtyard, round the side of the front entrance, and towards the gardens.

Footsteps resound on the cobblestones behind us—as well as confusion.

Before I can celebrate this minor victory, Julian's voice booms again. "Archard senses them that way!"

The footsteps resume towards us.

La Bête and I flee into the maze.

Lady Inanna must be looking down on us for though their sorcerer can sense the cardinal direction we are in, the mob of men must still navigate through the twisting paths and dead ends.

We pass the secret rose garden and come to a wall of high hedges—the outer border of the maze. La Bête simply reaches into the hedges and tears apart the branches.

Twigs and debris fly into my face but I barely notice.

"You're bleeding," I say, and I add with almost equal shock, "you're Bellamy."

La Bête turns and I no longer see the bloody hole in the back of his jacket.

"One of the bars from the gate pierced me," he explains. "I pulled it out and switched to my human form for I've noticed that shifting heals my wounds."

"I'm glad that's the case. But you're Bellamy," I say. I point up at the sky for La Bête only looks at me blankly. "It's still night."

He stares back at me in awe.

I hear the sound of another fireball—that roaring *whoosh* is a sound I will never forget—and this time it explodes with a flare that lights up La Bête's human features and continues burning.

"He's just burning through the maze now to get to us," I say. I turn back to the hole La Bête has made in the hedge.

"Go," I urge, "try it."

"You first," La Bête says. He grabs me and pushes me toward the hole but I twist around.

"Can you get through?" I demand.

I see the answer on his face.

"I felt the curse when I was tearing through the hedge," he says. "I cannot pass my hands beyond that."

He gestures towards the opening in the hedge, our only hope for escaping.

A brush of—yes, I will admit it, *dread*—passes through me. A perfectly logical term for the emotion inspired by the curse that plagues my lover.

La Bête grabs me in a tight hug. He plants desperate kisses on my face. Then he shakes me.

"Beauty," he says. I drown in his cinnamon eyes. "You must go without me."

The scent of burning roses overtakes me. The rose garden is on fire.

"The rose garden is on fire," I say.

"You must leave," he repeats patiently. "Now."

"The rose garden is on fire," I repeat. "Come on."

I tug on La Bête's hand.

"Let it burn," he yells. He shoves me toward the way out, out into the forest.

"Bellamy La Bête," I say, as I jab my finger into his chest. "Who is the smartest person you know?"

"You are," he says with no hesitation.

"Then trust me!"

I tug him towards the rose garden—the entrance is right before us.

He grunts his assent.

"Hold on," he grunts before I try to enter.

He transforms before my eyes. His hair lengthens, grows wild. His mass grows. His legs creak and bend toward the other direction, and his nose protrudes into a slight snout.

His eyes remain the same.

"I can defend you better in this form," he explains, and he enters the opening into the rose garden first.

Well, it seems now he can shift between his human and beast forms at will.

I follow La Bête.

23
BEAUTY

WHEN I COME out the other side, Julian and his sorcerer are already there. They stand in a burning gap where I presume their last fireball landed. Greedy flames slowly consume the garden. The gathering power calls to my ring: it's intense enough to make me stumble. I pray that the sorcerer's magic is too different to harness the roses' enchantment.

"Beauty!" Julian cries when he sees me.

I step around La Bête who tenses even further and edges back slightly in front of me.

"Julian," I say. "It was a mistake for you to come here."

"You steal my words, Beauty," he says. "But it's not too late before the others catch up. I can say you were tricked, kidnapped. Come back to me."

He reaches out his arm. His words are smooth as butter but I see the glitter in his eyes. Julian will never forgive me for poisoning him, even if I were so inclined to choose him.

Which I am not.

"No," I say clearly. I take La Bête's hand. He squeezes mine in solidarity. I feel the buzz between us and I know that the roses' enchantment is fueling his beast as well.

"You would choose a savage beast over me?"

"I've made my choice time and time again, Julian," I say. "It was never a decision between you or another man. Even if I didn't love La Bête, I would never choose to be with you."

Julian sneers.

"We'll see how you feel when your beast lies dead! Archard!"

Julian gestures sharply at the sorcerer at his side. The thin man raises his arms. I recognize the markings of his guild on his robes and think that Julian must have a lot of money at his disposal to hire from them.

The sorcerer mutters words under his breath—a dark enchantment—and I lose La Bête's grip from my hand.

He dives straight at the sorcerer.

The fireball releases wildly up and out, over me. I hear it land with an explosion and feel the tiny abrasions form when bits of twigs and rock hit my back but my focus is on La Bête.

More men have appeared in the burning gap and leap forward to help their sorcerer. Some even have swords.

One raises a blunderbuss and aims it at La Bête but La Bête wrestles with the three—four—five men who leap in to pry him off the sorcerer.

La Bête plucks one of the men off his back and tosses him easily across the garden. The man smacks into the stone bench and slumps like a rag doll.

La Bête's fury is fearsome to behold. Men throw themselves at him and he annihilates them one after the other. A man who stabs at him with a dagger gets his back broken over La Bête's knee. There's a woman too, and La Bête sinks his fangs into her with no hesitation, and rips out her throat in a gush of blood.

I think I finally understand what it is to be human and overtaken by my emotions. From a rational standpoint, the sight of La Bête's savagery should horrify me. It doesn't. Later, I will mourn the loss of lives. But right now, adrenaline courses through me. I glory in every kill. My bloodlust demands the death and destruction of all those who dared come after us.

A hand grabs my arm in a painful grip.

"Beauty," Julian hisses in my ear.

I struggle wildly against him as his other arm wraps around my waist and pulls me back. More wildly, I think, than he expected. I fling my head back and I hear a crunch, and Julian's grunt.

Julian's furious bellow deafens my ear. He holds on to me and presses his body against mine.

I throw my elbow back but his bloodlust is as high as mine and he has my arms pinned tightly to my sides. His manhood stirs against my bottom. For once I wish I'd spend just a little less time reading and more time with my siblings while they learned to dance and fight with grace.

Julian's hot breath laughs in my ear and makes me want to vomit. I feel a smear on my ear and realize that it is blood, and that Julian is high from the fighting.

"I thought you were smart, Beauty. But you're just a dumb slut like the rest, aren't you? I should never have aspired to marry you. The only thing you're good for is fucking, and when I'm done with you, I'll throw you to the rest of the men. You'll be known as the Whore of Orleans—if you even survive that long. I want you to think of me—"

Julian raises one of his arms to lift my chin as he speaks.

"—of what we could've had if—"

I think he wants to force my face towards his but the slack in his hold allows me to twist out of his arms.

I bring up the rosary—the whole remaining strand for I have no qualms about killing Julian—and I aim for his mouth.

But his ceaseless prattle aside, Julian doesn't have a great open maw like La Bête's. I end up hitting him in the mouth with the beads and then he strikes me.

It's open-handed but all that means is that instead of dropping me to the ground, it flings me aside.

Pain explodes above my right brow. I've hit a rock.

I throw my forearm up over my face: a survival reflex to block further attacks, but none come.

I feel the air above me move and I peer out in time to witness La Bête land on Julian.

He pins Julian to the ground.

La Bête's hands are on each side of Julian's head—I think he's going to rip his head clean off when the sorcerer Archard's voice rings:

"Beast! If you care for your slut you will unhand Montserrat at once."

I swivel my head and have to squint at the sorcerer with my blood-gummed eye. I wipe at the blood running down my brow and my vision clears.

Archard has a fireball ready between his hands, an angry knot of braided flames, and he is aiming it at me. Around him lie a score of wounded and dead townspeople— La Bête's doing.

La Bête snarls—but his hands come off Julian's head.

Julian scrambles to his feet as La Bête prowls to my side.

He helps me to my feet. We hold each other up, bruised and bleeding, and surrounded by an angry mob made angrier that we aren't dead yet.

"I've had enough," Julian says. His voice is shaky. He knows how close to death he came. "Archard, just kill them."

La Bête wraps his arms around me and envelopes me in his warm embrace. His head dips down.

"I will find you in the next life, Beauty," he whispers into my ear.

"You will have to wait a while," I say. "For I plan on living a number of years yet."

The huff of La Bête's laugh on my neck is filled with love, admiration, and probably an equal mix of resignation and hope. He holds me tighter.

From the corner of my eyes I see the fireball let loose from between the sorcerer's hands.

It arcs across the garden towards us.

I smell the burning roses and feel that same power gathered in the air as I did before when I burned the one rose, but multiplied a thousand, thousand fold.

It waits on baited breath, a monumental force that casts the magic of the sorcerer's spell in an insignificant light. I have all the time in the world as the fireball reaches the apogee of its trajectory and plummets toward us.

Take us home.

Take us home to Dar al-Sakan.

There's an absence of sound and then the fireball is right upon us.

La Bête crushes me to him. I hope my ribs survive.

A strong wind gusts. I no longer see the bright orange flame of the fireball, or the rose garden consumed by flames.

All is black.

A great roaring fills my ears.

Underneath the roaring, I can almost hear the whisper of a gossamer web as it burns away and smolders into insignificant ashes.

We drown in the scent of roses.

24
BEAUTY

ONE MONTH LATER.

"You'd better get out of the water before the sirens appear," I yell from my spot on the beach. "They come out at dusk, you know."

La Bête waves at me from where he stands in the ebbing tide.

For a moment, the fiery ball of the setting sun reminds me of when La Bête and I escaped from the Black Forest—but the expanse of the sea laid out before me is like nothing I've seen in my old life. A breeze blows over me, flecked with moisture, and I taste salt on my lips, and whiff brine in the air.

This is Kurys. The land Ahmed came from, the land where the sun sets in the west. The land that has accepted us, if not with open arms, then without prejudged hate.

After some initial chagrin at our method of arrival (we landed, blood-soaked and battered, in the middle of a staid conference), the university took me in as the protégé of a celebrated scholar.

I thrive under their tutelage, and the environment geared for learning.

La Bête works as a lowly gardener but his hard work and affinity for growing things is earning him a good reputation. At home he spends his time cultivating the garden he started in our tiny patio.

I'm sure he regrets the loss of his plants, as I regret the loss of my metal collection, and my notebook, and even Rattler. And I mourn for the loss of my family, but that is a different sort of grief, and one I suspect I would have felt regardless, had I stayed in Orleans.

La Bête and I have each other. We've been given the freedom to start over. And so we move on.

I tease La Bête about his new station in life: he who is accustomed to having an endless supply of coin at his disposal, to having people indebted to him, suddenly having to live off our small stipends.

He claims he's the happiest he's ever been in all his centuries.

Looking out across to where he bobs in the water, I believe him.

It's the happiest I've ever been too.

Things could be better. We could be rich. Julian could be dead. But men like Julian have a way of surviving in the world. For now, I will be satisfied with being on the opposite side of it: away from him, and others who would side with him.

Things could be better. But I couldn't be happier.

Another wave rolls over La Bête. He shakes his head when he resurfaces and even from here, I can see his wide grin.

He bounds out of the water and up the beach towards me.

"You better dry off first," I warn.

He stops a couple meters away—but too close.

I shriek and grab a scarf to protect me as he goes into a great shudder that sends water flying everywhere.

We have the beach to ourselves today. La Bête has chosen his beastly form to enjoy the water and the last of the dying sun's rays.

La Bête flops down on the blanket beside me.

He gathers me into a hug with his wet arms and showers me with wet kisses as I laughingly protest.

"I love you," he says happily as he plants a last tender kiss on the new scar that splits my brow. I finish my squealing and settle into his side.

"Yes," I say, "I have ascertained that from your actions."

La Bête bumps the side of my face with his snout.

"You love me too," he says teasingly. "Beauty *loooooooves* me."

"That, too, is obvious," I say loftily.

La Bête plants his mouth on mine and plunders me with a kiss.

I come up with a gasp for air when he pulls away.

"Say it," he insists. "Say you love me."

"I love you, Bellamy La Bête."

La Bête grins. "Then there is one thing I would demand from you if we are to continue in this relationship. Something you have yet to give me."

"But true love hath no conditions," I say with a mock scowl.

"Well, this one does."

I laugh. "Very well, what it is then?"

It is all a farce, of course. I would give La Bête anything.

"Give me your name. Your real one."

I look at him in surprise. His voice is serious and his brown eyes intent.

Well, here we are. We've come so far and somehow I've neglected to share that detail along the way.

I reach my arms around his neck and tug La Bête's face closer to mine.

I whisper my name into his ear.

FAUSTA BORJA'S FAIRY TALES

CINDERELLA

CINDERELLA was in the stocks again.

It was her fault of course: she was the laziest of Mistress Fiona's maids. Fiona Duale was renowned throughout the village—the kingdom even—for her exacting standards so it was a mystery why she kept Cinderella around. Some said it was because Mistress Fiona had a soft heart and had taken pity on the penniless maiden who had lost her parents when she was a child. But those who knew Mistress Fiona personally (and especially those who had felt her switch land on their backside) said the mistress liked to make an example of her troublesome maid to frighten the other servants into submission.

Certainly, the punishments Mistress Fiona doled out never had a lasting effect on Cinderella: no matter how the young woman whimpered, how prettily she squirmed, or how tearfully she pleaded throughout the actual ordeal; within hours she would be back to brushing off her chores, gossiping with susceptible maids, and taunting the guests at Mistress Fiona's inn.

But Mistress Fiona was nothing if not up to the task of disciplining the most irascible of her lot.

Just last week she had commissioned a special order from the blacksmith: a modified pillory stock which included the usual framework with holes for securing the head and hands, but also a horizontal beam to comfortably bend the subject over at the waist. (Mistress Fiona did not want employees with bad backs, after all.)

The mistress had received her order last Wednesday and installed the stocks in the inn's courtyard where servants and guests alike could witness the public shame of any offending servant.

Cinderella did not disappoint. It was now Friday, only three days since the stocks were installed, and for the third time in three days, Cinderella found herself helplessly bound to the stocks.

And it was only ten-o'clock in the morning.

"Ooh," chimed a voice. It was accompanied by the scent of fresh cut hay.

"What have we here?"

Cinderella closed her eyes. *Go away*, she pleaded in her head, *please, please, just go away*.

But Gracie did not go away.

Instead Cinderella felt light fingers reach out and caress her breasts through the cotton of her maid's dress. The scent of hay grew stronger.

Cinderella squirmed but the wood frame of the stocks trapped her hands and head firmly in place and she couldn't escape from Gracie's exploration of her soft mounds and— *oh*—sensitive nipples.

"No," she moaned softly.

"What was that?"

Cinderella's eyes flew open.

Gracie set down the wash pail she was holding with her non-exploratory hand. She put both hands on her hips.

"Not a peep from you, you know that, Cinderella."

"I'm sorry," Cinderella said.

FAUSTA BORJA

Gracie's hand whipped out and slapped Cinderella across the cheek. "Not a peep."

Cinderella pressed her lips closed. Her cheek burned where Gracie had slapped it.

Gracie smiled.

Cinderella suppressed a fearful shiver. Gracie was the best of Mistress Fiona's maids. A diligent young woman who never complained about the busy workload, and delighted in helping out her fellow maids, Gracie was everything that Cinderella was not. And for some reason, Gracie hated her.

Cinderella risked a look at the other maid.

Gracie's wide almond-shaped eyes, snub nose, and plump cheeks contributed to her general aura of a sweet-natured, innocent maiden. Her light, breathy voice only furthered this impression—an impression that from what Cinderella could tell, was mostly accurate—except when it came to Cinderella.

Just now Gracie had the most devious look in her eyes.

"Oh, Cinderella," she cooed. "We all know how hard it is for you to behave."

Gracie walked past the stocks and beyond Cinderella's limited view. She felt, but could not turn to see, Gracie's hand touch her shoulder and slowly trail down her back to the curve of her buttocks—conveniently propped up by the horizontal bar that she was bent over.

Gracie affectionately patted Cinderella's round posterior.

"I think you need some help. Would you like my help?"

Cinderella knew better this time than to respond.

Gracie chuckled. It sounded like a purr in her sweet, light register, and Cinderella could not help the tug of desire that pulled at the pit of her belly.

Gracie's hand clutched at Cinderella's skirts and slowly began to raise them. "A naughty thing like you will never be able to stay silent, and then you'll have Mistress Fiona's switch to answer to."

Cinderella's heart was thudding so hard she thought it would burst from her breast.

A light spring breeze stirred around her bare calves and then Gracie had fully exposed Cinderella's backside, clad only in her lacy drawers.

"Please," Cinderella squeaked.

"Oh, Cinderella," said Gracie.

Cinderella shrieked as she felt a sudden abrupt tug on her drawers—*oh no no no, not here, not in the public courtyard where anyone can see*—and the bare breeze was touching her buttocks.

Distantly, Cinderella heard feminine giggles and one deep masculine chuckle and the thought of the all those people looking at her—staring at her—was just too much and she began to struggle.

Gracie pulled her drawers all the way down as Cinderella kicked and screamed.

"Ow!" Gracie said as Cinderella's feet connected with her shin.

And then Gracie was pulling Cinderella's shoes off her feet and for some reason, the indignity of standing barefoot in the courtyard dirt was more than the troublesome maid could stand.

"Stop it! No! I hate you! You evil, vile, horrible..." Cinderella could hear herself shrieking shrilly but could not make herself stop.

Gracie came back into view with Cinderella's drawers in hand.

"...mean, low-down, dirty—mm—mrmph!"

Gracie stuffed the drawers into Cinderella's mouth, cutting off the tirade.

Cinderella screamed through the cloth and shook her head wildly from side to side as Gracie ruthlessly wrapped the drawer's lacings around her head and tied them off tightly so that Cinderella could not dislodge her flouncy drawers from her mouth.

"Mmmph," said Cinderella, pathetically.

"That's what you get," Gracie said, looking satisfied. "Although…"

Gracie's look turned musing. "It is getting a bit warm outside, isn't it?"

Cinderella stared sullenly at the ground.

"The sun is getting higher and—oh, your legs will be fine since they're bare to the world—but Cinderella, I just worry that you'll be too hot in that dress."

Gracie grasped the modest neckline of Cinderella's dress and yanked down hard.

The dress tore and Cinderella's breasts spilled out. She could feel them hanging like ripe morsels of fruit.

"Very nice," an admiring male voice said.

It was Henry, one of the stable boys.

Cinderella moaned.

"Aren't they?" Gracie did sound approving.

Gracie brought her palm to one of Cinderella's breasts and gently squeezed it.

"Like peaches and cream, she is," Gracie said. "And look at these rose-colored nips, would you? Touch them."

"Don't mind if I do."

Cinderella moaned again but this time it was desire she felt coursing through her veins and mingling with the humiliation.

She couldn't believe Henry was fondling her this way! He was relatively new to the inn and had yet to participate when Mistress Fiona punished Cinderella. He'd always been polite to Cinderella when she was going about her duties. But now...he took no heed as Cinderella pleaded with her eyes for him to stop, instead chuckling as she squirmed to get away from him one moment, and then squirmed with desire the next.

Henry smelled of more hay and of fresh manure but there was something delicious about it and the way his rough calloused hands massaged her breasts.

And Gracie...her palms were calloused from work as well but her fingers were soft as they glided lightly back and forth across Cinderella's peaked nips.

A breeze stirred across Cinderella's backside and she realized she was rubbing her bare legs together, squeezing her secret place which, to her horror, was growing moist for all to see.

"What's going on here?" A commanding contralto voice cut through the courtyard.

Cinderella froze. Gracie and Henry snatched their hands back and held them properly folded in front of them. They dipped their heads to the mistress.

The sight of Mistress Fiona never failed to stir Cinderella—whether it stirred fear, desire, love, or a mix of all three was a mystery to Cinderella who didn't like to look too deeply within herself.

The mistress wore an ivory colored dress today—it was a beautiful complement to her cocoa colored skin—and simply cut from quality linen. It suited her statuesque form.

"The poor thing couldn't keep her mouth shut, mistress," Gracie said. "She was drawing ever so much attention and distracting the servants from work."

"I see," the mistress said in her famously measured tones, "well, it's shut now. Good thinking, Gracie."

Gracie flushed with pleasure.

Cinderella flushed as well as Mistress Fiona slowly took a turn around the stocks to survey her in utter silence.

Cinderella had never felt quite so pathetic.

Her own drawers stuffed ignominiously into her mouth; her bare breasts tumbling out from her torn dress; her skirts rustled up about her waist while her buttocks, the crevice of her secret place, her thighs, her calves, and even her cursed bare feet were exposed to all.

She was a shameful spectacle.

"Very good," said the mistress. "A prince is visiting this evening and I despaired of finding the time to properly punish Cinderella today."

Cinderella's ears perked. Did this mean she wouldn't receive a punishment from the mistress today? Though at the same time the thought gave her a pang...but the mistress wasn't done speaking.

"Let all the servants and guests know that I will need their assistance in punishing Cinderella."

A pleased murmur traveled around the courtyard from all who had heard the pronouncement.

"Oh and—" Mistress Fiona stopped to look up at the sky, "for as long as the sun stays up, she is not allowed to come."

Cinderella nearly fainted.

To Cinderella's intense (and short-lived) relief, Gracie had to return to her chores. She was Mistress Fiona's best maid after all.

"I'll be back for you later," Gracie promised.

Henry rubbed his hands. "Not me. I got the whole morning off on account of having to work through this evening when the prince arrives."

Henry chuckled.

Unseen fingers pinched Cinderella sharply between her legs.

Cinderella's drawers muffled her cry. Her unknown aggressor flicked their finger against her lips as if to test their resilience.

"Marisol," said Henry. "Come to join the fun?"

"Oh, I consider it my duty when it comes to punishing Cinderella."

Marisol left off playing between Cinderella's lips and sauntered to the front of the stocks.

Marisol was another of Mistress Fiona's maids. She was not the best, like Gracie, but she had a cruel streak which Mistress Fiona found useful. Marisol often assisted Mistress Fiona when she disciplined one of the servants.

She wasted no time with hellos, simply reached out to Cinderella's breasts and pinched and pulled at them.

Cinderella wailed into her drawers.

Marisol laughed and slapped at Cinderella's breasts, setting them to jiggling in all different directions.

Henry looked like he felt a bit sorry for her but just when Cinderella thought he might speak up he reached down to rub his crotch where a prominent bulge had grown.

Marisol noticed too.

She jerked at the lacings tying Cinderella's drawers to her face and yanked off the drawers.

"What—" Cinderella tried to speak.

"Shut up." Marisol stuffed three fingers into Cinderella's mouth. She leaned down so that the maids were eye to eye.

Cinderella couldn't help but notice how very long and curly Marisol's eyelashes were, and how lovely they made her large hazel colored eyes.

Marisol moved her fingers in and out of Cinderella's mouth. Cinderella sucked on the citrusy sweet fingers and decided Marisol must have helped Cook make some honey lemon bars this morning.

"Have you ever had Cinderella in the mouth before, Henry?

"No."

Cinderella couldn't see Henry past Marisol but she could practically feel his excitement thrumming through the air.

"Would you like to?"

"Hell, yes."

Marisol smiled. "You're in luck. Cinderella is wonderful at sucking cock. Isn't that right, Cinderella?"

Cinderella nodded—she had to fight to move her head with Marisol's fingers pumping in and out of her mouth.

Marisol's free hand smacked Cinderella's breast. "You're a good cocksucker, aren't you, Cinderella?"

Cinderella nodded again.

Marisol smacked her breast again. "And you don't ever bite."

This was ridiculous. Mistress Fiona had standards for her servants: even Cinderella could never be so ill-mannered as to bite a cock in her mouth, like some Black Forest savage.

Marisol's fingers found one of her nipples and pinched tight. Tears sprang to Cinderella's eyes. "You never bite."

Cinderella nodded sullenly.

"Good." Marisol removed her hands and stepped away.

Before Cinderella could even breathe a sigh of relief, Henry eagerly stepped forward and thrust his cock into her mouth.

"Mmph!"

Henry was slim in girth but the tip of his penis hit the back of throat before it was halfway in. She swallowed the impulse to gag.

"Open up, love," said Henry.

Cinderella obliged and opened up her throat. Henry slid the rest of the way in with a groan. He must have washed recently—he smelled more of the inn's soap than natural man's musk.

Cinderella was just getting used to his pumping rhythm when a hand smacked her buttocks.

"Don't mind me," she heard Marisol say behind her.

Cinderella closed her eyes and concentrated on the silky smooth feel of Henry's cock traveling in and out of her throat.

Fingers dipped into her secret place and spread the moisture found there.

"You really are a slut, aren't you, Cinderella?" said Marisol admiringly.

More fingers shoved into her secret—well it wasn't such a secret at the moment now, was it?—into her pussy and squished around, stretching the entrance until Cinderella ached.

Marisol began thrusting her fingers in and out of Cinderella's cunt to the same rhythm as Henry.

Cinderella moaned around Henry's cock and he moaned with her. Henry was well-trimmed down there like all of Mistress Fiona's servants. His closely shaved thatch

FAUSTA BORJA

rubbed Cinderella's cheeks sharply with each stroke, making her feel—

SMACK.

Cinderella cried out and Henry moaned again, loving the feel of her throat vibrating around him.

SMACK. Marisol had removed her fingers from Cinderella's pussy and was smacking it directly on the lips.

Cinderella would've howled if she could.

"You were about to come, weren't you, slut? You just love having your cunt stuffed, it makes you come like a whore, doesn't it?"

SMACK. "Slut!" SMACK. "Whore!" Even Cinderella could hear how wet the smacking was.

Cinderella was keening around Henry's cock.

Marisol spread Cinderella's buttocks.

Cinderella tried to shake her head but Henry's cock made it impossible.

Marisol drew the moisture from Cinderella's pussy up to that other opening. Cinderella's skin prickled like electricity as Marisol massaged her slick fingers around her puckered entrance.

Then Marisol licked her tongue across Cinderella's cunt.

Cinderella sobbed as Marisol licked and nibbled and teased but never put enough pressure on her swollen pearl, nor gave Cinderella the deep plundering in her pussy that she truly craved.

Henry grabbed tightly onto her hair which had already half fallen out of the careless maid's bun she'd put it in this morning, and jabbed into her mouth over and over again.

Cinderella could only endure as Henry fucked her face with wild abandon.

184

Finally he thrust deep into her throat and went taut. At that moment one of the slick fingers exploring around her anus took the plunge and sank into her. Above her, Henry hooted out his pleasure as Cinderella felt warmth shooting into the back of her throat and Marisol gleefully skewered her from behind.

After a frozen moment, Henry slumped over and gently removed his cock.

Dazed, Cinderella licked ineffectively at the strands of saliva and cum that Henry had left trailing down her chin.

Another man had already replaced Henry in front of her and he lightly smacked his cock against her cheek till she opened her mouth and took him in.

More hands—large, rough hands—grabbed Cinderella's hips and hard flesh jostled her from behind.

"That's right," said Marisol. Her finger finally left Cinderella but Cinderella knew better than to be relieved. An unmistakable hardness pushed between her legs and nudged at her woman's entrance. Cinderella tried to thrust back at him, aching for release but Marisol—that hag!—interfered.

"Ah-ah-ah!" Marisol chastised the man behind her. Still his cock rubbed insistently up and down her slit. Cinderella prayed for him to shove the other maid aside and then plunge his cock into her pussy but a moment later his cock took all the slickness it had gathered from between her thighs and moved up to that dark passage. His manhood prodded insistently at her anus until she was stretched enough for him to pop in the head.

Cinderella whimpered.

She had stopped sucking the cock in front of her but the man—a guest she didn't recognize—didn't seem to care.

185

He was a fat mouthful but not long enough to gag her and he seemed content to simply have her mouth around him.

The man behind her went slowly despite Marisol's urgings but eventually he sank all the way in and then he gently pulled out, and pushed back in again.

Marisol eventually grew bored with the gentle man's slow gyrations and she couldn't inspire the unknown inn guest to any heights of cruelty either so, echoing Gracie, she promised Cinderella that she would return later.

Eventually the men fucking her face and her ass climaxed with little fanfare and walked away. The man who'd been behind gave her an affectionate pat on the buttocks. Cinderella never saw who it was.

A few more guests used her throughout the morning and the servants seemed to go out of their way to take a break and torment her whenever they could but everyone was careful to obey Mistress's Fiona's edict and no one brought her to climax.

The sun was high and hot on her skin when Gracie and Marisol approached Cinderella in the stocks again. Though her heart seized in fear, it turned to joy when the maids released her from the stocks.

"Just a break so you're not totally useless this evening when the prince and his men come to visit," said Marisol warningly. She pinched Cinderella's breasts and slapped her hands away when Cinderella tried to cover them up. "Don't bother."

They let her use the privy, cleaned her up a bit, (they left her in her torn dress), rubbed some balm into the chafed skin around her neck and wrists, and then put her in the stocks again.

Marisol and Gracie made sure to haul Cinderella's skirts up again before they left her.

Cinderella wasn't exactly happy to be in the stocks again but she had to reflect that her circumstance was more fortunate than this morning. The other guests had all left by now as the prince's men needed all the quarters the inn could provide, and the servants were too busy running around and preparing for the prince's arrival to visit her for longer than a few moments.

Unfortunately, a few moments was all it took for the servants to absentmindedly grope her buttocks, or roll her nipples between nimble fingers, or quickly dip into her pussy to test her slickness.

Cinderella sank into a drugged state of desire.

She had no sense of the passing time—only a drifting drowsiness that pervaded her limbs and slowed her heart.

She was shifting her legs together, concentrating on the slick rubbing of her lips and willing the friction to grow into release when she realized how cold the breeze was on her wet pussy and thighs.

Slowly Cinderella registered her surroundings. She was still in the stocks in the courtyard of the inn. She was alone.

And the sun had set.

Terror gripped Cinderella's heart.

She had been left in the stocks. Forgotten. Abandoned. It was a familiar feeling from long ago and Cinderella gave into it, shivering in her loneliness.

Footsteps sounded from the inn—sure, confident steps that resounded on the wooden floor inside.

Cinderella raised her head.

"Hello?" she called out. Her voice croaked with disuse. She cleared it and tried again.

"Hello!" This time the footsteps paused.

"I'm still outside! You left me here." Cinderella tried to sound accusing but instead she sounded weak and unsure.

The footsteps quickened, grew closer, then a soft thud sounded behind her as the person leapt down into the hardened dirt of the courtyard.

"Where did everyone go?" Cinderella said. She tried to twist her head around but of course still couldn't see behind her.

"They're in the bathhouse washing up after the journey," a man's voice said. He came into view.

The stranger stared at Cinderella and she stared back.

The lamps had already been lighted and he seemed an apparition looming out at her in the night. He had the look of a Black Forest savage: coarse dark that gleamed in the lamplight; strong brows over bright narrow eyes; a strong nose and a strong chin.

In fact everything about him looked strong despite his average height and slim build. His clothes were an eclectic mix: he wore a savage's embroidered vest but heavy kingdom boots; a kingdom broadsword and a savage's bow.

"Who are you?" she squeaked.

He was staring at Cinderella's bare breasts and had to drag his eyes back to her face.

"I'm Coal, of White Snow nation," he said, looking as surprised by the sight of her as she was by him.

"You're one of the visiting prince's men," Cinderella said, and couldn't help adding, "a Black Forest savage."

His face darkened.

"It's true that the nations have a bloody history," he said evenly. "And White Snow nation in particular. But we do not have a monopoly on savagery inside the Black Forest, I don't think."

"I'm sorry," said Cinderella. She licked her lips. "Where are the others? The mistress, and the servants, and the prince and his men?"

"Your mistress and the other servants and the prince's men are in the bathhouse," he said patiently.

Of course. Some clarity came rushing back to Cinderella and she remembered Gracie stopping to tell her that they were all needed to help the prince's men wash, and that they would release her when they returned.

Cinderella eyed the stranger who now had a strange smile on his lips.

"Do you think," she started nervously. "Do you think you can let me out of this? Please?"

The stranger named Coal shook his head slowly.

"Oh no," he said. "I know Mistress Fiona and her ways. If she had you put in there, I'm not letting you out without her permission."

"But..."

"No," he said firmly. He crossed his arms and grinned at her. Then his eyes darkened as they roamed over her dangling breasts again.

Her nipples tightened almost painfully in response and Cinderella whimpered at the reminder of the state her body was in.

Coal chuckled. "Seems you're in quite a predicament," he said.

He paced around her, taking in her form. It reminded Cinderella of Mistress Fiona earlier: they had the same air of staring at something that belonged to them, something that was theirs to do with as they pleased.

He disappeared behind her and Cinderella cursed him inside her head.

Savages! She didn't care what he said; it had been savages that killed her parents when she was a child; savages like him from one of those nations in the Black Forest—

Coal's hand reached out and covered her pussy.

189

Cinderella moaned. She didn't realize how chilled she'd become and his warm hand pressed against her womanhood until it pulsated with heat.

"How long have you been in the stocks?" Coal asked her casually. His finger gently squeezed itself into her cunt.

Cinderella couldn't help herself: she thrust her hips back at him. He obliged her by adding another finger and thrusting them in harder.

"All day," she said breathlessly.

"And have you been allowed to—" another finger brushed over her pearl, "come?"

"No," she said.

He withdrew his hands.

"But," she said desperately. "The mistress only said I wasn't allowed to come while the sun was up!"

"Good to know," he said.

Then his hardness was pressing against her.

"Oh, please," she said.

The head of his cock rubbed at her entrance, widened it, took its slickness and swirled it around her pleasure nub. The blood rushed into Cinderella's head, saturated her nipples, made her feel heady and faint.

"Oh, oh," she said. "Please, please fuck me! Please fuck me now!"

He answered by grasping her hips firmly. A hand pushed mercilessly on her lower back, forcing her to tilt her hips.

Coal's cock scraped her tight entrance and buried itself fully into her cunt.

Cinderella moaned. Her walls tightened even more around his cock and she heard him groan in response.

He pulled back and buried himself in her again. His cock brushed against her core: that, along with his sacks slapping heavily against her little nub was enough to set off the unfurling pleasure inside her that had lain in wait all day.

Coal had only gone three strokes into the strange girl he'd found trapped in the stocks when she screamed in climax.

"Merciful mother," he groaned as her walls threatened to swallow him with their pulsing. But he forced his cock through the tight passage and buried himself again.

He ran his hands over her pleasing posterior: the women in his retinue were fierce warriors with beautifully toned buttocks only a little more padded than his men, but this woman in front of him now was all roundness and softness.

He kneaded her cheeks with his hands and reveled in how plump and pliable they were.

SMACK. He slapped his hand against one cheek and it bounced pleasingly.

The girl whimpered. He decided the girl had had enough time to come down from her climax.

Coal pulled all the way out and then thrust in hard enough to knock the breath out of her. He spanked her buttocks again, addicted to the way the flesh reddened and bounced back.

He let himself go and pounded her pussy without care.

"Ungh—ungh—ungh—" the noises spilled from the girl's mouth as if coming directly from her pussy.

He kept pounding; the hard flesh and sinew over his pelvis crashed into her thighs; his scrotum flew wildly back and forth, slick with her desire; his hands spanked her ass cheeks and each time she squeaked as if surprised.

He was almost there. The girl's sounds had started rising again but he didn't slow down. His hips ground into her, his cock speared her mercilessly.

Coal's balls tightened into hard sacs and he shoved deeply into her: his essence rushed down his shaft and spurted out almost painfully. His semen flooded the woman's cunt.

She was squirming desperately and he found it in himself to twitch his hips.

It was enough. The girl climaxed again.

When the sound came flooding back to his ears he realized there were now others milling about the courtyard.

Mistress Fiona tactfully waited until he'd pulled out and tucked his penis back into his trousers before she approached.

"Your highness," she said. "Welcome to the inn."

Gracie and Marisol practically carried Cinderella to the bathhouse between them. They forced Cinderella to eat half a sandwich along the way and then thrust her into the showers.

"We didn't realize Prince Coal had left the bathhouse," Gracie chattered excitedly.

"He didn't tell me he was the prince," Cinderella muttered. The other maids ignored her as they pulled her out of the shower.

Cinderella moaned as they lowered her into one of the baths dug into the ground filled with fresh hot spring water. She settled onto the carved stone bench and sat there limply.

"He brought so many men with him—I counted at least thirty—" Gracie continued, "—and he even had some women!"

Marisol stripped off her own dress without ceremony and slid into the bath with Cinderella. She grabbed a sponge and dipped it into the warm lavender-scented water before starting on Cinderella.

Gracie joined them, chatting about the prince and his men as they soaped and lathered. Cinderella tried to help but the warmth of the water made her feel sickly.

"It took forever to get them all washed and clean. Most of them couldn't wait and started taking us aside before they were out of the baths," Gracie confided. "Of course then we had to wash them all over again but Marisol and I didn't bother getting ready since we knew we were going to get you."

Gracie playfully rubbed a sponge over Cinderella's nipple.

"Up now," Marisol dragged Cinderella to her feet. They dried with big fluffy towels.

They took her to the changing rooms where Cinderella sprawled onto a couch while the other two took turns rubbing scented oils onto each other.

Gracie laid out fresh maids' dresses while Marisol rifled through the oil jars.

"What do you think for Cinderella?" Marisol asked Gracie. She lifted the stoppers off a couple of the jars. "Vanilla? Neroli?"

"Neroli," Gracie said decisively. "It smells so lovely and delicate on her."

Marisol tugged Cinderella's legs out from underneath her so that she lay sprawled out on the couch facedown.

They massaged the neroli oil into her limbs, making her moan.

Gracie giggled as she ran her fingers over Cinderella's reddened buttocks. "The prince sure liked spanking you."

"Who wouldn't," Marisol said. SMACK. She whacked Cinderella's rear.

"Not fair," Cinderella mumbled into a pillow.

"Don't tell us you don't love it," said Gracie. Her fingers briskly worked the oil between her legs.

"That's right, we all know what a slut you are," Marisol said.

"I think the prince really likes you," Gracie said. "You know, I heard he's looking to recruit more Dwarfs for his sister."

"Who is his sister? Why does she need dwarfs?" Cinderella asked.

"His sister is the queen. She doesn't need actual dwarfs, she calls her men Dwarfs—"

"Why does she call her men Dwarfs?"

"Because she met most of them when she was serving in the Mines," said Gracie.

Cinderella shuddered. The Mines were a prison deep in the Black Forest where all the worst criminals from all the nations and kingdoms were sent. "Guess she really is a savage," she said into the pillow.

Gracie shushed her and Marisol smacked her rear.

"The queen was sent there unjustly," said Gracie. "Don't tell me you don't know the story of Snow White of White Snow nation?"

"No, and I don't care," mumbled Cinderella. "They're all savages in the Black Forest and they can all rot. I wish they'd never come to stay here!"

"Cinderella!"

"That's enough from you," said Marisol. She turned Cinderella over with rough hands.

"My mother was from Morning Calm nation," Gracie said, a reproachful look in her eyes. "I understand about your parents and all but the raiders that killed them were nameless outcasts. We're not all the same, any more than all the kingdoms surrounding the Black Forest are the same."

Cinderella looked away. "Sorry, Gracie. I just meant..." Cinderella trailed off. She wasn't sure what she'd meant.

"It's fine, I know it's hard. And you did lose your parents." Gracie said. Cinderella could tell Gracie was still hurt but didn't know what to say to make it better.

They finished oiling her in silence and then they all got dressed.

Gracie brushed out Cinderella's hair and looked her over.

Gracie fluffed Cinderella's loose hair and drew a pale tendril forward over her breast.

"Perfect," she said.

Marisol pinched Cinderella's nipple.

"Perfect," she echoed.

A few servants were already laid out on tables in various states of undress when Cinderella, Gracie, and Marisol arrived at the main hall.

People were still eating from the platters of roasted meats, cheeses, and fruits set on the tables and, of course, drinking.

Marisol and Gracie grabbed pitchers of ale from a tray. After a belated moment, Cinderella grabbed a pitcher from another tray and they split off into the room to get to work.

FAUSTA BORJA

Cinderella had grabbed a pitcher of cider and beelined for the mistress knowing that it was her favorite.

Mistress Fiona was seated at the center table. She was engrossed in a conversation of local politics with Prince Coal and a few of the Dwarfs when Cinderella approached. The mistress held out her cup without looking at Cinderella.

Cinderella carefully poured her cider into the mistress's cup and—avoiding eye contact with a few men nearby who held up their empty cups—she set up her post right behind her mistress.

"Excuse me," Prince Coal looked up at Cinderella. "I would like some more ale."

Cinderella shrugged. "I only have cider."

Silence fell at their table.

Mistress Fiona swerved around in her seat and pinned Cinderella with her sharp gaze.

"Is it made from apples?" asked the prince.

"It is. Cinderella will fetch you ale if you'd prefer, Prince Coal," said the mistress.

"Oh no, my family adores apples," said the prince. "A tart taste of cider is exactly what I want."

Mistress Fiona nodded at Cinderella.

Cinderella forced her feet to walk over to the prince.

She poured the cider into his cup but was not so careful as she'd been with the mistress and she sloshed some of it onto his hand.

"Oops," Cinderella said.

Mistress Fiona tsked.

The prince threw back the cider and set the empty cup down.

"Perhaps the prince would enjoy the taste of cider poured over a tart," said Mistress Fiona.

Cinderella shifted uneasily.

Prince Coal smiled. "Why yes, I would."

Mistress Fiona rose behind her. "Lie back on the table, Cinderella."

Cinderella turned and looked to her mistress pleadingly.

The mistress's look grew frosty.

"I said, lie back on the table, Cinderella," the mistress repeated softly.

Cinderella backed away from the mistress, clutching the pitcher to her chest. She bumped into the table behind her.

The look on Mistress Fiona's face was fearsome to behold.

"Prince Coal," said the mistress.

"Yes, Mistress Fiona?"

"Cinderella seems to have trouble understanding my words. Please make her understand."

"My pleasure, Mistress Fiona."

The prince rose and—first grabbing Cinderella's pitcher from her while she stared at him dumbly—he pushed her back onto the table.

Men rose and grabbed her arms as she flailed and kicked trying to rise again.

Other men—actually, one was a woman—grabbed her legs as the prince tossed up her skirts.

The woman helped the prince remove Cinderella's drawers. They knocked one of her shoes off in the process and Cinderella wondered wildly to herself why she couldn't keep her shoes on.

Then hands pushed her thighs open and pinned her knees to the table.

Prince Coal raised the pitcher of cider he'd claimed from Cinderella.

"A toast to the queen," he cried.

The Dwarfs cried back at him. "To the queen!"

"A toast to the Queen's Dwarfs!" he cried.

"Here, here!" "To Coal and Snow White!"

"A toast to tasty tarts," he cried.

"To tasty tarts!" The room roared back at him. Fists pounded tables.

The prince tilted the pitcher over Cinderella and she gasped as cold cider hit her cunt and splashed onto her thighs. Her body shook with the vibrations from the pounded table.

Between the torsos of the Dwarfs holding her down, Cinderella saw her mistress watching intently.

Mistress Fiona gave her a fleeting, wistful smile before turning her back on Cinderella and leaving the room.

Before Cinderella could decide what she was feeling or even really wonder at the expression she'd seen on Mistress Fiona's face—had she imagined that wistful twist?—a warm mouth landed on her pussy and brought her back to her situation.

Hands tugged down the shoulders of her dress and drew her arms out of the sleeves.

Someone else had grabbed the pitcher and they poured cider over her breasts as soon as they'd tugged the dress down to her waist.

Her nipples pebbled in the cold cider and then mouths latched onto her.

Cinderella lost herself in all the suckling.

She didn't know how long had passed when the mouths left her and by some telepathic consensus,

Cinderella was lifted and shifted over on the table so that her head laid back over the edge of one side, and her legs dangled off the other.

Mouths latched onto her again—teeth nipped at her breasts, tongues delved into the folds of her pussy—and then someone had climbed onto the bench behind her head and inserted his penis into her mouth.

She caught a brief glimpse of him and his stature before all she could see was the darkness between his legs and realized he was a dwarf—a Queen's Dwarf who actually a dwarf. There was nothing dwarf-like about his cock though and she was grateful for the tilted angle she was at that made it easier to open her throat for him.

Hands roamed all over her and she had a moment of claustrophobia, but the feel of the cock in her mouth (for all that it was a stranger's) was oddly comforting, and she relaxed again.

Cider was poured on her again and again until they ran out, or the Dwarfs grew eager to move on.

The dwarf removed his cock from her mouth and jumped down from the bench. Cinderella was lifted again.

This time they stood her up and lifted her dress off her.

Then they maneuvered her back to the table—but now a man, yet another unknown stranger, was already lying there. He fisted his own cock in a tight grip, and grinned at the expression in her wide eyes. His beard and thatch were a bright red she had never seen before.

The Dwarfs wrangled Cinderella over the man so that she was bent backwards over him, her back to his chest.

She twisted her hips away from the cock that prodded insistently at her buttocks but the Dwarfs held her in place and spread her buttocks and positioned her anus over his cock.

Cinderella gritted her teeth as the Dwarfs slowly impaled her on the man. Her wetness had already liberally moistened her crack and she was loose from the day's activities so it was not so painful when he finally sank in all the way, though she felt horribly full and skewered.

The prince was unlacing another man's trousers. A dark cock sprang out, and the prince pumped it a few strokes in his tight grip while he shared a passionate kiss with the man.

When they finally came up for air the prince pushed the black man toward Cinderella and he obliged by climbing onto the table.

The prince climbed the table as well and he stroked and tugged and guided the hard black cock to the entrance of Cinderella's pussy.

Cinderella gasped as she felt it nudge open her slick folds.

The cock pushed into her pussy.

Cinderella moaned. Redbeard stroked into her dark canal, and the black man continued to push into her pussy, assisted by the prince.

Her pussy adjusted and welcomed the newcomer.

The cocks dueled inside her, fighting for space as they dipped into their respective passages.

Most of the other Dwarfs had found other partners or grabbed servants to see to their pleasure but a few men remained around Cinderella's table, pumping their cocks in fists as they watched their fellow Dwarfs plunder her, and awaited their turn.

Cinderella's cunt was full of cock. Her ass was full of cock. She was on the brink.

Fausta Borja's Beauty and the Beast

Redbeard stiffened. Cinderella braced herself but he quickly slipped out of her—his semen shot up and hit the cock pillaging her cunt.

Cinderella unraveled and reached her climax.

The man on top of her stayed still as her pussy flexed around him but when she came down from her orgasm, he moved off of her though he had not yet come.

The black man got underneath and pulled her on top of him into the same position she'd been with Redbeard, with her back to his chest. To Cinderella's surprise, he quickly dipped his penis right back to where it had been and continued pushing into her cunt.

The dwarf hopped back onto the table, followed by another man.

The new man shoved his cock into Cinderella's mouth. He smelled of musky sweat which was not entirely unpleasant but after only a few swirls he pulled back and then climbed on top of her.

The prince put his hand on her breast and absentmindedly soothed her with smooth circles around her nipple. The dwarf put his face down to Cinderella's breasts and licked and bit them.

The musk-scented man pulled his trousers down to his knees and brought his cock to Cinderella's pussy where the black man was already sawing away.

Cinderella whimpered.

The new cock began to push into her cunt—where there was no room.

What do they think they're doing? Cinderella thought hysterically. Aloud, she could only squeak.

Cinderella shook her head from side to side and the prince gently murmured wordless noises of encouragement as her cunt slowly stretched to its limits.

201

Both the men were in her cunt. She had never accommodated two cocks there and couldn't believe she was doing it now. The fullness paralyzed her into shock and she could only lie there between them as the two men went to work using her pussy.

But the Dwarfs had more in store for her.

Prince Coal rose and went to the man on top of Cinderella. He undid his own trousers and massaged the man's buttocks.

Cinderella couldn't see what happened next but she gasped when she felt the next powerful push into her pussy.

Prince Coal was skewering the man on top of her. He took charge of the rhythm and made everyone below him move to his slow, inexorable pace.

The dwarf rose from Cinderella's breasts and returned to her mouth. She opened for him automatically and sucked when he thrust his cock in.

New hands and tongues took over her breasts, they mauled and teased and pinched her. The men inside of her and on top of her relentlessly thrusted into her, giving her no quarter.

Cinderella's nerves twisted and danced; she lost track of where her body ended and the next one began; she felt fully plugged on both ends; she felt her skin full of her tension, bursting to go somewhere.

The scream came up her throat and vibrated around the cock it found there.

Cinderella's nerves burst and rained back down on her.

Her climax blinded her.

She heard her own hoarse screams and realized the cock in her mouth had left her.

Cinderella hung suspended in her glorious orgasm for an eternity, and when she began to float down, she finally noticed—

Hot cum splashed onto her face. The dwarf.

Hot cum splashed onto her chest and stomach—her watchers who had stood jerking as their fellows used her.

The man beneath her gripped her waist and splurged his semen right into her.

The man above her pulled out. Behind him, the prince continued fucking him as he dropped to his knees and splashed his jizz onto her pussy with a heavy groan.

Cinderella noticed all this in a moment, a moment when she was still floating back to herself, and then the prince tore himself off the man he was fucking and came to her.

The others backed off and the prince grabbed Cinderella with a snarl.

He pulled her off the black man and flipped her onto her knees. Before she realized what was happening, he sank his cock into her ass.

His hand reached around slapped her clitoris and she screamed and came again.

He shoved into her ass in a frenzy of pounding till he stiffened and warmth gushed into her back channel.

He pulled out but kept her on her knees and slapped her buttocks and then shoved his fingers into her sopping cunt and fucked her with his hand till she came again.

His hand formed into a fist and invaded her snatch and she came before he could even move a few strokes.

The night was long and Cinderella came again, and again, and again.

Cinderella's body ached deliciously the next morning. She had taken a shower the night before—rather, she been carried into the bathhouse by the Dwarfs and been rinsed and sudsed and cleaned by them—but she headed to the bathhouse again after she woke.

Everyone who had worked the night before had the morning off and Cinderella wanted a long soak before the evening's activities.

It was close to noon when Cinderella sank into her own personal bath and sighed. The rest of the servants must have gotten up earlier than her and she had the place to herself.

Cinderella was lightly dozing when she heard footsteps echo in the stone bath chamber. She opened her eyes.

It was the mistress.

Mistress Fiona must have just come from the showers. Her skin glistened with droplets of water and she had not bothered with a towel to cover her transition to the baths. She was nude but for a delicate golden chain that hung loosely from her neck.

The mistress turned her head and murmured to the two servants that Cinderella had barely noticed standing behind her.

They shot Cinderella narrow looks but disappeared, leaving Cinderella and her mistress alone.

Mistress Fiona approached Cinderella's bath and stepped in.

Cinderella watched discreetly through her lashes and hungrily lapped up the vision of the mistress sinking into the hot water.

The mistress had the most highly arched of feet; the most deliciously sculpted calves; the most generous spread of thighs; the most beautiful thatch of tight curls crowning her pussy; the most lusciously curved hips; the womanliest of waists; the most succulent of breasts; the most delicately long neck; and of course, her face with its expressive mouth capable of both generosity and cruelty, its decisive nose, its direct eyes that stared directly into a person's soul...

Mistress Fiona was the most of anything and anyone that Cinderella had ever met.

"You were very good last night with the prince and his men, Cinderella," said the mistress. "Even though you had to be convinced to be good."

Cinderella bowed her head.

The mistress stroked her hands through the top of steamy water in slow, hypnotic, passes.

"Would you like to join the Dwarfs, Cinderella?"

Cinderella gaze darted up to Mistress Fiona. She couldn't speak.

Mistress Fiona continued stroking the water.

"Prince Coal normally only accepts warriors into his retinue but they lack women like you, women who enjoy being used as you do, and he's willing to make an exception to have you."

Mistress Fiona pronounced this matter-of-factly though her words made the blood leave Cinderella's face.

What did the mistress mean, women like Cinderella, who enjoyed being used? Did the mistress think less of Cinderella for being the sort that could fulfill this lack in the Dwarfs? Had she offered Cinderella to the prince because she wanted to be rid of her, this sluttish whore that was a blight to her efficient army of servants?

Cinderella turned away from the mistress to hide the tears that pricked her eyes.

"Also, one of the Dwarfs was enamored of your feet. Thinks they're the most beautiful he's seen in all the nations and kingdoms."

Mistress Fiona's voice was wry as she said this. Perhaps it was a jest. Though...her damn shoes did have trouble staying on her feet.

"Look at me, Cinderella," the mistress commanded.

Cinderella turned back to Mistress Fiona and looked at her.

"The choice is entirely yours," said the mistress.

Cinderella was silent.

The mistress waded closer to Cinderella.

"Did the men not please you last night, Cinderella?"

"They pleased me, mistress."

"And Prince Coal?"

"He pleased me, mistress."

"Does it frighten you, the idea of traveling with the Dwarfs?"

"Yes," Cinderella admitted, "it frightens me a little...but I think I would grow used to it, and that the Dwarfs would keep me safe from harm."

The mistress had waded so close to Cinderella, their breasts brushed beneath the water.

Cinderella watched the ripples from their bodies collide.

"Then what is keeping you from accepting the prince's offer?

"Mistress," whispered Cinderella, staring down into the water. "I belong to you."

The silence stretched for so long that Cinderella finally looked up.

Mistress Fiona was expressionless though she had a gleam in her eye that gave Cinderella hope.

"Is there..." Cinderella hesitated. Her mind flashed to all the ways in which she was a terrible employee. "May I remain with you here, as a maid?"

"As a maid," Mistress Fiona repeated. "I think not."

The mistress did not give Cinderella's stomach time to sink before continuing, "But I believe there is another role you are particularly suited to. A new position that has just opened up."

Cinderella held her breath.

"As my personal slave. You would belong to me. Totally. To use as I please. To punish as I please. To give to others to use and punish you...as it pleases me. "

"Yes," breathed Cinderella. "Oh, yes."

"You will have to serve Prince Coal and the Dwarfs tonight. Just as you will have to serve any guests that come through the inn, at my whim. But your duties will now be limited to serving in only a...personal manner."

"Yes."

"From now on, instead of saying 'yes,' you will always say, 'yes, mistress.'"

"Yes, mistress."

"Very well." The mistress unclasped the golden chain from her neck.

Mistress Fiona wound the long strand around Cinderella's neck until she had a tight choker which she left open so that it trailed down Cinderella's back like a leash

"Your duties begin now. Kiss me, slave."

Cinderella inched closer to her mistress, her heart pounding

"Yes, mistress."

LITTLE RED RIDING HOOD

MISS SCARLET was late.

The woodcutter looked at the sky. The sun would set within the hour and it was the night before the full moon. Werewolves would roam the woods tonight. Not to mention, every yahoo from miles around who fancied himself a hunter would be sniffing around the edges of the Black Forest.

Technically, it was illegal in every civilized nation and kingdom to hunt werebeasts, including werewolves, but the woodcutter lived out in the wilderness, subject to no king nor queen.

The werewolves preferred the wilderness as well; more so than other werebeasts, even if it meant yahoos trying to hunt them. Wolf pelts were always in demand, and kingdom buyers rarely questioned whether the unusually large pelts came from natural wolves, or humans who happened to turn into wolves for three nights out of the month.

"Mister Benjamin!" Miss Scarlet burst out into the back patio where he was loading chopped wood into his cart for another trip into the nearby village tomorrow.

"Miss Scarlet." The woodcutter threw in the last bundle of wood and ducked his head at the young woman.

Scarlet Dubois wore her scarlet red cloak as usual. The hood was thrown back at the moment, and her black curls flounced wildly as she approached him, breathless.

"Mister Benjamin, I'm so sorry if I kept you waiting," said Miss Scarlet. Her rich brown skin was infused with color. "I stopped to pick some mountain flowers for Gram."

Benjamin could see the merry burst of purple, blue, and red peeking out from the basket hanging from Miss Scarlet's elbow.

"No need to fret on my account, Miss Scarlet," Benjamin said gruffly. "But you ought to get going right aways to Gram's house before it gets dark."

Everyone hearabouts called Miss Scarlet's grandma Gram, including Miss Scarlet's parents who should presumably call her Ma.

Miss Scarlet's face fell. The woodcutter was sorry too: he treasured the moments when Miss Scarlet stopped by for a bit of tea, and chatted at him while he listened and nodded and smiled, and occasionally worked up the courage to share a bit about himself. But his worry trumped his regret.

"Here are the chains from the blacksmith," he said. Benjamin leaned down for the tightly wrapped canvas parcel.

He lifted it over Miss Scarlet's shoulder and she hoisted it without complaint.

"Maybe I ought to walk you to Gram's," he said, eyeing the parcel. It wasn't very heavy but he was a woodcutter, and Miss Scarlet only a tiny little thing, even if she was a tall, tiny little thing.

"Oh, no," she said firmly. "I couldn't ask you to do that, and leave you to hike back in the dark when *bzou* might be out."

Folks hereabouts called their werewolves *bzou*. The woodcutter wasn't from the hereabouts (or the nearabouts) originally; he'd come (or fled) here a few years back.

The woodcutter wasn't really worried about the bzou for himself. Most kept to themselves. It was only the young ones who hadn't yet learned control that might be dangerous. Which was why Miss Scarlet, a very dutiful granddaughter, went to spend the three nights of the fullest moons at Gram's house. Gram's house was *really* out in the wilderness, up a steep mountain path used mostly by deer. Miss Scarlet and Gram secured the isolated house with chains to protect themselves against werewolves at night.

"I doubt the bzou will find me a tasty morsel, Miss Scarlet, unlike you," he said, eyeing her trim, willowy form.

Miss Scarlet laughed and blushed. Benjamin ducked his head and rubbed the thick ruff of hair behind his neck. He needed a haircut, he thought, to distract himself from staring at Miss Scarlet.

It was rare for him to be so forward but Miss Scarlet had held his attention from the day he moved to the hereabouts. He knew she had gone out with a couple of different boys from the village just like he occasionally saw a girl from there but none of those boys had managed to tie Miss Scarlet down and make her his own, just like none of the girls had tied him down. And lately, Miss Scarlet seemed to be showing some interest in him.

"You don't have to call me 'Miss Scarlet' all the time, you know," Miss Scarlet said. "You could call me...Scarlet."

Was it his imagination, or had Miss Scarlet's voice turned a little husky?

"Well. Scarlet." He held her eyes. "Then I suppose you ought to just call me Benjamin."

They smiled at each other tentatively.

Benjamin turned stern. "And now you really ought to get going. Are you sure you don't want me to go with—"

"I'll be fine, Benjamin," Scarlet said. "I'll make it to Gram's just before the sun sets but you'd have to walk back in the dark if you came along. Or else spend the night with me."

"I would have no objections to that," Benjamin said, scarcely believing his own gall, "but I'm sure Gram would object to the goings on that would happen if I was alone in a room with you."

Scarlet laughed again. He loved it when she laughed. She would always start by throwing her head back but then she would catch herself and laugh quietly, as if to share some secret joke between them.

"You'd be surprised," she said teasingly. "Gram is a wild woman at heart, and encourages me to be wild too." She sighed. "I'll be off then."

She drew in closer to Benjamin and tilted her head up. Her eyes were a tawny brown. "Perhaps I'll come by tomorrow and visit you?"

"I got to go into the village again for another delivery," he said regretfully. "Likely won't be back until near nightfall. You ought to stay safely tucked away at Gram's."

"Very well."

Scarlet hesitated, then placed her hand on Benjamin's chest to steady herself as she went up on tiptoes. The smell of her—woods and spices and honeysuckle—made him feel heady.

Scarlet kissed him, chastely, on the lips.

She fell back on her heels. He gazed down at her, dazed.

Scarlet smiled. "In three days then. You'd better be ready for me, Benjamin Paquet."

She set off towards the dirt road next to his cabin. Her hips twitched becomingly beneath her flowing cloak.

Benjamin's mouth was dry. "Oh, I'll be ready," he promised.

Scarlet smiled as she reached the dirt road. She had deliberately sashayed her hips as she walked away from Benjamin, knowing he was watching her.

She had known the woodcutter for years, ever since he mysteriously moved into their neck of the woods without a word to say about his past or where he'd come from.

He had intimidated her at first with his stern way of speaking, and aloof demeanor. Chopping wood all day had blessed him with a lean, wiry frame rather than bulk and brawn, but anyone who looked at him could sense the lithe deadliness coiled inside, ready to lash out if needed. His straight black hair, golden skin, and narrow eyes declared his native nations blood, whereas most of the folk hereabouts were kingdom transplants.

Benjamin Paquet had his secrets but it quickly became apparent to all who lived in the wilderness nearabouts that he was also an honorable, hard-working man, and people learned to stop prying and simply accepted him.

He was also sweet, and very shy. Scarlet had recently begun to tease him gently, when she realized her feelings for him had grown beyond polite neighborly interests, or even platonic friendly ones.

Yes, Scarlet thought, swinging her basket full of goodies for Gram, in three days' time she and Benjamin would get to know each other even more, and she was certainly looking forward to it.

If she hadn't been so distracted thinking about the woodcutter, she would've heard them moving through the woods.

A group of men stepped into the road in front of Scarlet.

"Well, lookee here, boys, we've got us a bonafide little red riding hood."

There were five of them, young, and from the looks of their unscuffed boots, shiny new bows, and the ridiculous "accent" their leader was sporting, they were city folk, come to hunt bzou and taunt local women.

Scarlet's heart pounded.

"You boys move aside now and let me be on my way," she said, keeping her voice steady and unwavering.

"Now why would we do that, girly?" The leader, a skinny lad taller, even, than her, leered down at Scarlet. He aped her twang with exaggerated enunciation. "You's a fine looking little lady and we mean to have ourselves a fine time with you."

She almost laughed at how stupid he sounded. Did folks hereabouts really sound like that to him?

But laughing would only antagonize these so-called hunters, and she didn't have time to delay.

Two of them had already slinked around her so that she was surrounded on all sides.

Scarlet set down her basket.

"That's a girl," said the leader. "Don't give us no trouble, like, and we won't hurt ya too much and we can all have us a good time."

Scarlet let the parcel of iron chains slip off her shoulders and into her hands. She swung the canvas around herself in a wide arc.

The men shouted as they sprang back. She caught one square in the legs and he fell to the ground.

"Fucking bitch," he cursed. This one didn't bother with a fake twang. The other men snickered and laughed as he rolled in the dirt road. He had a paunchy belly, young though he was, and he staggered to his feet like a drunk boar.

"I'm going to fuck you until your cunt bleeds, you stupid whore."

Scarlet swung again. The paunchy man tried to catch the canvas but it escaped his clumsy hands and caught him in his thick midriff. He fell to his knees. The others roared with laughter at their chum.

Then someone bearhugged Scarlet from behind. She struggled as they lifted her off her feet. The leader pried the parcel of chains from her grip.

Scarlet kicked her feet and heard some grunts as they connected but then the ruffians grabbed her legs and wrestled her to the dirt road.

"Hunter's balls, she's feisty," one complained. He and another sat on her legs as the leader pushed up her skirts and groped her quim. Her drawers stopped him from touching her directly but his invasive fingers sought to find her as she wriggled about.

Gods, they were going to rape her right here in the middle of the road, right now. The sun was setting but not fast enough for a hungry bzou to materialize and eat these appalling men.

The leader flew back from Scarlet. She watched with stunned eyes as Benjamin punched him squarely in the jaw and he crumpled to the ground.

Benjamin grabbed the head of the man nearest him and yanked it down into his knee. Scarlet could hear the man's nose cartilage crunch noisily and then blood splurted out from it.

The remaining three men scrambled to their feet.

"We're just trying to have some fun," the paunchy one said, stupidly. "You can join us, you don't have to get all—"

Benjamin headbutt him and he staggered back, throwing his hands up as if that would calm the woodcutter.

"We'll go," gasped one of the last remaining two.

He grabbed his friend with the bleeding nose, and the last one grabbed the paunchy one, and they all grabbed their unconscious leader from the side of the road and disappeared into the woods, probably back to where their camp was set. Hopefully they wouldn't hunt any bzou tonight. Or, perhaps more hopefully, they would hunt for bzou tonight and get themselves killed.

Benjamin took a few steps as if to go after them but then he seemed to remember her. His eyes went down to Scarlet, sprawled inelegantly on the ground.

He made a sound and came toward her but Scarlet pushed her skirts down and scrambled to her feet before he could help her up.

"Are you all right?" she heard him ask. She avoided his gaze.

"Yes," Scarlet said. Her face was burning. She surreptitiously tried to straighten her twisted drawers through her skirts.

"Thank you," she forced herself to say through gritted teeth. This was *not* how she wished to appear before Benjamin!

The woodcutter picked up the fallen canvas parcel, her basket, and some bruised mountain flowers which he carefully laid back on the basket.

"I'll walk you to Gram's."

"Don't trouble yourself," Scarlet said. She tried to take back her basket but he did not let go. She had no choice but to follow him as he set off walking briskly down the road.

"You should've run, Scarlet," Benjamin said. "Or screamed. I was right down the road. If I hadn't decided at the last minute to follow you—"

"They shouldn't have attacked me," she snapped. "And you don't need to follow me around, Benjamin. I can take care of myself."

Ugh. Well, the last wasn't *always* true but the woodcutter was kind enough not to throw the events of the previous five minutes into her face.

"You're right," he said quietly. "It's them that shouldn't have attacked you. Who knows what difference you running or screaming would've made. I ain't leaving you to walk to Gram's on your own though, not after that. So let's just agree to disagree on that one."

She wanted to stamp her feet and roar but she knew that was unfair to Benjamin and she bit her tongue and kept her mouth shut so she wouldn't yell at him.

She was a mess of anger and embarrassment right now—and yes, a part of her was a teeny bit scared at how close those stupid boys had come to violating her. All the emotions whirled through her and made her dizzy with the need to lash out. Benjamin meant well but she was genuinely angry that he felt it was his duty to escort her to

Gram's like she was some helpless little fluff, and the fact that things had been going so well between them only made everything worse.

Gods, she needed to get to Gram's and down a tranquilizer potion.

Just a little while longer.

They finally reached the last path that would take them to Gram's.

The wind grew fiercer and numbed their cheeks.

Orange and pink streaked the horizon and a blanket of blue twilight settled over them.

"How does a woodcutter learn to fight like that?" she said. It came out more accusing than she intended and she followed up quickly with: "Never mind, you don't have to tell me."

But she was curious.

He was silent and she thought that was that, until he opened his mouth and said slowly, "I was a soldier once."

He paused, then the words all came out. Still slow.

"I was a soldier, and I was a woodcutter before that. From a wilderness not unlike our own. Then I was conscripted to fight in a queen's war. Not my queen, not my war, but it didn't matter. They were going to kill our families if we didn't join them. And after years of fighting, we lost, and the queen was overthrown. I went back to my wilderness...but everyone had died anyway. While we went to wage war against the enemy, the enemy came to us. Or, I don't know, maybe the queen killed our families anyway, so that we wouldn't have nothing to go home to. It don't matter. I had no one. So I left. And I came here."

He fell silent again. Scarlet's heart ached for him. She couldn't begin to imagine what it was like to lose your entire family.

She reached out and squeezed his arm, right above the elbow where he carried her basket. The woodcutter reached with his other hand and laid it over hers.

Then Scarlet remembered their situation and snatched her hand back. She quickened her stride.

The last sliver of sun was about to set. Gram's house came into view at the top of the path.

"Here," Scarlet said. Benjamin let her take the basket and the canvas parcel of iron chains.

"Hurry back," Scarlet said. "Maybe I'll see you after...after."

Benjamin nodded.

Scarlet ran up the path, huffing with the weight of the chains. She knocked on Gram's door and looked back down.

Benjamin, that stubborn man, stood there looking till Gram opened the door and let her in.

Scarlet hoped he got home safely.

The woodcutter wasted no time getting home after he saw Scarlet safely to Gram's door. He wouldn't have minded going after those men who had assaulted Scarlet but he wasn't foolhardy enough to tempt fate while bzou roamed.

The sun set before he got home and the howls that went up soon after chilled his spine.

Tomorrow he would set out for the village early, conduct his business as quickly as possible, and then return, hopefully early enough to track those men and ensure they didn't bother Scarlet ever again.

The woodcutter had been filled with cold fear that turned quickly to rage when he came upon those men trying to force themselves on Scarlet. He mentally rebuked himself again for not walking her to Gram's in the first place.

But Scarlet Dubois was fiercely independent—it was one of the characteristics that had drawn him to her—and he knew he had to respect that if he was to woo her.

He would give her time after this to settle down—even if she wasn't ticked off at him, Benjamin wasn't insensitive enough to try and court a woman right after she'd been accosted. And he hadn't missed the fact that her promise to visit him in three days had turned into a "maybe I'll see you."

It was time to back off, give Scarlet some time, and let her come back to him when she was good and ready. Maybe they could start up again from there, or maybe she would forever associate him with the incident and shun him romantically (he squeezed that thought quickly out of his mind), but he hoped she came back to see him in any case. He missed her presence already.

As it turned out, the woodcutter didn't have to wait long before Scarlet came running back to find him.

"Benjamin!" Scarlet screamed. She ran towards the woodcutter's cabin, desperate to find him.

It was the next day, the sun was about to set, and Scarlet could feel the weight of the hanging moon above her.

She picked up the scent of a sweaty horse, and then her keen ears heard Benjamin's soft voice, and some splashing water. No doubt he was wiping the horse down after the trip into the village.

Scarlet ran harder.

She knew it was useless to shout when the wind whipped against her but she did so anyway. "Benjamin!"

Scarlet gasped when she turned round the corner and saw him.

The woodcutter's horse neighed and pranced in his shack.

"Whoa," Benjamin calmed the horse. But Scarlet scarcely paid attention.

Benjamin was stark naked and dripping with water. He had just finished pouring a bucket of water over himself and was using some rags to towel himself dry.

"Miss Scarlet!" The woodcutter swore, cut himself off, then snatched the trousers hanging from a line. He hopped into them quickly and turned to her.

"Scarlet, what's this about?" He ran a quick eye over her to ensure she wasn't hurt and his eyes widened with he saw the torn skirt of her dress.

"Did those hunters...I'm gonna kill them! That cursed tanner kept me at the village with his count! I was gonna—"

Benjamin cut himself off and grabbed Scarlet by the shoulders. "Are you all right, Scarlet? What did they do to you? It'll be okay, I promise."

He looked a little wild as he pulled her tight into a hug. Scarlet spoke into his neck.

"I'm fine! I got away. That's not important—"

Benjamin pulled back to look at her face. "It is important, and you can tell me if anything—"

"Benjamin, please, they didn't hurt me, and I don't have much time."

The urgency in her voice reached him.

"What's the matter?"

"Do you have any iron chains left from the blacksmith?"

"Iron...no, I only ordered enough for your Gram and gave it all to you yesterday—"

Scarlet groaned. "Do you have any sort of iron shackles, or—or a cage or something—"

"A cage?" He gave her a sharp look. "No, I don't have anything like that just lying about somewhere. What's this about?"

"All right," Scarlet said, "all right. She squared her shoulders and pushed him towards his cabin. "I'll run on to Gram's. You lock yourself up inside and don't come out tonight."

"Scarlet! The sun is setting now. It'll be nightfall in less than ten minutes. You ain't got time to run to Gram's, you need to come inside with me."

"No, I can't, I—"

Benjamin grabbed her hand and dragged her with him. "Scarlet, please, it's not safe for you out here."

Scarlet dug her heels in. "Benjamin, no."

"Look, I promise I'll be a gentleman—"

"Benjamin!" she growled so that he turned to look at her.

"I am bzou."

He just stared so she reached up and put her hands on his cheeks.

"I am bzou," Scarlet repeated. "I'm a werewolf. I get cranky and turn into a wolf for three nights out of the month. I'm young so I can't control myself yet. Gram tranquilizes me and chains me up before the sun sets but I knocked over the tranquilizing potion this afternoon and had to run back to my house for more herbs. That's when those hunters found me. I might hurt someone. I might hurt you. You need to go inside."

"You are bzou," Benjamin said, dazed.

He took her hands from his face and pulled her toward his cabin.

"Yes."

The woodcutter blinked down at her. Then his brows drew down. "But the hunters are out. And they're even more of a danger to you than I thought."

He took her hands from his face and pulled her toward his cabin.

"Benjamin, what do you think you're doing?"

"Putting you inside. You can't be out here. What if the hunters find you? They'll try to kill you for your pelt."

"Benjamin," she said. She was a little stunned (and ecstatically happy) that he was not angry or afraid of her. But she had to focus now.

"Your cabin can't contain me. I'll jump out a window or break down a door to be free."

They reached the cabin and Benjamin quickly shoved her inside. He came in behind her and shut the door.

His cabin smelled of hearthfire, and pine, and of him.

"What do we do then?" he asked her. "Tell me there's something else I can do besides leave you outside to be hunted and killed, because I ain't doing that."

Scarlet stared at his bare chest and it came to her.

"Gram used to be able to stop the change," she said slowly. "When I was young—when the change first started."

"How?"

"She'd pin me down," she repeated. "Yap at me. Nip at me. It was enough then, to establish her dominance. But as I grew older, she was unable to stop the change."

"Gram ain't dominant to you no more?"

"It has nothing to do with that. Not quite. There are only so many things you can do to establish dominance, and she couldn't do anything more drastic than what she was doing, so she couldn't stop the change."

Scarlet stepped away from him. His cabin was one large room. The hearth was built into one wall, set with stones. A tidy made up bed was pushed into the corner. A bear rug covered the middle of the pine floor.

"I think," Scarlet said, "I think if you establish your dominance over me, that it will stop the change."

"I am dominant to you," he said. He said it plainly, like it was a fact and he didn't understand why she couldn't see it.

Scarlet glared. "It's not about who is dominant over who. You need to demonstrate...your dominance."

He was still looking at her quizzically. "Pinning you down stopped working for your grandma."

"You have to fuck me," she said.

The woodcutter blushed the color of her name.

"Well, that is..." He cleared his throat. "Well, Scarlet, if that's what it takes then I guess—"

"I will put up a fight."

He shut up.

"I'm too close to the change and it's in my nature to fight anyone who tries to dominate me."

"Scarlet...I don't see how I can force myself on you."

"You're not forcing yourself on me," she said patiently. "You're establishing your dominance. I don't have super strength in human form, just some heightened senses. I shouldn't be able to hurt you too badly."

His look turned laconic. Then troubled.

"This is the only way," Scarlet said. "This is the only way to stop me from changing into a wolf and attacking you or some other innocent person."

An innocent person...he hadn't even thought about her getting out and hurting others besides him. His mind took a dark turn and he fantasized about letting her kill those so-called hunters that had tried to rape her... But that would be wrong. Not because they didn't deserve to die but because if she killed them, she should be in control of herself and making a conscious decision.

He thought of Scarlet turning into a wolf, and accidently killing him, and never forgiving herself. He thought of her getting out, and killing some innocent person, and never forgiving herself. He thought of hunters shooting her dead so they could skin her, and sell her fur, and of him never forgiving himself.

Benjamin undid the clasp on Scarlet's cloak.

"What are you doing?"

Scarlet clutched her red cloak but he tugged it from her grasp and hung it up on a peg.

He grasped her arms and turned her around. His fingers went to the buttons on the back of her dress.

"Benjamin!"

Scarlet tore herself away from him and whirled to face him. She stepped back. Her loose dress gaped at her neckline and her hands pressed it tighter to her bosom.

He eyed her.

"I've made my decision," he said. "We're doing this."

"All right, I'm glad we can agree but...I mean look, the sun hasn't even set yet—"

He turned her around again and undid a few more buttons. She wrenched herself away and stepped back from him. She moved till she hit the wall and couldn't move anymore.

"Hang on just a moment..."

Scarlet trailed off as Benjamin pressed his hard body against hers and crowded her against the wall. She was tall enough for him to put his forehead to hers without leaning down much.

His lips were right next to hers, close enough she could feel his breath on her lips when he murmured to her.

"Scarlet, you can keep talking all you want, but nothing you say now is going to change my mind."

His lips didn't kiss her. She closed her eyes in trepidation and anticipation and felt his breath move down her face and over her neck.

He bit her neck. She yelped.

He picked her up.

Scarlet kicked and struggled—it was like she had said, she just couldn't seem to help herself.

He dumped her on the bed. She tried to worm away immediately.

Benjamin grabbed her leg and yanked her back. She kicked at his hands and twisted out from his grasp.

Scarlet fell off the bed and landed on the soft bear pelt. She tried to scramble to her feet but found no purchase on the fur. Benjamin grabbed her and flipped her around.

He straddled her.

Scarlet felt the instant the sun disappeared behind the horizon. She moaned. Her skin tightened. She ached with a power that demanded to burst out of her flesh. Shred it to pieces. Crush her bones and reorganize them into a form more suitable for the predator within.

The woodcutter reached for her dress which was already falling off her shoulders, and drew it down.

Scarlet's breasts were visible through her thin chemise. Benjamin bent his head and put his mouth over a dark nipple that called for his attention.

He breathed through the chemise, covering her nipple in hot air.

Scarlet arched. She thrust her breast into his mouth, scraping it against his teeth. Then her arm snaked up and boxed his ear.

Benjamin grunted as his ear blossomed with pain.

He grabbed her arms and pushed them back down. He pinned her to the bear rug and stared down at his woman. Because that's what she was.

At least for this one night when she needed him.

Scarlet stared back up at him. Her face looked the same yet was somehow different. The planes of her cheeks seemed sharper. Her chin more angular. Her eyes lightened to a tawny amber.

She looked like a wild predator.

She looked like she wanted to eat him.

And not in a good way.

The woodcutter bent his head to her breasts again. He breathed on Scarlet's nipples, nuzzled her flesh, and bit her when she snarled.

The flesh and bone of Scarlet's wrists trembled and vibrated in his hands. He didn't dare loosen his grip.

He caught Scarlet's chemise in his teeth and yanked it down. The chemise ripped. He used his face to brush aside the ripped sides of the chemise, agitating Scarlet's nipples in the process.

Scarlet was growling continuously.

He nibbled slowly up around one breast, and then the other. He avoided her nipples and started again.

Closer, he drew to a nipple, then avoided it to nuzzle her flesh.

Scarlet's growls turned to whimpers.

Slowly—achingly slowly—he drew his tongue from the underside of breast, up, up—Scarlet arched into his mouth—up till it found her areola and licked all around it.

Scarlet gasped. He let go of her arms to seize her breasts. Her arms went immediately behind his neck and drew him down to her breasts. He let her draw his head down. This time his mouth latched immediately onto her nipple.

Scarlet moaned.

Her flesh was hot—dangerously hot.

The woodcutter massaged Scarlet's breasts with one hand as he suckled her, and the other explored her skirts.

He felt where Scarlet's dress was torn and had a jarring moment when he remembered that the hunters had torn it, and he remembered how she had looked when he came upon them yesterday. That skinny stripling had his hand right where Benjamin was going now.

The woodcutter bit Scarlet's nipple and she moaned again. It erased the image of the hunter from his mind and he continued to pull up Scarlet's skirts.

Scarlet struggled against him.

Benjamin sat on her legs as she tried to kick. He pushed her skirts up but she twisted round and round. Finally he grabbed the dress and yanked it down. The last buttons popped off and he tugged the dress off of her.

He grabbed her ankles before she could crawl away, sat on her again, and pushed her chemise up, completely revealing her breasts.

He had wanted to take his time with her, the first time they did this, and treasure every moment. But that was impossible now.

He slid the chemise up her arms and quickly wrapped the shreds of it around her wrists till they were bound.

He scuttled down her legs and went for the ribbon of her drawers. The sight of her sweet pussy and its wreath of tight curls almost made him lose his grip but he jerked the drawers all the way down to her ankles. Benjamin wrapped the drawers around her ankles and tied the ribbon around so that they were bound as well.

Then, ignoring the snarls coming from Scarlet, he pushed her legs up so that she was doubled over at the waist, caught her hands, and pulled her bound wrists over her feet so that she trapped her own knees.

He had once seen Scarlet blush when she exposed too much ankle as he helped her off his cart.

Now she glared at him, naked, panting, seemingly unaware of the way her bare breasts were crushed by her knees, or how her pussy was open and displayed for him.

He could see the wetness of her glistening folds and didn't delay any longer. He shoved his trousers down and mounted her.

"Get off me!"

She rolled side to side trying to dislodge him but his cock found her entrance.

He didn't waste time with preliminaries.

The head of his cock stabbed in. Her tight sheath coated him with its juices. He pushed relentlessly till he was all the way into her pussy.

Scarlet screamed.

The woodcutter covered her mouth with his own. She bit his lip and he reared back and slapped her across the cheek. Her teeth gnashed at his fingers.

He grasped her hip with one hand, her ankles in another, and went to work.

Benjamin set up a slow, relentless rhythm. Scarlet had no choice but to accept his fucking.

There was no escape in the position she was in.

The woodcutter had his knees splayed wide, his chest pushed forward, and his head tilted back as he thrust. He was hitting parts of her inside that dismantled her being, made her mouth fall helplessly open.

Benjamin grabbed her hips and jerked them down. He shifted his hips and bore down on her, angling his thrusts so that they rubbed against the little nub at the top of her slit.

Scarlet could no longer tell the difference between the power of the bzou spiraling up inside her, or her climax building to a release.

She burst.

Benjamin rode on as she cried out her climax.

Her cries died to whimpers and still he rammed into her.

Scarlet grimaced and begged, "No more. No more!"

"Yes, more," Benjamin grunted above her.

"No, please. I can't take anymore..."

"You will take it," he said.

His thrusts came quicker; hard jerks with longer pauses in between.

"You're mine," he said.

"Mine." His hips slammed into the backs of her thighs.

"Mine." He slapped her buttocks—the sound was sudden and loud in the cabin.

Scarlet couldn't respond—she was coming again. This one was silent. Her mouth just opened and her breath caught and tears sprang to her eyes.

She gasped for air as the orgasm continued.

Benjamin slapped her buttocks again.

"Mine," he growled again. His hips jerked and he squeezed inside her one last time, somehow fit his whole being into her, stuffed his soul into her along with his cock, possessed her, filled her with his cum.

The cabin was silent but for their gasping breaths.

He eased out from her and untied her limbs.

229

Scarlet sprawled out onto the bear rug. She was covered in sweat. She couldn't move. She couldn't think. She couldn't transform into the bzou.

Benjamin slid his arms beneath her and carried her to the bed. He crawled in under the covers with her, threw a possessive arm around her waist and tugged her in close to him.

"When did you know you were bzou?"

"I was thirteen. All the girls I knew in the village had started their monthly bleeding already but I hadn't started mine."

"Is it...connected to that?"

"I don't have a monthly bleed, just the bzou transformation."

"What happens to men?"

"I don't know. We don't know any bzou men. For all I know, there's no such thing."

Silence.

"My parents never told me about Gram, that she was bzou, and I might be too, so I had no idea."

"That must've been hard. Your ma ain't bzou?"

"It skipped her."

He stroked her back in small circles.

"I almost killed my parents. Literally, I almost killed them. My father has scars running his arms and chest from when he protected Mama."

"How did they stop you?"

"Gram showed up. She had suspected for a while that I might have the bzou in me, and she would hang around our house on the nights around the full moon. When I attacked

Papa, she leapt in through a window and sat on me. It was enough to make me change back."

"But that stopped working."

"It stopped working. But Gram never meant to stop me from changing altogether. Even when she still could, she only forced her dominance over me once a moon. Mama wanted her to keep me that way but Gram refused. Said I'd been born with the bzou in me, and to take it out completely was to destroy who I was."

"Why did she keep doing it at all, stop you from changing, after that first time?"

"It was to help me learn control. If she had been able to continue, to stop the change from happening once in a while, then I would've learned to do it for myself. Eventually, I would've learned to control myself in wolf form too. That's why I still can't control myself even though it's been ten years since I first changed."

"Will you be able to control yourself now? If we do this on the regular?"

"Probably. We'll see."

She snuggled into him.

"I knew a werebear once. A fellow soldier. He accidentally bit his mate when he was in bear form."

"What happened to her?"

"Him. His mate was another man. His mate turned into a werebear too. Can that happen with bzou? Or is it passed down?"

"It's passed down. You can't pass it to someone when you bite them. I'm sorry—I should've told you that before we started."

"It doesn't matter. I would've done this anyway."

He was dozing when he felt her weight on him.

The woodcutter opened his eyes.

Scarlet's yellow eyes stared into his. She growled softly.

It was the dead of night now.

He took hold of her arms to move her off of him and felt it. Her flesh rippled beneath his hands.

Her arms flew up abruptly and knocked his hands off her. She crouched over him. Laid her hand on his chest. She curved her fingers and dragged her nails into him. Her hands were still human and they gouged his skin, but didn't draw blood.

The woodcutter caught Scarlet's hand. She shook his hand off and slapped him across the face. It was open-handed but she'd curved her fingers again and he'd felt the sting of her nails against his forming beard. He hadn't shaved in a couple days.

Scarlet leaned over him and sniffed his cheek.

Benjamin had a feeling she'd drawn blood. Her tongue darted out and licked his skin.

"That's enough." He grabbed a fistful of hair and pulled her head back. She strained against him and shook her head wildly.

"That's enough!" He rose and shoved her off him.

She landed awkwardly and tried to shoot up again.

Benjamin stuck his knee in her stomach.

Scarlet screamed and flailed.

Her skin was hot again, and he could swear he saw little ridges of her flesh undulate out in wavelets.

She was still naked. He was already hard.

He moved off her stomach. She kicked out at him and kneed his ribs. He grunted and yanked her ankles down and climbed on top of her and pushed apart her thighs.

She fought him, and clenched her legs together.

He gripped her knees and wrenched them open. He moved swiftly between them and fell on top of her before she could dislodge him.

Scarlet bucked and writhed but he had her pinned to the bed.

He grabbed her arms and bore them into the bed as he ground into her. He raised his hips and his cock bumped and collided against her slippery entrance.

He found her warmth and ravaged it.

She shuddered around him as his cock plunged in.

He didn't know if she was changing or already coming, but he kept going 'cause he was going to be inside of her either way.

Her pussy contorted around him and he groaned as his cock was held hostage in her vise-like sheathe.

His balls tightened and he was already coming.

She shuddered and shuddered as she came, and he came, and her pussy squeezed and wrung him dry.

He didn't remember falling asleep, or anything after he'd come, so he decided he must've passed out.

She dozed sweetly next to him, with her fingers curled up in his chest hair, right next to where she had gouged him.

He maneuvered the edges of the blankets on top of them and fell back asleep.

"When you were a woodcutter...before you were a soldier. Did you have someone?"

"Did I have a lover, like you?"

"Yes."

"No."

"Nobody?"

"I was fifteen when the army came to take us. As much as I would've loved to have gotten under Miss Melodie or Miss Clarissa's skirts, I never got the chance."

He grew quiet.

"I'm sorry."

"I'm sorry too. Miss Melodie was always twitching her skirts at me."

"I meant I'm sorry they're not there anymore!"

"Well. I like to think they found some other boys—or girls—they were willing to let under their skirts, and moved to another village somewhere."

She sighed.

"You want to ask me about the girls in the village nearabouts too?"

"Why would I?"

"Since you're so curious about my past lovers."

"I'm not curious! I was just..."

"I've had some interesting lovers, Scarlet, but none like you."

"Well!"

"Well?"

"Well good for you."

"Ask me about the girls in the village nearabouts."

"...What about those girls you went out with in the village nearabouts?"

"They're not like you, either."

"Hmm."

"What's the matter?"

"Aren't you going to ask me about the boys I've seen in the village?"

"Nope."

"Why not?"

"They don't matter now."

"Huh! Well, maybe I want a polygamous relationship!"

"That's fine if that's what you really want."

"It is?"

"Honey, you can fuck whoever you want as long as you know you belong to me."

"Well! I don't want *you* fucking anyone else but *me*."

He chuckled. "I had a feeling it would be that way for you."

"And *I* am not...fucking...anyone else either! Not for a while, at least."

"Deal. We're monogamous. For now."

"That's right. For now. So you better not make me angry, Benjamin Paquet."

"Oh, I plan on making you real angry, Scarlet Dubois."

He could see she was actually getting angry. The talk of seeing other people had upset her, the way it did some women—and some men too.

Or maybe that was the wolf in her. He remembered hearing wolves mated for life.

Foolish woman. Couldn't she see that she belonged to him now, no matter what? Just like he belonged to her. But he could keep his cock in one place if he had to. For the rest of his life, if that's what she needed.

She was making angry little noises in her throat now.

Faint light had brightened his windows. Dawn was coming, though night still held its grip on the sky.

The woodcutter threw off the covers and turned Scarlet over.

"What are you doing?" she huffed. He put his hand on her neck to keep her face against the bed. She rose to her knees, giving him an enticing view of her firm buttocks, and a peek at her hiding quim.

"The night ain't over and you're getting fussy."

"I am not getting—oh!"

He slipped into her from behind. She was slippery from their previous matings.

He put both hands on her hips and set up a slow rhythm.

Her hands bunched up the bed covers in her fists. She rose to all fours and tried to crawl away from him.

He pulled her hips back so that she settled back around his cock.

"You're mine," he said.

She growled and wriggled her hips.

"You're mine," he growled back at her. "Say it."

She huffed and puffed as he thrust into her.

"Say it!" He gritted his teeth as he rocked his hips. He knocked his pelvis against her buttocks. His balls swung and slapped her mound.

Her pussy was hot, pulsating, and wet around him. She collapsed flat onto the bed.

He moved over her and kept sawing into her.

He thought he would break her body with his ramming but she was strong.

"I'm yours!" she cried out. "I'm yours...aah!"

Scarlet climaxed.

The woodcutter slipped out and turned Scarlet onto her back.

She lay sprawled and open as he mounted her again.

He rammed his cock back into her wet pussy.

His cock was throbbing, sore, ready to burst. He could not remember a time when he wasn't inside of Scarlet. His memory of life began and ended inside her.

He tensed over her and then his cock exploded. She clenched her pussy around him and milked him and milked him until every bit of the cum that had been inside him was now inside her.

The woodcutter fell on top of Scarlet, and lay still.

Light seeped in through the windows now. Dawn had arrived.

Scarlet raised her hand and drew her nails slowly up Benjamin's back—lightly, lightly.

He shivered and she placed her hand on the back of his neck. She maneuvered him to face her.

"You're mine too." She kissed him.

A *few moons later.*

Scarlet loped to Benjamin's cabin.

Her paws hit the dirt of the road and she paused to sit back on her haunches and howl into the night.

She was close enough now that he should've heard her. She howled again, and once more.

Benjamin looked up when he heard the howls split the night. Scarlet.

The moon was bright and high.

He brought out the second bucket of heated water and set it on the patio.

It wasn't long before Scarlet trotted into view.

She came to him with her tongue lolling out and licked his hand. There was blood on her muzzle and on her fur. More than the usual amount from a rabbit or even coyote.

Scarlet sat at his feet and shuddered. Her fur rippled. Bones slid around underneath her flesh.

Scarlet the woman sat in front of him—she fell over, off balance and Benjamin hurried to help her up.

"Are you hurt?" he demanded.

"No," she said. She cupped some water from a bucket and rinsed her mouth out and spat.

"The blood is all theirs."

"You found them."

"Yes."

"All of them?"

"Yes. They won't be bothering anyone any more."

"Good."

Benjamin picked up a bucket and poured warm water over Scarlet. She scrubbed herself with honeysuckle soap.

Those five hunters that had accosted Scarlet had continued to cause trouble. They killed a farmer's goat and raped one of the village girls.

No nation nor kingdom rules in the wilderness of the hereabouts and the nearabouts.

Outsiders who think to take advantage of the lawlessness need to be reminded.

Think twice before hunting bzou, lest the bzou come hunting for you.

The woodcutter helped Scarlet dry and lead his woman inside.

THE RED SHOES

CLARA BLAMED it on the red shoes.

She had burned herself three times now while baking apple pies for the church bake sale and she thanked God she was almost done.

Clara stuck the last pie in the oven and slammed the oven door shut.

Phew.

Clara set about cleaning the kitchen, trying very hard not to think about the red shoes. Noah would be home soon and she wanted to have dinner ready.

Clara stopped to wipe a finger along the pot she'd made the apple pie filling in. She stuck the filling in her mouth.

Mmmm. She closed her eyes. It was just the right amount of sticky and sweet and tart.

Her mind wandered to her morning at the Black Forest farmer's market. She'd been picking through a bushel of apples when she saw *her* stalk through the fruit stalls like some exotic creature from another world—which, if Clara thought about it, she was. Emily Choi. Emily wore a red dress that clung to her body in the most indecent way and a pair of red stiletto heels to match.

Clara gaped. The apple vendor was going on about the harvest but Clara brushed past him. Clara didn't know why but she found herself scurrying after Emily as she stalked through the short brown grass arm in arm with a handsome man who kept flashing Emily...indecent looks.

And right before Clara's eyes, the man reached down and caressed Emily's posterior, right there in the middle of the market. Clara looked around wildly but no one else seemed to notice, or care. Well.

Clara was from Chastebury, a small hamlet in the Black Forest. Chastebury hadn't always been a part of the Black Forest. Clara had been born into a world with modern electricity, hospitals, and telephones. She met her husband, Noah, in college, married him, and eventually helped him settle Chastebury, a community that revolved around their church where Noah was pastor.

There were no telephones in Chastebury, and no televisions, and no automobiles. So no one could really pinpoint when it happened. The changes had been gradual. The woods surrounding them grew wilder. The stars shone brighter. Eventually no one could find the modern roads or highways that used to lead to the big city. And then the bears started talking—that was when they knew.

Chastebury had moved to another world. The Black Forest.

Noah and the congregation prayed about it and they determined that it was God's will. Who else could've performed such a feat?

Strangely, being displaced into the Black Forest made Chastebury more connected to the world outside. Noah had set up deliveries in that other world, deliveries of any goods that the hamlet couldn't produce on its own, so that their hamlet could continue in its isolation.

Now they had to travel outside their hamlet, which they did with the help of magical talismans that prevented them from getting lost. (Donated to the church by pagan pilgrims.) Noah had once even stopped in the middle of a village square and given one of his favorite sermons on the sinful nature of lust, and the villagers had stopped to listen breathlessly with wide eyes.

Unfortunately, a few people left Chastebury permanently to explore the new world outside. Emily Choi was one of those.

That morning instead of buying apples, Clara followed Emily and her man as they wandered the farmer's market. She never called out to Emily. What would she say?

The man kept his hands on Emily's lower back, (or rear), and every once in a while when Emily stopped to examine some produce, he would pull her close and run his hands all over her.

It was absolutely indecent but Clara couldn't help feeling a little jealous. Noah wasn't even that affectionate in private.

And then they were in a secluded part of the market, a makeshift alley behind the stalls. Clara hung back in case the couple had grown alert but she needn't have worried. When she finally managed to peek her head around the last stall the man had pushed Emily against a wall and neither of them were paying any attention to their surroundings.

The man nibbled on Emily's neck while she moaned. Clara's face flamed as she realized the man was fondling Emily's breasts with one hand and the other...the other hand looked as if he was undoing his trousers.

Suddenly, he grabbed Emily behind her knees and hoisted her legs up and around his waist. Emily's dress was short enough that it rolled up her hips.

Then he pressed himself against Emily and Emily was screaming and he was muffling her screams with his mouth.

He kissed her—devoured her, it looked like to Clara—while below...

Clara's face flamed now just remembering.

Clara looked down at the pot she'd meant to wash in the sink. She had licked it clean while she thought of Emily and her man in that alley. And the shoes.

Clara looked around her kitchen. Apple pies lay cooling on a rack and there were still pots and pans to clean up.

Noah was due home any minute. He wouldn't harangue her about not having dinner ready but still, Clara would feel so guilty if she couldn't do that for him. She loved being a good wife.

Nevertheless Clara found her hand wandering up inside the skirt of her dress—a modest cotton sundress, nothing indecent for the preacher's wife—and reaching inside her panties for the wetness found there.

Clara moaned.

She knew it was a sin to touch herself but surely...surely that didn't compare to Emily. Clara remembered how the man had maneuvered himself against Emily after hoisting up her legs, and she wondered what it would be like to have sex while standing.

She backed herself against the warm cabinets next to the oven and leaned her head back as she dipped her fingers inside her sex and spread the moisture all over her folds and up to her clitoris. She was so wet.

Clara thought of the way that man had pushed Emily against the stall while Emily moaned and moaned.

Clara brought her fingers up and licked them. Sticky. Sweet. Tart. Her hand traveled back down. She dipped her finger into her sex again. Her other hand traveled up to her engorged nipples where they pressed against her sundress.

Clara let herself think of the image her mind had been flashing back to all day ever since she first saw...

Emily's red shoes digging into the man's back as he thrust into her.

Clara moaned. She stuffed another finger into herself and felt her sex widen and stretch as she pumped her hand against herself.

Clara stepped away from the cabinets and bent over the kitchen island. She laid an elbow down to prop herself up while her hand worked away at her...pussy.

The thrill of thinking that dirty word to herself—pussy!—was almost enough to make her come right there but she held back.

She imagined Noah behind her now. Imagined he had come home early and caught her bent over the middle of the kitchen frigging—frigging!—herself.

SINNER—he would cry at her. Then he wouldn't be able to help himself, he would grab her hips and shove into her from behind. Perhaps she would be wearing a pair of red shoes that hitched up her butt and angled her sex at him. Perhaps he would grab Clara's neck and ground her face into the floured counter as he fucked her. Fuck!

Clara imagined her husband fucking her while she frigged her pussy and suddenly the warmth in her belly exploded. Clara arched her back and moaned as even more wetness flooded her hand and her pussy walls clenched at her fingers.

The oven beeped at her.

The last apple pie was ready.

Noah came home late so Clara was able to clean and set out dinner for him in time.

"I saw Emily Choi at the farmer's market this morning," Clara said as she cut into the braised short rib leftovers she'd reheated.

"Oh?" Noah didn't like being reminded of wayward members of his congregation but he also tried not to be a petty man. "How was she?"

"I didn't get a chance to talk to her—" because I was too busy watching her get fucked, Clara thought, "—but she looked good."

Well she *had* looked good. Clara had been unable to look away from their coupling. Even when Emily's heavy lidded eyes spotted Clara and widened.

Clara had gasped but stood there frozen. Emily's eyes stared into Clara's while the man pounded her against the stall. Then Emily threw back her head and moaned and came. That's when Clara had finally fled.

"Good," Noah said perfunctorily. He dug into the side of broccoli she had made. Noah was always very good about eating all his vegetables.

They talked about the work Noah had done at church today—he'd spent the day counseling some married couples—and about who they thought would bake what for the bake sale tomorrow.

After dinner Clara curled up on the sofa as she read a book and Noah sat next to her with his notebook and his scripture and worked on his upcoming Sunday sermon.

Clara's feet were cold and she wriggled them against Noah until he obligingly let her slip her feet underneath his thighs.

She stared at her husband over her book and underneath her lashes. The sight of him never failed to stir her.

He was a large man whose charisma only made him seem larger. His black hair was trimmed close to his head and he kept a trim beard too, little more than a stubble. It gave him a military look that suited his stern face. His eyes were so dark they looked black, and they would flash out from under his hooded eyelids with fiery passion as he spoke about God and the sins of man.

Right now his brows furrowed and his eyes flashed with vexation as he flipped through the pages of his scripture.

"What's the matter?" Clara asked.

"Nothing," he said quickly. "I'm just having trouble finding something—ah."

He landed—seemingly randomly to Clara—on a page. "I found it."

Clara went back to reading her book. The red leather bound volume was one of Clara's secret treasures. She had discovered it in the church library one day, sitting innocuously between a tepid "clean" romance and a book about birds. *Fausta Borja's Fairy Tales*, gold letters proclaimed.

Clara had taken the book home, expecting to relax while reading some familiar stories but she'd been shocked instead. The stories were not how Clara remembered them. Snow White was used by depraved criminals who labored in the mines all day. A woodcutter kept Little Red Riding Hood captive in his cabin all night. Beauty's family gave her to the Beast as his concubine in exchange for five chests of gold.

At first Clara had kept the book in the back of a drawer but she grew bolder with time and placed it on the shared bookshelf. Now she was reading the book right in front of Noah for the first time, and he seemed none the wiser. Clara blamed the red shoes for her recklessness. She trembled when she thought of how her husband might react if he only knew the filth she read, but at the same time, the wicked part of her was excited.

The tops of her feet had warmed and she moved them onto Noah's lap. He covered her feet with one of his warm hands.

He rubbed absentmindedly at the arches of her feet as he made notes. Clara stifled a moan. His touch sent an electrifying thrill up her legs and right into her pussy. She shifted in her seat and felt her slick pussy lips rub against one another and she had to stifle another moan.

"Are you all right, Clara?" Noah looked at her with concern.

"Yes," Clara said. "My butt was just falling asleep."

Noah went back to working on his sermon.

Clara moved her feet around in his lap. Today, even these wicked fairy tales couldn't hold her attention. Soon Noah was shifting in his seat too.

"I think it's time to go to bed," he said and abruptly closed his notebook.

"Oh, okay," said Clara. It was only nine o'clock but it wasn't rare for them to go to bed early and rise with the sun.

She followed her husband to the bedroom where they changed into their nightclothes—boxers and t-shirt for him, and a modest nightgown for her.

They turned off the lights and got under the covers.

Clara felt Noah's hand seek her out under the blankets and she wriggled towards him in response.

Noah removed his boxers while staying under the covers, then he climbed on top of her. He lifted the hem of her nightdress up. His hands felt her bare skin and he stopped short.

"Where are your panties?" he whispered to her.

"I didn't wear them to bed," she said, and held her breath. She wasn't sure if Noah would categorize this act as a sin but after blinking down at her he continued with his lovemaking.

His penis—it was already hard which was almost a perpetual state with her husband—nudged at her entrance and slid in through the tight wet warmth.

He let out a strangled groan. "You're so wet," he said.

Clara didn't know how to respond, and didn't. This was the most they'd ever said during their lovemaking act. Noah usually just climbed on top of her, did the deed under the blankets, and rolled off.

Noah liked to preach to the congregation that even if you were married, it was unseemly to have sex in any position other than missionary, nor was it seemly to do supplementary acts like fellatio or cunnilingus, nor was it seemly to take too much pleasure from sex—even married, missionary sex. It only led you to think more about sex, and such preoccupation could only lead to sin.

Clara rarely came during sex with her husband but she didn't mind submitting to him and she hoped he took some pleasure from it, even if he wasn't supposed to take too much.

Tonight was different though. She was so slick and the memory of those red shoes was so near. When Noah sped up and really pumped into her, Clara couldn't stop herself from drawing her legs up and around his waist.

He looked down at her in surprise but she closed her eyes and stifled a moan. His chest moved over her breasts and rubbed her nipples. He rarely touched her sensitive peaks so this bit of contact was almost too much for Clara.

She felt the orgasm uncoil from her belly. She tried not to move too much or make noise but she couldn't stop her pussy from clenching at Noah's cock—cock!—and he let out a fierce groan that was almost a yell and froze against her.

Clara felt his sperm coat the inside of her pussy and the added slickness only lengthened the pleasure of her orgasm. She tried not to shudder.

Noah rolled off her with a gasp and flung himself onto his back.

He stared up at the ceiling until his harsh breaths calmed and then Clara averted her gaze from his bare butt and legs when he got out of the bed to clean up.

When he was done, she rose from the bed and did her own clean up.

She came back to bed feeling some trepidation but when she slipped under the covers Noah's breathing had already smoothed out.

He had fallen asleep.

Clara felt her own eyelids grow heavy and as sleep pulled her under, she had one clear thought blossom through her mind.

She was going to buy a pair of red shoes.

The bake sale took up all of Clara's time the next day, and then she had choir practice the morning after that and chores to do in the evening so she didn't have a chance to go to the cobbler until the third day after she'd seen Emily at the market.

Chastebury had its own cobbler but going to Mr. O'Leary to commision the sort of shoes Clara had in mind was out of the question. Clara double-checked to make sure she had her talisman to guide her through the woods and set out for the next village over.

Clara was no artist but she designed and made her own simple clothes so she'd drawn up a few sketches of what she wanted.

The cobbler pored over the sketches—he marveled over the thin lined paper in her notebook, and the metal spiral that held it together—and snorted.

"Ye can't walk in these," he said. "Not far anyway. Although..."

He gave Clara a speculative look. "Perhaps it's not walking ye had in mind?"

Clara flushed. "Can you make them or not?"

"Och sure," he said. "I can make 'em. And I'd like to see ye wearing them too."

He chuckled.

Clara thought about telling him the shoes were for someone else but he was about to measure her feet so she saved herself the trouble.

The week while Clara waited for her red shoes was excruciating. She missed her section's cues during choir practice and burned Noah's dinners. She caught Noah giving her odd looks and she prepared wild excuses in her head but he never asked her what was wrong.

At night he seemed to watch her closely during their lovemaking but Clara was careful not to read any fairy tales or think too hard about the red shoes and she managed not to come for most of the week. There was one exception when her husband grabbed her wrists and raised them over her head, then locked his eyes on her while he moved inside of her and she couldn't help the shudder that came over her.

Finally, the week was over and her red shoes were ready.

"Mrs. Rhee! Mrs. Clara Rhee!"

Clara pretended not to hear the strident voice calling her name. She clutched the velvet satchel in her hands and hurried down Chastebury's main street.

"Mrs. Rhee!" A plump hand grabbed Clara's arm. Clara looked down at the baker, Meena Park. Meena was even more petite than Clara was, and appropriately curvy for a woman who baked bread and pastries for a living.

Meena thrust a warm cloth-wrapped bundle at Clara. Clara managed to grab it without dropping her precious shoes.

"Some croissants and pastries for you and your husband, Mrs. Rhee," Meena said breathlessly. Her round cheeks were rosy and her pretty black eyes were bright.

Clara managed not to roll her eyes. Meena was in love with Noah. She was always calling Clara "Mrs. Rhee" and giving her pastries to share with her husband.

"Thank you, Meena," Clara said. "They smell lovely."

"Oh," Meena's cheeks grew even rosier at the compliment. "You're too kind."

Meena looked Clara over. She did this every time she saw Clara. Clara figured she was checking out the competition though as far as she knew, Meena had never gone so far as to actually flirt with her husband.

"Your dress looks very pretty on you today," Meena said. Her eyes dropped to the satchel. "What's that you got there, Mrs. Rhee?"

"Oh just some new shoes," Clara said casually.

"Ooh," Meena said, "can I see?"

"No," Clara said. She added quickly when Meena's face fell, "I still need to add a few touches."

"Oh," Meena trilled. "I'm intrigued."

Clara smiled. "I have to get dinner going for Noah now."

"Oo-kay then, Mrs. Rhee. Say hello to the preacher for me."

"I will," Clara tossed over her shoulder. She was already walking away. She wanted to get home and try her new shoes on already!

"Maybe I'll see those new shoes at church on Sunday," Meena called after her.

"Maybe," Clara responded. *Fat chance*, she thought. Noah would have an aneurism if she wore her red shoes to Sunday service. God, he would just...why, he would...Clara's mind couldn't even contemplate.

Finally!

Clara locked the door behind her and drew the blinds closed downstairs. She didn't normally wear shoes in the house but it wasn't as if she could leave the house in her red shoes so she planned on wearing them in every room.

Clara set the pastries down on the kitchen counter and rushed upstairs to the bedroom where there was a full length mirror.

She sat on the bed facing the mirror and slowly opened the satchel.

Clara took out the red shoes and caressed them. The heels were long, tapered, and exquisitely narrow. The cobbler had wrapped leather around the narrow heels and underneath as well, so that the shoes were entirely blood red except for the inside soles where they were undyed sheepskin.

Clara bent down and slipped the shoes on one at a time, savoring the feel of the supple leather as it molded to her feet. She had tried them on at the cobbler's of course, but the cobbler's lecherous gaze had prevented her from enjoying the experience.

Clara raised her eyes to the mirror. She wore another cotton sundress, a blue one with puffed sleeves and flared skirt that came down to her knees.

The red shoes propped up her calves and brought out their sleek muscle tone.

Clara reached up and undid her tight hair bun. She loosened the waves her hair came down in and spread them around her shoulders and looked at herself again.

Yes. The woman that stared back at her was almost unrecognizable to Clara and it excited her immensely. Her hair was all mussed as if she'd never brushed it in her life. Her eyes were bold. Her erect nipples pushed against her dress.

She leaned back and spread her knees wide and slowly lifted the hem of her skirt so that she could see her own soaked panties. God, she looked like a wicked, sinful woman.

Clara rose abruptly and unzipped her dress. She shrugged it off and let it fall to the floor and she stepped out of the dress puddle and stared at herself in the mirror wearing only her underwear and the red shoes.

She liked her cotton underwear but Clara decided it wasn't appropriate right now. She unclipped her bra and threw it on the bed. Her small pert breasts bounced with their release.

Clara turned her back to the mirror and slowly drew her panties down her legs. She kept her knees straight and stared at her reflection as she bent over and exposed her pussy to herself. Clara stepped out of the panties and turned to face the mirror again.

She had never seen herself like this before. Her red shoes made her legs seem to go on forever till they reached her trim thatch of hair. Clara rarely looked at herself naked but she gave herself a long look now and liked what she saw.

It was time to walk about in her new red shoes.

Clara grabbed the rail as she descended the stairs, not wanting to twist her ankle.

She practiced stalking back and forth in the linoleum floor of the kitchen and watched her breasts jiggle in the reflection of the oven door glass.

She walked on the rug covering the living room floor and tried bending herself over the back of the sofa. She tried to imagine what her butt looked like stuck up in the air like that.

Then she plucked her secret book of fairy tales off the bookshelf and sprawled on the sofa with one of her legs flung over the back.

She started reading in the middle of a story she'd already read.

> *The prince rose and pushed Cinderella back onto the table.*
> *Men rose and grabbed her arms as she flailed and kicked trying to rise again.*

Other men—actually, one was a woman—grabbed her legs as the prince tossed up her skirts.

The woman helped the prince remove Cinderella's drawers. They knocked one of her shoes off in the process and Cinderella wondered wildly to herself why she couldn't keep her shoes on.

Then hands pushed her thighs open and pinned her knees to the table.

Things were just getting interesting when Clara heard the footsteps.

Noah!

Clara's eyes flew to the clock on the wall—it was only five o'clock and Noah shouldn't have been home for another hour.

That doesn't matter, her mind screamed at herself. *He's here now, get up! Get up!*

Clara slammed her book shut and scrambled to her feet. She kicked off the red shoes and pushed them under the sofa.

The sound of footsteps had retreated which meant Noah had passed the front of the house and would enter the kitchen door at any moment.

Clara stuck her book back on the shelf and ran across the living room, kitchen, and fled up the stairs.

She heard the kitchen door open as she tugged her sundress on.

"Clara?" Noah's voice called out. "Where are you?"

"I'm upstairs!" Clara called.

She tugged her panties on but had to toss her bra underneath the bed since she hadn't had time to put it on. Frantically she worked her hair into a quick ponytail.

Noah appeared in the doorway.

"Hey," Clara squeaked. She cleared her throat and tried for a casual tone. "You're home early. I'm sorry I don't have dinner going yet."

"That's all right," Noah said. He leaned against the doorframe and studied her. "I saw the pastries downstairs. I can make some egg croissant sandwiches and give you a night off."

"Oh, that'd be nice," Clara said. When Noah didn't speak and kept looking at her she said inanely, "Meena Park says hello."

"You were in town today?"

"Yes, I had to—I had to run some errands." Clara said. "To—ah, the library. To return some books."

Noah's face darkened for some reason. He advanced toward Clara.

Clara had an urge to bolt. She told herself that was ridiculous—this was her husband and he had every right to be in their bedroom.

Noah looked down at Clara.

"Clara," he said quietly. "I know what you've been up to."

Clara's mind went blank.

Finally she stuttered, "Wha—what do you mean? I haven't—why, I haven't been up to anything, Noah."

"Don't lie to me, Clara."

Noah looked—oh, he looked angry. He had the face he wore at church when he went on about sin and wickedness but now he was directing it right at her.

Noah grabbed Clara's shoulders.

"Look at you," he said roughly. Without warning his hand grabbed her breast. "You're not wearing a bra, Clara. What's gotten into you? I can see your nipples pointing at me."

His thumb and finger pinched Clara's nipple and she gasped. Still, she couldn't speak.

"You've been acting strangely all week. Did you think I hadn't noticed? Did you think you could hide your lustful, wicked thoughts from me, your husband?"

Oh my god.

He knew about the shoes.

"Noah, please," Clara babbled. "I can explain, I promise I haven't done anything terribly sinful—"

"LIAR!"

Noah grabbed Clara by the back of her neck.

"Noah!" Clara cried. "What are you doing?"

He had never handled her this way before. Her husband forced her out the door and down the stairs.

"It's time for you to confront your sins, Clara," he said grimly.

They got downstairs and he dragged her to the living room and threw her down on the sofa.

Clara righted herself and watched helplessly as her husband went to the bookshelf and snatched a book. A red leather bound volume. *Fausta Borja's Fairy Tales.*

Oh my god. It wasn't the shoes. He had discovered the book.

"I found this last week."

Last week?

"And I read through some of these so-called fairy tales. Tales of filth!"

Clara flinched.

Noah opened the book.

"This page is bent," he said, eyeing her suspiciously. "Were you reading this story when I got home? Cinderella?"

Clara nodded mutely.

He thrust the book in her hands. "Read it."

Clara stared down at the page she'd left off on.

"Read it aloud to me," Noah said.

She stared up at him in horror.

"Don't give me that look, Clara," he said. "I know what sort of smut you read. That innocent act isn't going to work on me. Read it."

Falteringly, Clara read aloud. It was the passage she'd read earlier. Her face flamed red as she described how Cinderella was used by multiple men. Still, she couldn't help but distractedly wonder why Noah hadn't said anything about discovering her secret for an entire week.

"Stop," Noah said.

Clara stopped.

Noah paced back and forth. Clara risked a glance up at him and to her shock, noticed the large bulge in his pants.

He caught her looking and glared.

"Get up."

Clara rose unsteadily to her feet.

Noah sat down on the sofa.

"You know what this means, Clara," he said. "You're my wife and it's my duty to punish what's mine. Bend over my lap."

Clara stared at her husband.

"Bend over my lap," he said softly. "Now."

Heart pounding, Clara obeyed.

Her head and arms hung over one side while her legs dangled on the other. For some reason Noah pulled at the band in her hair and pulled it loose from her ponytail. Then he lifted the hem of her skirt.

Briefly his warm hand skimmed over her panty-covered buttocks, then without warning he spanked her.

Clara cried out.

His hand cracked across her backside again. And again.

Clara squirmed and—she couldn't help herself—she tried to stand but Noah shoved a large hand into the small of her back and forced her to stay. Noah's erection pushed into her stomach like it wanted to come out the other side.

Smack!

Clara felt tears prick her eyes.

"Please," she whimpered. "Please, I'll be good. I promise not to think lustful thoughts anymore."

"LIAR!" Smack!

Noah's hand cupped her core. Clara moaned.

"Your panties are wet," her husband said. "Is this from earlier? When you were reading your filth?"

Clara didn't answer.

"Let's get this out of the way." To her horror, Noah pulled her panties away and down her thighs. He left them around her knees and cracked his hand across her bare butt.

Clara groaned in mortification and agony.

Noah went on with her punishment, switching from one cheek to another.

"Your ass is red from my spanking, Clara," Noah said.

His hand grabbed one cheek. He kneaded it with his strong fingertips. The movement rubbed her folds together and Clara held in a moan.

He switched to the other cheek and massaged that one too. Clara squirmed but this time it was not in pain.

Noah spanked her again. "Is this turning you on, Clara?" Smack.

"No!"

"Are you wet for me?" Smack.

"No! Please, Noah, I'm good. I'm a good wife!"

"I'll be the judge of that."

His finger drew slowly down her slick folds.

"Don't!"

SMACK. "Are you not my wife, Clara?"

"I am. I am your wife."

"Then by law you will obey me. And you will accept any punishment I dole out to you, do you understand me, Clara?"

Clara nodded tearfully.

"I want to hear your answer, Clara."

"I understand!"

"What do you understand?"

"I'm your wife. I must obey you. I must—I must..." Clara shuddered.

"You must accept my punishment," Noah sounded encouraging now.

"I must accept your punishment," she repeated.

Noah drew his finger up and down her pussy.

"I'm going to have to see how wet you are, Clara. I need to know how much of a slut my wife really is. Remember that you brought this upon yourself. "

Noah's finger intruded into her pussy. She was so lubricated he slid in with no effort. He slipped in another finger.

"You really are a filthy whore, aren't you, Clara?"

Clara shuddered with shame. And something else.

"You love this, don't you?" Noah's fingers thrusted into her harshly now. She could hear the squelching as her wet pussy sucked at his fingers.

God help her, it felt so good.

"Is this what you do to yourself while you're home all day? Do you touch yourself?"

Clara could only shake her head.

"Answer me!"

Clara struggled.

"What do you think you're doing, Clara?"

He wrestled with her to the floor. Clara shook her head. She didn't want to answer him, didn't want to admit her shame aloud. To Clara's surprise, Noah suddenly rolled off her.

"What's this?"

Clara sat up and saw her husband reach under the sofa.

"Don't!" Clara cried.

It was too late.

Noah pulled his hand out and her red shoes dangled from his fingers. He rose slowly to his feet.

She expected rage but her husband looked truly shocked—almost dazed.

"They're...they're..." Clara stuttered.

Wild thoughts of proclaiming that she'd never seen them before in her life, or that she had found them on the street and took them home to donate later, or that they belonged to Meena Park—these thoughts ran through Clara's head, and then they died.

Her breathing calmed. Her situation had gone past the point of anything she had imagined or fantasized and now that she was here, now, she couldn't be terrified of the unknown.

"They're mine," Clara said clearly.

Noah looked down at her. Clara felt very exposed sprawled out on the floor, braless in her sundress with her panties twisted around her knees, while he loomed over her. But she also noticed that the bulge in his pants was as big as ever.

"They're yours?" he repeated incredulously. "You admit to it?"

"Yes," said Clara. "When I saw Emily Choi at the market last week she was with a man, and I followed them to a secluded part of the market and then I saw them..." Clara flushed. "I saw them...coupling. Fucking. And Emily wore red shoes. Like these. I saw them digging into his back. And I decided I wanted a pair of red shoes. So I commissioned them from the cobbler."

"Mr. O'Leary made you these?" A dangerous note entered her husband's voice.

"No!" Clara cried. "No, I couldn't go to him with something like this. I went outside Chastebury."

Noah loomed over her, his face inscrutable. He tossed the shoes on the floor.

"Get up," he said curtly. "Put them on,"

"What?"

"Now!" he barked.

Clara scrambled to her feet and stumbled as her panties tangled around her ankles.

"Take those ridiculous panties off," Noah said.

Clara stepped out of the panties.

"Now put on the shoes."

Clara wobbled while stepping into the shoes but Noah did not help her. She stood tentatively before him in the red shoes.

"Take off the dress."

Clara hesitated.

Noah lunged forward and grabbed her waist. Clara shrieked. He bent her over, flipped up her dress and smacked her bottom quickly three times in succession.

He released her and moved back, folding his arms as if nothing had happened. Clara straightened up slowly, and eyed her husband with wary eyes.

"Take off the dress," he repeated.

Clara reached up and unzipped her dress. She could not look at Noah's face as she struggled to unzip the dress and then let it drop to the floor.

"Good," Noah said. He was breathing hard. "A slut like you shouldn't get to wear clothes."

Clara shuddered. His words made a part of her cringe but that part was growing smaller. The other part of her, the wicked, sinful part, was rising to the surface and could feel the slickness coat her thighs.

"Turn around, slowly. Let me see your nakedness in the bright light of day."

Clara turned, slowly, all the way around. All the while she could feel the flush on her face and breasts.

"Sit on the sofa."

Clara walked past her husband and sat on the sofa.

"Not like that," her husband said. "You're sitting like a lady. I want you to sit like a slut."

Clara stared at him.

"You know what I mean."

Slowly, Clara opened her knees and exposed her pussy to her husband's hungry gaze.

Noah knelt between her legs and pushed her knees wider.

He stared into her glistening sex as if mesmerized.

"What have you done to me, Clara?" he whispered. "What have you done to us?"

"Noah," Clara breathed. The look on her husband's face stole her breath. She reached forward to touch his face.

He took her hand—gently—and set it on the couch. "Keep your hands at your sides, Clara," he said. "I have to taste you. And you will not stop me."

Then he leaned forward and pressed his face right into her pussy.

Clara froze.

The tip of his tongue prodded at her folds, tentatively at first. Then he pressed his entire tongue against her and lapped in slow, long strokes that made Clara throw her head back and moan.

His hands were between her thighs now too. His thumb drew lazy circles around her clitoris while his fingers delved into her sex.

Clara couldn't believe this was happening. This was her husband! The pastor of her church! The preacher! The man who stood on the pulpit every Sunday and raged about how sinful it was to give into lustful desires. And here he was with his head between her legs, lapping up her juices like it was nectar from the pagan gods, and he a supplicant.

Clara's thighs tightened around Noah's head and he shoved them open again with his hands. He used his tongue now to breach her sex, slid it in and out, licked around her entrance until she shook and begged.

"Please, Noah, please!" she cried.

"What are you begging for, Clara?" Noah came up for air. His hands worked between her legs as Clara shook her head back and forth.

"Please, I need...I need..."

"Tell me what you need." His fingers worked her relentlessly.

Clara could not bring herself to say the words.

Noah withdrew his hands.

"Please!" Clara screamed. "Please make me come!"

"Are you a slut, Clara?"

"Yes! Yes, I'm a slut. I'm a whore! Make me come! Make me—"

Noah dived back between her legs. His tongue pressed against her clitoris while his fingers impaled her over and over again.

Clara screamed. "Yes! I'm coming! I'm coming! I'm a filthy whore and—oh my god—!"

Clara writhed. Noah kept his mouth firmly latched onto her and his fingers stuffed her pussy as she rode out her pleasure.

Finally she stopped flopped back on the sofa and Noah raised his head.

"You taste like heaven, Clara," he said. He put his fingers in front of her mouth. "Lick," he said.

Clara glared at her husband.

"You better watch how you look at me, Clara," Noah said. "Fact, I better teach you a lesson right now. Get on your knees."

Clara's glare turned to into a look of fright. She rose unsteadily from the sofa and then dropped to her knees.

Noah put his fingers to her mouth. This time she opened her mouth and tasted herself on his fingers. He forced her head back so that she had to look up at him like she was the supplicant now. She had tasted herself before of course, but it was different when her husband forced her to lick her own juices off the fingers he had fucked her with.

Noah withdrew his fingers. "Undo my pants."

Clara's nipples tightened with anticipation. Was he really going to let her taste him?

Her hands shook as she undid her husband's belt. Then she unbuttoned his pants and unzipped them.

The outline of his cock bulged against his boxers. Clara stared.

Impatiently Noah pulled the front of the boxers down so that they sat beneath his balls. Noah's cock waved at Clara. It looked bloated and angry.

"Taste me, Clara."

Clara didn't need to be told twice. She eagerly leaned forward and put her lips to the head of his cock. Tentatively she licked. Salty precum coated her tongue. Clara moaned and swirled her tongue all around the head of Noah's cock.

"God," Noah prayed above her. He looked down. "Touch me. Take me in your mouth."

Clara grasped the base of Noah's cock. She squeezed because she could, and rarely had the chance. Noah gasped. Clara stuffed his cock into her mouth, ran her tongue along the underside, closed her lips tight around his shaft.

Tentatively at first, and then growing more sure of herself, Clara moved her head back and forth on Noah's cock. She marveled that something that was so hard could be so velvety smooth. Clara squeezed her hand around his base to make up for what her mouth couldn't cover.

"Deeper," Noah said.

Clara tried. But it was her first time sucking cock after all. Noah's cock hit the back of her throat and she could not control the gag or her recoil back.

Noah grabbed her by the back of the head. He clenched her loose hair through his fingers and jerked her face forward. Clara gagged and coughed as Noah's cock rammed into her throat.

Tears sprung to her eyes. She made awful noises as her throat tried to close but was prevented by the large obstacle of Noah's cock.

"Tilt your head." He tugged on her hair. "Open wider. You can breathe through your nose. Breathe, Clara!"

"Ungh!" And then Clara could breathe.

Noah pulled back, providing a brief respite to her throat, and then he slammed into her throat again. Clara was ready this time, but it was still difficult. She couldn't help her hands on Noah's thighs, pushing back at him while he pushed into her but he didn't seem to notice.

Noah fucked her mouth, all while keeping his merciless grip on the back of Clara's head.

Tears ran down Clara's face, a purely physical reflex to the treatment she endured.

"Enough!" Noah yanked her head back and stepped away from her.

Clara gulped for air and stared at her husband in trepidation. Was it over? Was Noah going to change his mind now and leave her unfulfilled while he prayed to God for forgiveness?

Clara sent up her own silent prayer to God. She didn't care what Noah shouted on Sundays, this could not be wrong. Clara loved Noah. Noah loved her. How could this be a sin? *Please, let him see the light*, she prayed.

Noah removed his pants and sat on the sofa. "Come here, Clara. I want you to straddle me."

Clara's heart sang as she obeyed. She climbed onto Noah's lap with her knees spread on either side of him.

Noah clenched his cock in one hand and put his other hand on the small of her back as he guided himself into her.

She was wet and able to impale herself on her husband's cock in one downward push.

Noah put his hands around her waist. He guided her up and down on his shaft until Clara moaned and lolled her head back.

"God, Clara," Noah whispered. "You're beautiful."

Noah's hands rose to her breasts. Clara gasped. His thumbs caressed her nipples as she rode him. He flicked her sensitive peaks then moved his hands to her back and forced her to arch back. He bent his head and scraped his tongue across her nipples. Clara's breasts bounced and her nipples slipped in and out of his mouth but Noah didn't seem to mind.

He thrust up into her with low grunts while his hands bore down on her hips. Clara bucked her hips against his tight grip and Noah gave up a harsh groan. Warmth flooded Clara's pussy and still she bucked. Noah hugged Clara tight and latched onto her breast. His teeth bit down on her nipple.

"Fuck!" Clara screamed. "I'm coming! Fuck me, I'm coming!"

Noah's breathing was strangled as he thrust up into her and prolonged her orgasm.

Finally Clara slumped against Noah. Her head fell into the warm nook where his neck met his shoulder and she breathed in the comforting scent of her husband.

They stayed that way for a while.

Clara wondered where they would go from there.

Clara lifted the hem of her choir robes and daintily stepped across the stones in the grass that led to the church.

She was late for service. She normally would've waited to put her choir robes on till she got to church but the outfit she wore underneath her robes was not fit for the eyes of their congregation.

Actually the outfit was just a bra and panties. They were a demure ivory color but made of delicate layers of sheer lace that exposed her dark nipples and the newly bare slit between her legs. Clara had shaved her pussy for the first time that morning after Noah left early for church and her folds rubbed together as she walked.

It had been almost two weeks since Noah discovered Clara's red shoes. To Clara's disappointment, he never brought up the incident again and they returned to having sex under the covers with the lights off.

But Clara felt like a different person ever since that day and she couldn't go back to the person she had been before.

When she and Noah were out on main street together, she would imagine them turning into an alley and Noah ravaging her against the wall.

When they walked into a shop, Clara imagined her husband making her strip and letting the shopkeeper and patrons sample his wife's goods.

At home Clara would put on the red shoes and touch herself and imagine herself leaving the house in her shoes and walking around town dressed as she pleased. As slutty as she pleased.

"Hello, Clara!" Julia and Teddy Jackson waved at Clara.

"Hello Julia, hello Teddy," Clara said as she rounded some jasmine shrubs to join the couple on the walk to Sunday service. "How are the children?"

"On the church field trip to the Woodland kingdom with all the other kids," Julia said cheerfully. "It's wonderful to be free of..."

Teddy had stopped short and Julia trailed off as she followed her husband's gaze down to Clara's feet.

"...of—of—them." Julia finished with a stutter. Her flushed face swiveled to meet her husband's and they exchanged a look.

Clara calmly caught up to them. Her red shoes made definitive clicks against the brick road that led to the church.

"You...you look pretty with your hair down, Clara," Julia said.

"Why thank you, Julia. You look very pretty today too; that dress suits you. Shall we?" Clara gestured towards the church. "We'll be late if we don't keep going."

"I—I—yes, of course. We might be late..." Julia slipped her arm into Teddy's and she managed to keep up the conversation with Clara about the weather, and the lake picnic next week, all while her gaze kept darting down to Clara's red shoes. Teddy remained silent but he darted looks too. Not just at Clara's shoes, but appraisingly, up and down her body till Julia elbowed him.

It was a gorgeous day full of sun and billowy clouds, perfect for a walk. The church stood next to a small lake where a breeze blew in like the breath of God and set all of Clara's nerves atingle.

She carefully rearranged her choir robes so that they would not open and expose her secrets to the wind.

They made it to the little stone church and Clara said her goodbyes to Julia and Teddy. She made her way down the center aisle to the dais in front of the room where the choir box was.

She heard conversations die out as she clicked past in her red shoes, and then furious whispers start up in her wake.

Clara ignored all this as she stepped onto the dais. She paused in front of the altar and looked up at the large metal circle that represented their unity with the one true god.

Some of the Black Forest folk who visited had hypothesized that that symbol was the reason Chastebury had found its way into their world. They thought that perhaps the congregation's prayers had imbued the circle with power, just like the talismans that people used here, but much bigger: big enough to move an entire hamlet.

Clara offered up a brief prayer and traced a circle over her heart with two fingers.

"Amen," she said quietly and made her way to the choir box. The other members made room for her. Some stared and some avoided her gaze.

Clara took her seat. They were a small chamber choir of ten people and the silence around her was deafening. Clara looked around and determinedly gave the others polite nods and smiles, forcing them to acknowledge her. Everyone slowly went back to talking amongst themselves while they waited for Noah to show up and begin service. No one breathed a word about her red shoes.

Clara reflected to that day she first met her husband. Her college choir had just given a holiday concert and Clara had a solo. Her voice was a low contralto which always surprised people because she was so slight and petite. It surprised Noah.

He came up to her after the concert, full of intense passion that made him more awkward than handsome at that age, and earnestly told Clara that God had spoken to him through her voice. It should have frightened her but she loved him almost immediately. She had felt an instant connection which she had always attributed to God's grace in showing her to her future husband.

Something was bothering Noah lately.

At first Clara had thought it was the incident with the red shoes but she'd come to realize that it was something that had been bothering Noah before that.

The evenings when Noah worked on his sermons and Clara read or sewed used to be their quiet time together. But these days looking at scripture agitated Noah.

He thumbed through his book like the words kept changing on him which was funny because Clara could've sworn he had most of it committed to memory. He used to love spouting the holy word but that had stopped almost completely. She could hear the silences in his sentences where his scripture quotes used to go.

Clara asked him what the matter was but he only grew more taciturn.

Clara was at her wit's end when something inside her had whispered that she should wear the red shoes to church today. That it would give Noah the final push he needed to confront his demons.

Clara hoped it was the good in her that whispered, and not the wicked.

The congregation rose.

Clara belatedly rose to her feet and saw Noah striding to the pulpit.

In those last breathless moments before everything changed, Clara prayed that she had made the right decision and that God was still with her.

Noah made the usual announcements and then took a seat on the side of the dais while the conductor rose and led the choir through their first hymn. An ethereal and haunting piece about God's love. Clara gave herself over to the music but she still noticed the moment Noah stiffened.

She didn't dare break her gaze off the conductor but she felt the heat of Noah's look travel from her red shoes peeking out beneath her robes, up to her face.

The song finally ended. The conductor gave them an approving nod and took his seat. Clara risked a glance at Noah.

He was furious.

He rose from his chair. Noah walked toward Clara with slow menacing steps.

Clara's heartbeat fluttered in her throat. Surely he wouldn't pull her out of the choir box in front of the entire adult congregation...?

No.

At the last minute Noah gave her a searing glare and swerved to take his place behind the pulpit.

"Friends," Noah's voice boomed. "Loved ones," his voice caressed. "I stand here before you today to preach to you about lust."

Noah walked out from behind his pulpit and paced in front of the altar.

"We think we know about lust. We think we have struggled with it. We think we have won. After all, we are a small and respectable hamlet. No scandals here. We are all respectable citizens."

Noah's gaze traveled over the congregation.

"That's what we think," he said. His words dripped with menace. "But we are wrong."

A susurrus of unease spread through the congregation.

"A siren lives among us. Tempts us to sin. She comes to our services. Bakes pies for our bake sales. Sings in our choir."

Clara's hands bunched up her robes in her fists and she struggled not to hyperventilate.

"My brothers and sisters, I have a confession: I have sinned mightily. I have lusted. I have craved. I have yearned for carnal pleasures...and I have acted upon my lust!"

A gasp when up through the church. Noah raised his voice.

"Worst of all, I have harbored this siren of temptation in my own home, sheltered her even as she showed me her true carnal nature!"

The blood left Clara's face. She could feel every eye of the congregation locked on her.

"Clara Rhee, I call you to the altar!" Noah cried.

Clara couldn't move.

"Clara Rhee, as you are my wife and you have sworn to obey me, I call you to the altar!" Noah's voice was harsh with demand.

The congregation erupted into a clamor that was entirely too loud for the thirty or so members present.

Clara rose. She held her head high and walked out of the choir box.

Silence fell over the church.

Her red shoes clacked loudly against the hardwood floor of the dais as she walked up to Noah.

"The audacity of sin!" Noah cried. "Look how she saunters over, confident in her power!"

Noah grabbed Clara's arm as she reached him and thrust her at the congregation.

"I want a show of hands," Noah said. His eyes looked out at them piercingly. "I want to see a show of hands of those that have lusted after this siren."

Clara could hear her own shuddering breaths. What was happening?

"There is no need to be ashamed. There will be no repercussions. I want to see an honest show of hands of those who have looked, heard, smelled, or been near this woman, and felt lust."

A hand went up.

Clara gasped. The hand belonged to petite and round Meena Park. Other hands rose, tentatively at first, but then quite a few. Most of the congregation, in fact.

Noah nodded. "That's more like it. Though I think some of you are still holding back. Clara!"

Noah turned to her. Clara locked eyes with her husband. Something flashed between them, a moment of intimacy that was shocking right then, in front of all these people.

"Take off your robe, Clara," Noah said quietly.

Clara licked her lips. Without quite willing it, her hands rose to her robe and efficiently undid the buttons. When she was done her hands fell to her sides. Her robes were so voluminous that the folds still hid her from the congregation's sight.

Noah walked behind her. He snatched the robe off Clara. It flew off in a thunder of silk and fluttered to the ground where Noah had flung it.

Clara's world tilted and shifted: she felt almost dizzy from it.

Clara stood before the congregation in only her sheer lingerie and red shoes.

It was dead silent.

Still behind her, Noah's arms reached inside Clara's. One hand stole up and cupped a breast and the other stole down and cupped her mound over her panties. Inside Clara, the dark beast of desire reared its head.

Clara melted back against Noah and she mewled into the silence.

Noah withdrew and Clara had to brace herself to stand on her own.

"Now," Noah said, his voice silky. "May God strike you down if you lie to me now: I want a show of hands from those who feel lust for this woman right here, right now!"

Clara looked out at the sea of raised hands, dazed. Every hand was in the air except for...Gregory Stone's husband, Andrew.

"Does it count if I feel some mighty lust for you, preacher?" Andrew called out.

Noah nodded. "That's perfectly natural, Andrew. And Clara and I are as one so yes, it counts."

Noah addressed the entire congregation. "It is as I suspected. Our sin is deep. It affects us all. But God has spoken to me, shown me the way. Join me at the altar, friends, and I will show you how God will cleanse us of our sins. Join me now."

People obeyed immediately. They all rose and eventually they stood around her and Noah in a large circle.

"Meena Park," Noah nodded at the baker. "Come forth, friend."

The voluptuous baker stepped forward with gleaming eyes. Meena's dress prominently displayed her plump bosom which fairly trembled with anticipation.

Clara might have thought that Meena had a crush on Noah but it was obvious now that all the excitement in her eyes was for Clara. How could Clara have been so blind?

"Meena, what do you want to do when you see this slut that stands before you?"

Meena's pink little tongue licked her lips. "I want to touch her. I want to see all of her... I want to see what she tastes like."

"Touch Clara then, Meena Park," Noah said.

Meena drew close to Clara. Clara was short but the top of Meena's head only reached Clara's chin. Clara stepped back instinctively but Noah's firm body was behind her.

Meena's hand rose and caressed Clara's cheek. Her fingers skimmed down Clara's long neck, and lingered at the slope of her breasts. Meena's thumb played gently with Clara's nipple through the sheer lace and Meena leaned her face into Clara's neck and inhaled deeply.

Noah's hands unclasped Clara's bra.

"See Clara," Noah said.

Meena pulled down the straps of Clara's bra and peeled it away from her. Clara's nipples pebbled into stiff peaks.

Clara was intensely aware that Meena was not the only one looking at her. The entire congregation stood around her, entranced.

Noah and Meena grasped Clara's panties and pulled down together. Clara stepped out of the panties and Meena tossed them out of the way. Clara saw Wesley Harrison pluck them off the ground and surreptitiously pocket them.

Clara heard the strangled gasp Noah made as he saw her bare mound for the first time.

His voice was a low rumble when he spoke again to Meena.

"Taste Clara."

Meena splayed her hand on Clara's ribs and bent her small head to Clara's breast.

Meena took Clara's nipple into her mouth. She tongued the nipple till it was good and wet and then delicately manipulated it with her thumb and forefinger while her mouth moved to the other nipple.

Clara squirmed and Meena took firm grasp of both her small breasts and massaged them while she continued to lick and tease the peaks.

Meena's hand stole down to Clara's bare pussy.

"Wait," Noah said.

Noah picked Clara up and moved to the altar. He laid her atop the cold marble and Clara shivered. Her feet shod in the red shoes hung off the edge, facing the congregation.

Noah nodded to Meena.

He moved aside as Meena darted forward. She weaved her arms around Clara's thighs and plunged her face into Clara's pussy.

Meena smashed against Clara, her cold little nose poked into Clara's folds, her mouth opened wide, and she lapped frantically at Clara's sex.

The baker's enthusiasm triggered the desire that had laid ready to explode within Clara all week.

Already she felt the tension pooling in her nether regions.

Meena's tongue covered Clara's clitoris like a small blanket and Clara whimpered.

Meena's tongue fairly vibrated on top of Clara's clitoris.

"Please, it's—it's too much," Clara gasped.

Clara tried to kick her legs. Meena only took a firmer grasp of her thighs—God, the baker's hands were strong—and pressed her tongue against Clara's nub of pleasure.

So many eyes on Clara. It was still so silent. Only Clara's ragged breaths and Meena's slurping disturbed the quiet.

Her tension unraveled.

Clara arched her back.

She wanted to scream out but she was shy in front of so many and it came out as a strangled sob.

Meena stumbled back in triumph.

Clara tried to close her legs but Noah pushed her thighs wide so that everyone could see her wet cunt tremble and clench as she came down from her orgasm.

"Behold!" Noah's voice boomed. "Behold the whore of Chastebury!"

Clara shuddered.

"Do you want to see her come again?" Noah shouted.

"Yes!" "Aye!" "Amen!"

"Do you want to see her so overtaken by her lustful nature that she screams out filthy words?"

"Amen!"

"Do you want to see this sinful slut be used like she deserves?"

"Amen!"

Noah pulled Clara off the altar. Her limbs were limp and loose as he maneuvered her around and bent her over the altar.

Clara laid her cheek against the hard marble and was grateful that it had warmed somewhat. Though her nipples were still painfully peaked as her breasts were smushed against the hard flat surface.

Noah kicked her red shoes farther apart.

There was some rustling which Clara guessed was his pants loosening.

Clara flashed back to that day she had first seen Emily Choi's red shoes and imagined herself with her own pair of red shoes, bent over by Noah.

Clara had her own pair of red shoes now.

Noah was about to take her for real.

In front of all the citizens of Chastebury.

Noah dipped his fingers into her slit and scooped up the moisture there.

Clara twisted her head and looked down through her veil of tussled hair to Noah.

He held his glistening fingers up for the congregation. "Witness how her body begs for this."

Then Noah positioned himself behind Clara and reamed his cock into her swollen pussy without further ado.

Clara's sex stretched painfully at the sudden intrusion. Noah didn't allow her time to grow used to his member, nor did he reach around to play with her clitoris.

He just grabbed her hips and pounded his cock into her pussy mercilessly.

Noah's cock split her pussy open with every thrust.

Noah's cock punched her cervix with every thrust.

Noah's cock pushed Clara closer to the brink of her sanity with every thrust.

He thrust so hard Clara was sure bruises were already forming on the front of her thighs as they banged into the edge of the altar. Not to mention her poor sex.

Clara's open-mouthed grunts and groans misted the marble next to her face. Her palms pressed down into the altar as Noah's cock punished her, broke down every barrier and allowed for nothing to stand between them.

Low, guttural sounds fell from Clara's throat.

"What do you want, Clara?" Noah's voice matched hers for its roughness.

"I want…"

"Shout it out, Clara! Shout it out to the heavens so that all may hear!"

"I want you to fuck me! Fuck me hard, Noah!" Clara screamed.

"Yes," Noah hissed. "That's my filthy slut."

Noah slammed into her faster. The sounds of their mating filled the church.

Clara no longer cared that everyone witnessed her shame. She no longer felt shame. Only a glorious tide of pleasure that she labeled as "sinful" to bring herself to greater heights.

"Fuck me! Use me! Fill me with your cum!"

Noah pounded into her with short, sharp thrusts. The spirit filled her. Sanctified her.

Clara came.

Noah jerked his hips so fast against her Clara's body vibrated from the constant, quick, motion.

"God!" Noah cried out. His cum spurted into Clara, gobs and gobs of it.

Noah froze against her and bellowed, "Holy God! Witness my use of this whore you've sent down to us from heaven! The slut you've bestowed upon us as our savior! She will consume our lust, cleanse our sins, and we will use her without shame!"

Clara slumped against the altar as Noah pulled out of her. She missed his cock already. Her body hummed. Clara felt awake for the first time in her life.

She pressed her hands against the altar and rose to stand on her trembling legs.

Noah helped her and took her hand as she turned to face all the glittering eyes of their congregation.

"Who's next?" Noah demanded.

The congregation surrounded her. Hands reached for Clara's breasts and between her legs. Clara surrendered as she was lifted and laid onto the altar once more.

Skirts covered Clara's face and then she saw Meena Park lift her dress and step to either side of her head.

Meena knelt and lowered her cunt over Clara's face. The scent of the other woman made Clara's nose flair and she opened her mouth eagerly to lick Meena's pussy.

"Wesley Harrison, you will fuck my wife," Noah's voice boomed. "You will stuff her cunt with your cock and fuck her without mercy."

Hard hands lifted Clara's butt and a hard body came between her legs. A cock slid into her pussy and a wave of Noah's cum gushed out of her as the new cock forced its way in. Noah's cock was the only one she had ever had in her pussy.

Clara had never felt so wicked in her life.

Those that didn't join in using Clara used each other.

They fucked and mated in the church until every last member had sated their lust, then Noah moved the entire congregation outside to the lake. The children weren't due back until tomorrow and everyone left their clothes inside and emerged from the church naked as the day they were born.

The sun was low by then, and diffused by clouds that illuminated the sky and lake with soft shades of pink and gold.

Noah held Clara's hand and tugged his cum-streaked wife with him as he walked into the lake. He stopped when she was waist deep and he was immersed to his thighs.

Completely nude, Noah addressed his congregation.

"God bestowed a great gift upon us today."

"Amen!"

"The hamlet of Chastebury will no longer live in ignorance and shame."

"Amen!"

"Let us be baptized in the lake to commemorate this day."

"Amen!"

One by one the members of the congregation approached and Noah and Clara dipped their heads under the water.

When they emerged, breathless and gasping, they kissed Clara and they kissed Noah.

And then they all went home, never to be the same again.

"What made you change your mind, Noah?"

"Mm?" Noah looked up from his study of scripture later that week when they cuddled together on the sofa. "Change my mind about what?"

"About lust. About sin."

"Oh." Noah looked down at his book. He paged through it—confidently like he used to when he knew where all the words were—and landed right where he wanted.

"Here," he said as he passed her the scripture and pointed at a highlighted passage. "Read this."

Clara read the passage, frowned, and read it again. She checked the front of the book where the familiar symbol of the circle was etched in gold.

"Did it always say that?" Clara was not as familiar with the scripture as Noah was.

"I don't know," Noah confessed. "My memory...ever since we came here. I'm not sure if my memory changed or the scripture changed. It's what it says now. More importantly, it's what I believe in my heart to be true, Clara."

Clara looked down at the words again.

> *Beloved, let us love one another, for love is from*
> *God, and let us lust after one another for lust is*
> *from God as well, and whoever loves and lusts*
> *has been born of God and knows God.*

Amen.

ABOUT THE AUTHOR

Old Fausta Borja
Wrote about hoo-hah,
Hemming and hawing at romance;
Little did she know
She'd be struck by arrow
And tangle the two in a dance.

Made in the USA
Middletown, DE
30 July 2017